Back to Jack

I0685667

A Time Synchers Adventure

Written by

Bill Applewhite

ISBN-13: 978-0989890908

Back to Jack/Applewhite, Bill/Juiced Publishing (2013-12-01).

1

Jack woke to the crashing together of his teeth. Jarring. Bouncing. Opening his eyes was a chore, but it would be worth it if that meant he could see the guy bouncing his head into the wall, and make him stop.

"Okay, Okay, I'm awake." He lashed out at the cruel torturer causing his pain, his hand thrusting wildly through the air. The shaking didn't stop. He was looking up into a piercing bright blue sky, the clouds jumping all around. No, that was his vision jumping around with all the jarring. He leaned his head over to each side. He was on his back, hemmed in on all sides of a wooden box.

"I'm in a casket?" he asked himself. "Whoa! Bizarre dream, Jack." His thoughts rambled for a moment. Open casket. Funeral procession? Whoever had sprung for the funeral had only paid for an old, weathered pine box. Cheapskates! But if this is my funeral, I'm dead, so why does my head hurt so much? There was music, if you could call whistling music. Another funeral cost reduction? Whoever paid for this shindig must not know about his life insurance coverage. Jack recognized the tune, but couldn't place it. Da Da, dada da dadada. It was an oddly cheerful tune for a funeral. He was having some trouble fighting through the pounding in his head. "Plus," he thought, "I deserve a little slack for being dead!"

"You awake yet?"

It was a man's voice. Didn't sound like God booming out commandments from a burning bush or anything. Just an ordinary man's voice. Dreams. Go figure.

"Hey. I see your eyes are open. Can't you hear me?"

The voice sounded a little annoyed now. Jack tilted his chin up to look back over his head at where the voice was coming from. There, high above him, but upside down, sat God on his throne, talking to him. Wait, Wait, Wait. Jack pushed himself up into a sitting position and looked back.

The gray hair and short beard was about right, but since when did God have a pot belly?

"Hey, you're not God. You're just an ordinary old man."

"Whoa!" the man yelled. Then he pulled back on, what, some leather straps? The coffin stopped moving.

"Who are you calling old?" the man asked.

"Anybody twice my age is old in my book," Jack answered weakly, "and I'd say you had already celebrated fifty." He closed his eyes and tried breathing through the headache. The man turned and dropped into the back of the wagon to look closer at Jack. There was a nasty bump rising out of Jack's dark hair.

"Doesn't look too bad. I'm the closest thing to God you've got. If I hadn't come along, I doubt you'd have made it to thirty. You'd still be out their lying in the brush, Indian bait or bear food. Either way, the outcome for you ain't so good," he laughed.

The old guy was laughing at him from under a big black Stetson, and completely outfitted in western wear.

Why was Cowboy God presiding over his funeral? This was gonna take years of therapy to figure out. Wagon. Bears. Indians. Cowboys... That was it! The dude ranch. It did make sense. Just not the Wiley Coyote bump on his head and the headache.

"I go by Mark. People just call me Doc. You have a headache? Blurred vision? Seeing double, or anything crazy like that that?"

Jack answered, "I thought I was riding to my grave in a pine coffin and God was talking to me...no, nothing crazy. Just this headache." He thrust out his hand. "Jack Banyan."

"Well, Jack, toss your hat down there and lay your head on it. That might help the headache some. I'll get you some medical attention in no time."

Doc started up the team of horses as Jack lay down to watch the clouds jump across the sky some more. Jack gently fingered the golf-ball sized lump on his head.

"What happened?"

"I didn't see it, but you must have hit your head on a rock. Fell off a horse maybe..." Jack couldn't tell if that was a statement or a question. Doc just continued to drive the wagon, whistling his tune. Jack was sure he knew the song, but there was no chance he was going to get the title in his aching head. Doc seemed to be aiming the wagon at only the biggest bumps and boulders, each one pulsing a shot of pain right through his brain. Closing his eyes helped limit the pain.

After a while of riding prone in the back of the wagon, Jack sat up against the sideboard and looked at his surroundings. It was late afternoon, and the wagon was just passing the first few wooden buildings of what looked like an Old Western town. There were people walking in the streets, horses and chickens. And what was that smell? Jack was surprised but impressed. He knew he was at a first class dude ranch, but a complete Old Western town with character actors, animals? It had all the sounds and smells he imagined, plus a few unpleasant odors that he should have expected, given the livestock roaming the streets.

"Hey, I thought you said you were taking me to a hospital?"

"No. I said I was going to get you some medical attention. My office there," he pointed to one of the small plank buildings ahead of them, "is the closest thing to a hospital around here."

People began to take notice of Doc and his wagon load. There was a lot of pointing, and a few followers. They had formed a small procession by the time they pulled up in front of Doc's office. Doc hopped down off of the seat and around to the back of the wagon. He made a shooing motion with his hands.

"Move along. Move along. Nothing to see here." There was some murmuring in the crowd, but nobody went anywhere. Jack was still unsteady, so Doc helped him down out of the wagon and into his office. The crowd shuffled forward to look inside, but Doc swung the door closed and pulled the curtains.

3

"Sorry about that. It's a quiet little town. Somebody new creates quite a buzz."

Doc wet a cloth from a wash basin and laid it across Jack's bruised head. Jack wanted to ask him where the faucet was.

"Okay. No real bleeding. I don't even think you'll need a bandage. Probably will help to keep this wet cloth on it, though. Do you know how to keep it cool?" he asked.

"Wave it through the air a few times," Jack answered with an incredulous look. "I didn't get hit that hard."

"Sorry. People nowadays seem to have forgotten some of the old tricks."

There was a knock at the door.

"I guess they didn't move along."

Doc pulled opened the door, and a small crowd of people nearly fell into the room as they leaned in the doorway to get a look at the handsome stranger.

"Say, Doc. Who'd ya bring in?"

Someone else asked, "What's the matter with him?"

"He fell off a horse and bumped his head, that's all," Doc answered.

One of the men up front got right to the point. "I never seen boots like that before. If'n he dies can I have 'em?"

"I'll give three dollar for 'em," someone else offered. The bidding was up to seven dollars before Doc broke in. "Nobody is going to die today, and nobody is going to get his boots."

From the back of the crowd, Jack heard, "Well, I don't trust strangers. And we know Decker don't like strangers. Maybe you ought to fix him up and send him on his way." The general murmur of the crowd seemed in consensus with that opinion.

That would be fine with Jack. He was starting to feel left out of the situation, like he was floating above the entire scene. Everyone had been talking about him as if he weren't there. Who was Decker? What did he have against strangers, especially a likable guy like Jack? And what was that they were saying about getting his boots if he died. Surely he wasn't going to die from a bump on the head?

"Hey, Doc, maybe I should get to a hospital. Just to be sure, you know?"

"OJ, get in here. The rest of you can go on home," Doc told the crowd as he pulled a sandy-haired boy of about eleven through the door and pushed it shut behind him.

"Jack, I told you, you're not hurt that bad. Mine is the only medical facility within miles. Besides, there is nothing anyone else can do for a concussion than I am doing right here. OJ, go fetch me some water and get it boiling."

"Concussion? That sounds bad! I want you to take me..."

Gunshots from down the street stopped Jack mid-sentence. Doc opened the door a crack and peered out into the fading light. There was some shouting and another gunshot. Jack tried to stand, but the wooziness pulled him back down.

"What's going on out there?"

"Those darned Bowe brothers have a pretty skewed idea of fun," Doc cursed. "Stay here. I'll be right back."

There were more gunshots, and the sound of glass breaking. The back door opened and OJ returned carrying two buckets of water. He set them down by the fireplace, then stole a peek out the front door. Jack asked the boy what he saw.

"Zeke and Elijah and someone else are shooting stuff in the street. I think they're drunk, because they ain't hittin' much. At least not what they're aiming at. Doc is trying to get them to stop."

OJ took off toward the melee, leaving Jack alone. Curiosity got him up to the doorway to watch the altercation. Doc was indeed trying to get three drunken men, teenagers really, to holster their weapons and go home.

"But Doc, I ain't won the bet yet," said the biggest one while he clumsily waved a pistol. "Throw another bottle, Davey." One of the other men tossed a bottle about ten feet in the air, then ducked down into a defensive crouch. The shooter took three shots at the bottle, which fell to the dirt unbroken. Wood chips flew off of the face of one the buildings across the street, however. The other two drunks burst out laughing.

"Damn, Zeke. Looks like you've gravely wounded them stables!"

"Too bad we weren't betting that you could hit the broad side of a barn!"

"Listen, boys. I am going to be digging one of those bullets out of somebody if you don't stop. Now go on back inside and finish your drinks, or head on home."

An angry woman burst out of one of the recently perforated buildings.

"Ezekiel and Elijah Bowe! You boys put those guns away before someone gets hurt. I've got children in there. One of those bullets just went through my kitchen." She was Irish, angry and brandishing a rolling pin.

"Yes, ma'am," the smallest of the three answered. "Come on, Zeke. Let's go back inside. You win. You CAN shoot a bottle out of the air. At least you can when you ain't drunk." Zeke looked around for several seconds, then holstered his pistol and turned back to the others.

"Then you owe me a drink, Lij." As they started to walk back toward the saloon, the woman lowered her rolling pin.

"Aye, what has happened to this town? Strangers rolling in, shooting contests in the streets, bullets flying through my kitchen! It is not safe anymore." Zeke stopped in his tracks. He turned and advanced toward the woman.

"What strangers?"

She had only started to talk when Doc leaned over to whisper to OJ.

"Get him out the back door of the office. Put him on a horse and get him to Hope's ranch. Hurry!" OJ took off running.

OJ and Jack had just slipped out the back door when the three men burst into the office, followed by Doc.

"Where is he, Doc? And who is he?" Zeke demanded.

"I don't know who he is. I found him unconscious out past the creek fork. I bandaged him up, that's all. He's probably already gone on his way."

"He better be. You know what Bart thinks of strangers around here."

"Yes, we all do. Say, doesn't Elijah owe you a drink?"

Zeke looked at his little brother.

"What about it, Lij? Are you trying to get out of buying me that drink I won?"

"I ain't trying to get out of nothing. We came over here looking for someone, that's all."

"He ain't here, so get back to the saloon and buy me that drink." Zeke shoved Elijah back out the door.

Jack was a little wobbly, but he and OJ made it onto a couple of horses.

"Follow me," OJ called out to Jack as he spurred his horse out the back door of the stable. Moments later he walked his horse back inside, where Jack and his horse had not moved.

"Mister, you need to follow me."

"I'm trying, but the horse doesn't seem to want to go anywhere." Jack was shaking the reins, moving back and forth in the saddle, gently tapping the horse with the heel of his boots. The boy sidled his horse up close to Jack's.

"Go left out the door and out of town. It's up the road a ways to Miss Hope's ranch." With that said, the boy reached out and swatted Jack's horse on its hind quarter. The horse bolted out of the back door with Jack's arms and legs flailing wildly. The horse immediately veered off to the right. Maybe it was the disorientation, but Jack had that 'Deja Vu all over again' feeling of having been on this wild ride before. The horse continued through the alley way, then right out into middle of the main street, where they slowed to a casual walk as they passed by the gathering of people. To Doc, it looked as if Jack had purposefully sprinted right into the middle of disaster, and then decided to slow down and taunt the Bowes. Which is precisely what it looked like to the Bowes.

"Hey, you! Come over here," Zeke yelled at Jack.

Jack looked over at him silently, working the reins in all sorts of motions but achieving nothing in the way of changing the direction of the horse. To Zeke, Jack's confused look was just another taunt.

"Hey, I'm talking to you!" Zeke pulled out his pistol. Jack's eyes locked onto what appeared to be a cannon in Zeke's hand. He tried to will the horse to turn. Stop. Do anything other than just continue sauntering by the bad man with the large gun.

"There's nothing I can do," he weakly answered. Zeke ran over to a position astride Jack and his horse, and walked along beside him. His drunken mind was unable to process why this stranger had a death wish.

"What's your name, mister?" The horse continued plodding forward.

"Jack. Jack Banyan." The crowd was torn between pity and laughter. It really was comical to see Jack's ineptitude causing so much consternation in Zeke. Elijah and Davey were trailing along, as was most of the crowd by now. Finally Zeke reached out and grabbed the horse's bridle, pulling it to a stop.

"Don't you know nothing about riding a horse? Get down off of there before you hurt yourself." Zeke was talking in a pathetic tone, which really started to get Jack's ire up. This was a dude ranch. Of course Jack didn't know much about riding horses. That was the ranch's job, to get him more comfortable around horses.

"Nice boots," Zeke admired when he saw Jack's foot in the stirrup.

"Great, another comedian," Jack thought as he lifted his leg over the horse and dropped out of the saddle. His right foot had only touched the ground when Zeke lifted up and away on Jack's left foot. Jack tumbled backward onto his butt, pushing up a cloud of dust. Elijah and Davey were laughing, while the rest of the crowd was holding its collective breath. Jack was speechless. Had he just been assaulted? That was a crime. There was no way this guy was going to get away with that crap. Jack put both hands on the ground and pushed himself up. He was about half way up when Zeke placed his hand on Jack's forehead and pushed him back into the dirt. Another cloud of dust. Elijah and Davey were doubled over with laughter now.

Jack's face was hot now. That definitely qualified as assault. This guy needed a course in customer service. Looking up from the dirt, Jack asked, "What do you think you're doing?"

"What do you think YOU'RE doing? I never told you to get up."

After a short pause, Zeke reached his hand out to help Jack to his feet.

"Now, I'm telling you to get up." As soon as Jack was again halfway up, Zeke let go of his hand and Jack went back down into the dirt. Elijah and Davey were having trouble breathing. "Get up, I said," Zeke taunted him. For Jack's part, he refused to be humiliated again. He just sat there. Zeke stopped laughing and growled the order again. "I said Get Up!" This time it was accompanied by a pointed pistol.

Jack was tired of this game.

"Yeah, right. I heard you. I want to know who your supervisor is," Jack said indignantly as he managed to finally get to his feet.

"What did you say?" Zeke was unfamiliar with that term, so he looked to Davey and Elijah for clarification. They shrugged.

"Who is your boss? I want to make a complaint to your supervisor."

Still confused, Zeke was at least back on familiar bullying terms.

"Why don't you make your complaint to me, and I will pass that on to my boss for you?" Zeke fed off of the supporting laughter from Elijah and Davey.

Between laughs, Elijah managed to address Jack.

"Mister, you better stop making Zeke so mad."

"Or what?" Jack said scornfully. "He's gonna shoot me?"

The collective gasp that came from the crowd surprised Jack a bit. They sure seemed to fear this bully.

"Not a bad idea," Zeke said. He lowered his pistol and squeezed off a shot between Jack's feet.

There was a full second between the impact of the bullet in the dirt, which Jack could actually feel in his feet, and the short hop Jack made when the realization registered in his mind. The delay only angered Zeke, who fired off two more shots. These got instant jumps from Jack. Jack's mind was racing, but he couldn't translate any of the thoughts into words. This clown was shooting at him! People were standing by watching him get shot at! This just didn't happen in a civilized society. Jack finally blurted out, "Hey! You're..y...you're gonna hurt someone!"

Zeke had no idea how to respond to that. Of course he was gonna hurt someone. That was the point.

Doc tried to intervene.

"All right, Zeke. You've made your point. Let him go."

Zeke's pistol moved from Jack to Doc.

"Shut up, Doc. I ain't done yet. I want those boots."

Jack snapped his eyes down to his boots, then back up at Zeke.

"I'm not giving you my boots."

The gun came back around to point squarely at Jack's chest. Jack quickly saw the wisdom in giving up the boots, but didn't get the chance to make that call himself. Elijah and Davey had come up from behind him, each locking down an arm. Zeke put his gun away, then put all of his 220 pounds into a sledge hammer of a stomach punch that crumpled Jack back down into the dirt. With his head spinning and his lungs screaming for oxygen, he barely noticed the boots being ripped from his feet.

Zeke sat down in the street to put the boots on. It took a moment for him to work the laces. He had no idea how to tie them sober, and his drunken fingers didn't have a chance. He managed to get them knotted up and stood up admiring his new boots.

"How about letting me have them boots, Zeke?" Elijah asked his brother. "Mine barely have any soles left to em."

"Shut up and get the horses," Zeke growled back at him. "You can have my old ones if you want." Elijah walked right by the old boots that were as bad as the ones he had on, and several sizes too big. He and Davey retrieved three horses from the front of the saloon, and the three men mounted. Zeke turned to the crowd.

"You better convince your friend here to be on his way. Bart don't want no strangers causing trouble around here."

As they rode off, Elijah looked back.

"Maybe I should've gotten those socks he was wearing." Zeke and Davey just laughed at him.

Jack looked and felt pitiful. He wanted to throw up. His head was pounding. He was lying barefoot in the middle of a dirt road in front of a crowd of strangers. This had been one bruising, confusing day. Doc and a few of the crowd offered to help him up. Jack pushed them away at first, but since he couldn't get up and walk away on his own, he quietly accepted their help out of the street.

2

Jack was deposited on a bench under the porch of the saloon. His shock and disorientation was complete. He just could not figure out why the dude ranch would go so far as to hire people to kick his ass! He hadn't really done anything to them anyway. He was just minding his own business. Which is what he was going to continue to do until he could figure out just where he was, why he was getting the shit kicked out of him, and who to start the complaint process with at the dude ranch. Hell, those had to be real bullets these peckers were shooting at him! Sure, they might be well trained to miss, but what if one had ricocheted and hit somebody. Jack thought the insurance company would be interested in what kind of risks these yahoos were taking. And damn it if these actors didn't just keep on going along the script. The whole time he was laying there in the street, and while they were helping him over to the porch, they were going on about the danger, and the gall of those gunslingers, and what was this stranger doing stirring up trouble.

Once he was on the porch, and someone had brought him a metal cup of water, the confusing talk continued. The mass of people had gathered around the front of the saloon, and Doc was trying to engage them one at a time. The crowd was having none of that, with shouts coming in from all directions about lawlessness, piracy, and general skullduggery. He heard somebody complain about Indians stealing horses. It was a lot of information to absorb, and Jack was only catching some of it. It was damn hard to think with his head hurting so much to begin with, and with all these people shouting he was in genuine pain.

"Hey! Would you people stop yelling and let me get my thoughts together!" Jack looked around for a few seconds before he realized the order had come from his mouth. The surprised crowd quieted down but Jack was too grateful that the pounding had stopped to break the silence. Doc went on the offensive. He addressed the crowd and got them to shout their complaints one at a time. The town apparently had a litany of grievances about this Bart fellow and his hired guns. Jack heard from the crowd about all of the wrongs that they had suffered. Bart had been running roughshod over the town since he and his gang arrived several months ago. Every time they tried to hire a lawman, Bart had run him off, bought him off, and in one case, apparently killed him off. According to the authorities, though, that had been a clear case of suicide. Someone in the crowd voiced his disagreement with the official cause of death.

"Don't know how he managed to stab hisself 17 times, and in the back, too. Weren't no suicide." That had put a stop to anyone volunteering to wear a badge in the town. Each attempt someone made at resisting the gang was being met by an increasingly violent response. It started with small things, like threats, broken windows and fences torn down. The last person to fight back was old Ben Riley.

"They poured kerosene on his outhouse and set fire to it ... with him in it!" Ben piped in, "They blocked the door on me, too. I ain't been able to drop trou inside one of them smelly deathtraps since!"

Someone in the crowd pointed out that Bart had been buying up all of the property in the county. He had resorted to bullying and cajoling when someone was reluctant to sell, at prices usually dictated by him. No one had a specific reason why Bart was acquiring the land, other than pure greed. They all seemed to believe he had plenty of that. Someone highlighted his recent political activity. It seemed Bart was spending a lot of time with the political players in territorial politics lately. Bart had just about gotten all the land that was available. The most notable holdout, and just about the last, was a poor widow named Hope Sugar, who had refused to succumb to Bart's heavy-handed tactics. They all agreed that she wouldn't be able to hold out forever. Jack peered into the crowd, but couldn't tell if the old gal was present.

Jack was moved, but he sure didn't think he had anything to offer in the short time he was going to be around. He got a little lost in the story, and for a while thought that the events had actually been happening to these people. They were good. They must have gotten a lot of practice.

"Doc, you got some aspirin to help with this headache?" That was Jack's first order of business. Doc sent a man into the saloon for a shot of whiskey.

"Sorry, Jack. All out of aspirin. Whiskey will have to do."

Jack tried to remember what brought him to this place, but could not get any further back in his mind than Doc's wagon. He knew that he didn't belong here, unless this was all part of the dude ranch treatment. But what those men had done to him was clearly outside the lines of any regular dude ranch experience. Hitting him, knocking him to the ground, and shooting real bullets at him. Stealing his boots! Even when Jack had gone through Army boot camp he'd not been treated so badly. His head injury alone should have been enough to call time out for medical treatment in whatever dude ranch production was going on. He had read that the Bar None was an immersive experience, at least that is what they claimed in their brochure, but this was above and beyond anything he might have expected.

3

Jack was tired, sore, and confused. He was mad at the dude ranch and its hired thugs for beating him up. Most of all he was angry about being humiliated in front of the town. And those creeps had taken his boots! If this was a game to be played, he would need to play it better. Well enough to win; at least well enough to get his boots back. He wasn't sure why, or how, but maybe this was some kind of a test. There had to be a logical explanation for what was going on. Long ago he had learned that the best way out of a bad situation was to take action. Any action. It didn't matter what that action was; simply taking the offensive would change the dynamic and give him some control of the situation. The nexus of this game seemed to be the Bart problem. Someone had expressed fear that just his presence would add to the long list of problems Bart was causing the town. Besides, that was where he was going to find his boots.

He was going to need some intel on this Bart problem.

"Look, as long as we are going to play this little game, or take this little test, or whatever, I am going to need some information." The faces in the crowd stared back in silence and confusion.

"Really, I need to know where to find Bart's ranch, who are these Bowe brothers, how many men work for Bart..." Perhaps no one believed that his help would be worth all that much, because the crowd was hesitant. The first answers came reluctantly; just a trickle at first. Once the floodgates were opened, however, people long tired of repression began pouring out the answers to Jack's questions.

Jack was surprised to learn how few men it took to bully a town full of people. He surveyed the crowd, and roughly estimated sixty people. That was probably only a fraction of the town. Estimates of Bart's gang ran from fifteen to thirty. He asked the crowd why they didn't work together to stop

Bart. That was when it got real quiet. Crickets chirping in the night kind of quiet.

"That's it," he thought. "This is one of those leadership excursions that companies send their employee teams on. This might be a little more involved than zip lines and building a bridge across a creek, but he was sure the basic tests and lessons were the same. Fail alone, but succeed when everyone learns to work as a team." Jack just couldn't figure out where the rest of his team was. It would have been nice had they been around to help him with that catastrophe in the street earlier.

Jack had only received in the mail last week the gift certificate for the Bar None. There had been no indication it was from his work, but he was certain that the rest of his team must be around here somewhere. He hoped not Steve from accounting. That blowhard was always jumping in and taking charge, whether he had a clue what was going on and how to fix it, or not. Steve knew very little about leadership. He would have been the first officer fragged in the Army. Maybe Stephanie is along for the trip. He didn't actually work together with the curvy little redhead. In fact they almost never had any contact unless Jack could find a reason to go by the finance office. That didn't stop Jack from dreaming a little. She would be a great asset on his bridge-building team. A mischievous grin came across his lips as he pictured her getting soaked in some cold creek water. This might be a fun little adventure after all.

The townspeople sure seemed to have their panties in a wad over a few bullies. Most of them just wanted to avoid the trouble that they were certain was coming their way. Doc was trying to keep everyone calm, and was advising a passive approach. He cautioned that Bart's gang hadn't gotten really violent yet. Nobody had been seriously hurt. A few broken windows, a couple of scrapes, a little dancing in the street. No real harm had come.

"Sure," Jack thought. "Old Ben Riley is too scared to take his morning constitutional anymore, and the whole town had watched Zeke and Elijah make a fool of me. And what about the faux suicide? All that, and Doc wanted everyone to take the high road. Well, maybe that was just the plot line. Whatever it took to get the leadership exercise started.

Doc managed to convince the crowd to go home for the night.

"We need to get you cleaned up and fed, Jack. I don't really have a place for you to sleep, though. I have a cot and OJ sleeps on some blankets on the floor." Doc asked a smallish man named Adolf to take Jack in. Adolf, in a very German accent, offered his barn and breakfast in the morning. As the crowd thinned and walked off, Jack saw a beautiful blonde woman standing quietly by herself and taking it all in. He hadn't heard her speak during the gathering. He wished she had. One look at her and he wanted to know what she sounded like, what she thought, who she was and everything else about her. He said a quick silent prayer that she had somehow missed his performance in the street with Zeke. She came up closer to the porch. In the flickering glow of the lanterns she was positively angelic. Jack was trying to think of something witty to say before he lost his opportunity.

"Doc, you better keep an eye on this tenderfoot. He is liable to get himself, or somebody else, hurt. I'm not so sure he is completely stable, mentally speaking."

That ended the search for something witty to say. Jack looked down at his socks.

"Here one day and I've already lost my boots," he muttered, a little louder than he intended.

"I sure hope you get those back. You dance a very nice jig in them," she said on her way past Jack. So she had witnessed his embarrassment. She smiled a little when she said it. Seeing that smile was almost worth the stinging shame...almost. His cheeks flushed red.

"Come tomorrow, I am going to kick some Bowe brother ass!" he thought as he watched her fade into the darkness.

4

Zeke was getting tired of hearing it. They had only been riding for fifteen minutes, but he'd heard Lij ask for those boots six times. Whine, whine, whine. That was all Lij had been doing since before he could remember, and tonight Lij was at his worst...

"Why do you get the boots?"

"You already have a good pair of boots"

"Please, can I have the boots?"

It was making Zeke's head hurt to hear it over and over again. That crap might have worked when they were growing up and Ma always came to his rescue, but Zeke wasn't about to let him get away with it now.

"Quit yer belly aching, Lij. I ain't giving you these boots." Sometimes growling was all it took. Other times it took an ass-whoopin'.

Zeke turned to Davey.

"You ever seen a pair of fancy boots like these?" Davey didn't talk much, but he always wore nice clothes and had a real fine saddle. He had been to St Louis once, so he definitely knew more about the world than they did.

"Nope, never have," was all Davey offered.

Zeke felt like rubbing a little salt into Elijah's wound.

"They sure are the nicest thing I ever put my foot in. They wrap right around your feet and make them feel like two babies all swaddled in blankets. I swear it's like putting your toes into a tub of butter!"

"Now what would you want to go sticking your feet into butter fer?" The salt was stinging Elijah. "You'd just get your feet all slippery and you can damn well bet you just ruined the whole tub. I ain't eating anything that's had your nasty toes a'wigglin' in it!"

"It don't matter anyway, Lij. Your foot is way too small to go into this here boot. They fits me perfect, like they was made for me. The way I see it, I am just like that story gal that gets to marry the prince cause her foot fits into that fancy slipper. And these are MY fancy slippers, Lij. Got it?"

Davey spoke before Elijah could answer.

"What's that in the road up there?" The three stopped their horses and peered ahead at a shadowy figure in the darkness. It was a single mounted rider coming toward them. The silence was broken by the sound of weapons cocking on all sides of them. They had to fight their natural inclination to draw their pistols. The rider was an Indian, carrying a rifle pointed at Zeke. Three more Indians appeared on the sides of the road.

"Guns down on ground," was the first order issued by the mounted Indian. Their hands went slowly to their waists and unlatched their belts. The Indians on the ground quickly snatched up the gun belts and grabbed the reins of the horses.

"Off."

The men got off of their horses, and the Indians climbed on. The Indians were speaking in their own language and laughing. Zeke was certain they were making fun of Elijah whining. That was probably how the Indians knew they were coming. If they got killed, it would be that whiner's fault. One of the Indians looked into his saddle bags and let out a whoop as he pulled out three bottles of whiskey. That seemed to make the Indians happier than the guns and horses they had captured.

"Walk."

The men started to walk off, hearing more taunting and laughing from the Indians. Elijah leaned over to Zeke.

"At least they ain't' taking them fancy boots."

Before they knew it, they were again surrounded by Indians, this time staring into the barrels of their own guns. The lead brave looked down at their feet, then back at Zeke's tortured face. Zeke could see the Indian's boots were stolen cavalry issue. They were worn through and the sole flapped at the toe. He was praying under his breath.

"Don't take the boots. Don't take the boots. Don't take the boots." He knew it was hopeless, though. The Indian simply pointed his gun at Zeke's feet and, as before, uttered a single command.

"Boots."

The Indians rode off, leaving the three of them standing in the road. Elijah was trying to hide his glee that Zeke didn't get to keep the boots. He knew better than to press his luck on this one. One look at Zeke confirmed that he had more to fear from Zeke than he had from the Indians.

"Ohhh Zeke, I am sooooo sorry. Them Injuns got no right to take them fancy slippers of yours. We'll get em back for you. You and me and Davey. We'll hunt them Injuns down and get back what they wrongfully took from ya. They's gonna pay, Zeke. We'll make em pay."

It wasn't going to work. Zeke advanced on Elijah.

"Somebody's gonna pay, all right. Somebody's big mouth is gonna pay for them boots! What you gotta go shooting your big mouth off for about them boots anyway, damn you." Zeke gave Elijah a two handed shove that sent him sprawling back into the dirt. Zeke went on, mimicking Elijah's whiny tone.

"Hey Mr. Injun, are you sure you wanna leave without stealing them fancy slippers my brother's wearing? You sure would look mighty powerful dancing around them wigwam fires in those fancy boots my brother's wearing!" Elijah's eyes darted back and forth, looking for a place to run. He would need trees or bushes to dart in and out of. Elijah was quicker than Zeke, but Zeke would catch him in a straight footrace. Especially when he was mad as he was now.

"You got an ass whoopin' coming, Lij. An ever-loving' ass-whoopin'. Only right now you're gonna get your ass up off the ground and fetch us some fire wood, cause it's gonna be a cold night and we've got us a long walk back to the ranch come morning."

Elijah got up slowly. He hated those 'ass-whoopings to come.' They always popped up out of nowhere, and he would be worried sick about when he was going to get it.

"And you better come up with a good story for why Bart's whiskey is getting drunk by an Indian raiding party of thirty braves."

"But I didn't see no Injuns but them four that robbed us, Zeke?"

"I ain't going back to the ranch and telling all them fellas that I walked right into an Indian trap and let four braves steal everything I own, and Bart's whiskey to boot! How many Indians did you see, Davey?"

"Hard to tell, Zeke. Coulda been forty."

Elijah stepped slowly into the brush to find some firewood. When he returned, Zeke was forcing his feet into the Indian's old cavalry boots and muttering about butter. A long, slow smile spread across Elijah's lips.

5

Jack slept right through the crowing roosters and buzzing flies. It was the goat licking his face that finally woke him. That and ... a deep-voiced German woman singing opera? That certainly fit the model for how his conscious periods had been starting lately. He had slept pretty well for a guy in a stable. That was probably due to the two large glasses of homemade beer that he and Adolph drank last night. Once they had gotten back to the stable, Adolph asked Jack if he wanted something that would make that headache go away. Thinking he meant Ibuprofen or Acetaminophen, Jack was pleasantly surprised when Adolph emerged from a storage room carrying two glasses full of brew.

"Family recipe I brought wit me from de old country. It is even bitta here in America."

Even at room temperature, it was surprisingly refreshing. Jack asked for a second, telling Adolph how much he enjoyed the first one.

"Can you imagine how good this would be cold?" Jack asked.

"Cold beer?" Adolph thought for a moment.

"Ya, I think so," he decided. "But for now I must keep hidden out here. Frau Coors does not know of my little hobby."

That got Jack's attention, but since he had no idea what to think of the historical reference to the brewing company, he left it alone.

This morning's singing was coming from what had to be Frau Coors. The large woman was sitting on a stool next to the goat squirting milk into a pail. She looked up, feigning surprise that he just happened to be awake. She spoke very little English, but she managed to get her point across.

"You work," she said, leaving the chore to Jack.

Jack sat up, then took her place on the stool. He remembered doing this once as a kid at the petting zoo, so most of the milk made it into the pail, with only an occasional squirt across his pant leg. He even got in a shot at the cat, which he figured was payback for all the cat indifference throughout history. The cat didn't seem to mind. When he took the full pail into the kitchen, Jack was invited to sit down to breakfast with Adolph's family. After he had his fill of sausage and eggs, Adolf sent him out with one of his boys to get the lay of Dawson's Creek and its people.

Few of the establishments were open, and the streets were mostly empty. What impressed Jack about the Bar None and its replica town was its complete authenticity. He could see a dusty cowhand sleeping in the dirt at the bottom of a staircase. The stairs led up the side of a two story building. The sign in front read Dawson's Creek Saloon and Hotel. There was a general store next to the saloon, and a barber next to that. They walked by the open door of a church. Jack poked his head inside, causing the preacher to take notice. Jack slipped out and kept moving along the walkway, not wanting to invite a sermon. He had spent less time with preachers than he had with cats in his lifetime, and that was about right in his book.

"Pardon me, Sir. Jack, wasn't it?" The preacher had popped outside behind Jack. Jack's shoulders dropped a little before he turned and greeted the preacher. They spent the next fifteen minutes locked in conversation. Locked, because as much as Jack tried to move along, he was held in the preacher's invisible, but all too real, grasp. Jack did learn a few things about the town, but mostly he got the standard recruiting pitch and start times for Sunday Mass. He also got some sage advice on walking softly around Bart and his gang.

After they had cleared earshot range of the church, Adolph's son offered, "Ma says those Cat Lickers drink too much, and that's why they sleep so late. 'Alcohol is the devil's brew' she is always sayin'." Jack figured that explained Adolph's little secret, and he wondered how long Adolph would be able to keep up his private venture. They passed by other storefronts along the street. A livery/tack shop, hardware store, candle maker, a couple of general stores. There was a law office and another church for the

Baptists. The town had a restaurant where Jack stopped inside to meet the owner, Mary Scoggins. Jack got four words in, "Hi. I am Jack," before Mary started off on a monologue. In the space of ten minutes, Jack knew Mary's life history (Scotland, married, Ellis Island, wagon train out West, widowed, available), the lowdown on those Baptists (no fun, always sticking their nose into other people's business), and the town's history. Mary told him how the town and creek got its name. Dawson was the English pronunciation for an Indian name. She went on to tell the story of Little White Dove and Running Brave. Legend held that the two forbidden lovers from different tribes on opposite sides of the creek drowned in the center of the Spring runoff-swollen creek as they swam to their first kiss. Da Sun was the Indian phrase for young love.

Before Jack left, he had an invitation to dinner any time, a picnic or 'whatever'. He was beginning to feel as trapped as he had in front of the church. He was saved by the sound of a bell ringing, and Adolph's boy saying that school was starting. Mary assured him that she would see him later as Jack backpedalled out of the door with the boy.

"Whew! Thanks for pulling me out of there, kid."

"Sure, Mister. Ma says that once Miss Mary gets her hooks into a man, her feet are constantly floating up to the ceiling. I didn't want to see no hooks in you, Mr. Jack, nor Miss Mary walking on the ceiling."

Jack laughed.

"No, that wouldn't be a pretty sight."

The boy went into the school house, and Jack continued with his tour of the town. There were many houses on this side of town, if that is what you would call them. They were mostly single room shacks built from planks. There were also homes made of mud bricks stacked up. Some were logs mortared together with mud. There sure weren't any building codes. The people he met were friendly for the most part, but they did harbor some reservation about opening up to him. He wasn't sure if their resistance was their fear of strangers and Bart, or if they didn't think Jack was going to last long enough to bother getting to know.

It was talking to some women washing clothes in the creek where Jack got a different story on the town's history. This one was based on a legend of an Indian attack on a wagon train here. The entire Dawson family was killed or taken captive by the raiding Indians. The captured men were tortured and killed, and the women were still reported to be alive as slaves in some far off Indian village. The town was only about eight years old. Doc had been there from the beginning. Most of the others came with wagon trains and mining rushes. Everyone had great expectations with the coming of the continental railroad and the opening up of the West. Jack found it interesting that while the authenticity of the Bar None was top notch, they had flaws in the backstory. Maybe there was supposed to be a few differences, so that it seemed more realistic. He couldn't see how that would matter, but he would ask Doc later to see which version he corroborated.

Whatever the dude ranch was up to, and whoever put them up to it, this had to cost a fortune to set up and run. Even reusing the facilities and storylines each week, the operating costs had to be enormous. Dozens of salaries to pay, animals all over the place, and there had to be insurance costs, what with all the risks this place took. That sure pointed to corporate sponsorship for his little adventure. Maybe today would provide a few answers.

OJ ran by him on his way to the school house.

"If I don't get in there quick, Mr. Johnson is going to tan my hide."

Corporal punishment? It had been a long time since Jack had heard of students getting spanked. That wasn't such a bad idea.

Before OJ took off in a rush for the little wooden school building, he told Jack that Doc had gone off to Denver, and left instructions that Jack should ride out to Hope's ranch and see if she could use a hand with anything. That worked for Jack. A little time away from this confusing arena might help him clear his head. If he could help a little old widow lady with a project or two, all the better. He walked back in the direction of the stable, grinning as he imagined the frightful image poor Werner held of Miss Mary, with her hidden hooks and ability to walk on the ceiling.

6

Jack started off in the direction of Hope's ranch. He got some very specific directions from the stable boy before he left.

"Take that there road up yonder a piece."

That was about all the information he needed, since Doc's horse, Charley, had his own plan for the trip. Charley mostly went where and when he wanted to. He stopped at his whim, and no amount of prodding from Jack could get him started again. When he was inclined to start up again, he did so with no particular hurry. When Jack finally appeared coming up the road to Hope's ranch much later in the morning, he was walking ahead of Charley, leading him by the reins. Hope's dog Biscuit announced their arrival as soon as they were within sight.

Jack's pace picked up when he saw Hope standing on the porch. This was no little old widow. This was a beautiful blonde woman in her twenties. His heart leapt as he realized it was the same beautiful woman he had spoken to last night. Well, she had spoken to him, anyway.

"God Bless Doc," he thought as he waved and shouted "Hello there."

He tied Charley up to the porch rail, not bothering to take off the saddle or blanket. Hope invited him into the house for coffee. Jack learned a lot about Hope in the short time that they spoke. Her trusting personality was apparent right from the start. She had no problems opening up to him, telling him her short history as a rancher in the territory. She had been married, and came out West with her husband James. They put down roots at Dawson's Creek about 4 years ago. There were Indian troubles early on, until she and her husband learned to trade with the tribe. James succumbed to a fever after only a year. She didn't give returning to Philadelphia more than a passing thought. Philadelphia was downright stifling to a woman who spoke her mind. Although it was rough going for a while, and it was a mostly solitary

31

existence, she had been living alone and running the ranch by herself since. Doc looked after her, and OJ helped her out sometimes. Jack noticed that she never seemed to be complaining about any of the difficulties, just stating them as facts. He was impressed by her toughness and independence, and he couldn't stop thinking about how beautiful she was. It felt completely natural sitting and talking to her over coffee. He realized he was lost in fantasy and not listening to her. When he tuned back in, she had gone from stating history to expressing her dreams to him.

"To be truthful with you, I've been thinking about packing up and heading for San Francisco. It sounds so pretty from the stories I've heard."

Hope was startled to hear herself say these things to a stranger. She hadn't even allowed herself to complete those thoughts to herself. There was something about talking with Jack, though, that made her open up. She felt as if she could confide in him. She shrugged that off to his being a stranger, but knew that there was a bit of denial in that explanation. She really enjoyed talking to Jack, and that was what scared her. She stood up and announced that she had work to do. It wasn't that she didn't want to continue talking with him. There just didn't seem to be a point to it. There really was work to be done, and sitting with Jack didn't seem to have much of a payoff. She did admit to herself that she was attracted to him, though. She wanted to be with a man something terrible. It had been three long years since her husband had died, and increasingly she missed the companionship, and the intimacy. That had been one of the best parts of being married. Living on her own all this time had adjusted her thinking in many ways. What was so important about being married to someone before having sex with them? She was ready for sex, but with someone she chose, someone she wanted. Her affection was a valuable commodity and she was not going to just sling it around. Jack suited the "want" requirement. He was a good looking son of a gun, with his chiseled features and lean build. He wasn't much in the "manly" category, though. He couldn't ride a horse, and those Bowe boys had made him look silly. That was ice in her veins. She needed much more than that from a man.

Jack saw the gesture for what it was. She had seen him helpless, humiliated and pitiful in the street yesterday. Of course she didn't see much in him. But that had all been just an elaborate stage play, and she knew that. Jack decided that this had to be part of the exercise. The story wasn't even all that original. Hadn't he seen this episode on TV, where the drifter joined forces with the tough, prairie woman to stand up to the rich, powerful cattle baron? Or was that Dukes of Hazard, and the pretty lady was standing up to Boss Hogg? Wherever he'd seen it before didn't matter. What did matter was that when they were done with the play acting, Jack wanted to get to know this pretty lady much better.

This was his make or break point. Story line or not, if he walked away here he had no shot. Not now, not later.

"Maybe I can move whatever this story line is in my own direction," he hoped. "Maybe it is only a rough draft, and I can direct it more than follow it?" Jack tried a little self-degrading humor.

"Well maybe the next time you're in town, we can have a dance together. Only this time nobody will be shooting at us." There was only silence where Jack was expecting at least a gratuitous laugh.

"Note to self: Self-deprecating humor is not appreciated by women in the Old West," he chided himself. She just looked at him in a way that made him doubly uncomfortable. Then he realized what it was that she needed. She needed to see him as a man. He was going to have to impress this girl. Showing off by picking up something really heavy passed through his mind. He felt the clock ticking on his opportunity, but he could think of nothing. Come on, Jack. How are you going to demonstrate some value to her?

"Maybe I can give you a hand, then. Surely you have some jobs that you need an extra set of hands to get done?" She would see that he was trying, which he hoped was at least a small positive in his favor.

Hope did have some things that needed doing, some things that it would take more than her and a boy to do. And it wouldn't hurt to let him earn that cup of coffee.

"Sure, you can help," she said. "We can start with that old stump in the front."

They spent about an hour digging at the base of the stump. Hope rigged her horse up to some tackle blocks and lines that she attached to the stump. The horse was resisting the work with turns and kicks, but she managed to get it pulling in the right direction with some effort. It was slow, exhausting work, but after a while the stump was ripped from the earth. They walked over to the stream for a cool down.

"This is a beautiful stream," Jack told her, trying to make conversation. "Does it run all year?"

"It slows to a trickle by the end of summer. There is a perfect place for a little pond right down there." She pointed to a spot where the stream ran through a low lying area and exited through a rocky crevice beneath a thick trunked tree.

"I have tried to dam it up several times, but my dams just wash away in the spring runoff."

"Why not move that boulder into the crevice?" Jack asked without a moment's reservation.

Hope had no immediate response. She stared in disbelief at the mammoth boulder that Jack so casually thought could be moved thirty yards.

"That would take a team of four, maybe six horses to drag that boulder through the dirt. And that is only possible because it is on a downhill slope."

"But it would work?" he asked.

"I suppose it could," she nodded, somewhat reluctantly. She mentally added that to the growing list of large projects that her ranch required. Maybe in the Fall she could get some of the other ranchers to bring by some extra pulling horses, and there would also have to be a harness worked out.

Jack jumped up and went right to work. He pulled an axle and the four wheels off of Hope's wagon, and set her to work wiring metal scuppers all along the outside of the wheels. He took the pulley off of the rail hoist over the barn and tied it around the trunk of the tree near the creek. They built a sturdy stand next to the running creek and mounted the water wheel. Jack designed a frame and sled runners from extra wood lying in the barn, and placed it in an area that they dug out around the base of the boulder. After much prying and pushing, they got the boulder to slide down onto the sled. Finally, he attached a rope to the wheel and to the sled after threading it through the pulley. The rope tightened and the sled started moving. They had to use all their strength to guide the sled, but in a matter of moments the boulder crashed down into the crevasse and the water began back-filling into a pond. They stood under the tree, clapping and shouting together.

"I can't believe you just did that! I never knew water could be so powerful."

"WE just did that. Easy Peasy," replied Jack with a smile.

"Easy Peasy?" asked Hope. "Who says that? What does it mean?"

"I don't know who else says it, but whenever I have a job that seems impossible that I am somehow going to get done, I say Easy Peasy. It puts me into the right, positive frame of mind," he answered. "And," Jack added with a triumphant smile, "We didn't have to deal with any smelly, kicking horses." He held his right hand high over his head.

"High five!"

Hope looked at him for a moment, then reached up and grasped his hand in hers. She jumped up and down and shouted.

"Oh Jack, I love it!"

It wasn't exactly the reaction he was expecting, but Jack was beaming. He was embarrassed at how much her few words of praise had made him feel like a hero. She had a way of making him feel important like no one else. He really liked this girl. He wanted to be her hero.

7

The arrival of the gift certificate via Next Day Mail had Jack perplexed. There was nothing in the From block and no accompanying letter. Had he won 2nd prize in that annual magazine clearing house sweepstakes? Someone else gets the big, 3 foot check for a million dollars and he gets a week at a dude ranch? Maybe it was from Brittany...or was it Bethany. Damn it, he was going to have to start writing these girls names down the next day. Unlikely, whatever her name was. Sure, the sex was great that night a couple of weeks ago, but slipping out in the morning and not calling was, as usual, not going to be rewarded. Unless this was some sort of reality TV revenge show! Actually, that possibility had merit...a reality show of paybacks to one-night-stand artists and cheaters. Maybe there were cameras everywhere, taping the complete ass kicking he'd gotten, his mounting confusion and the coming mental breakdown. Finally, when the poor bastard is in some dusty corner of the saloon, all broken and curled up in the fetal position, the girl marches in with a camera crew and a microphone.

"That's why you shouldn't be such a pig! Would it have killed you to stay through breakfast? Maybe call like you said you would?!!!!"

A swift kick in the nuts and ratings through the roof...possible!

If it had been four years ago, Jack would have put money on the gift certificate coming from Mr. and Mrs. Bradford. Better known as Rachel's parents; his future in-laws. Only the dude ranch certificate would have been their way of finding a way to kill him. Maybe falling off a horse, crushed in a stampede, rattlesnake bite, getting shot by a drunk cowboy...whatever would keep him from marrying their daughter. Never had Jack run into anyone that disliked him so much. Not so much dislike as distrust. And they were right all along. By the time Jack realized all the reasons he was getting married didn't include love, Rachel was trying on wedding dresses and narrowing down the guest list. When Jack last saw the Bradfords, their frosty dismissal let Jack know that, although they may have harbored a desire to see him dead, they were no longer compelled to act on the impulse. The look of relief in their eyes was like that of hurricane evacuees watching television in some inland hotel as they see the eye of the storm take a sudden turn and spare their evacuated home from certain destruction. No, the gift certificate hadn't come from them.

Jack still wasn't entirely sure why he decided to validate the certificate and make the trip to the Bar None. Things went wrong from the beginning. The brochure had suggested bringing western wear. That meant a trip to one of those stores with a huge boot for a sign. Several hundred dollars later he had all the straight-cut, button-fly jeans and shirts with pearl snaps on them that he could shove into a suitcase. What he did not have was a pair of boots. No matter how many boots he tried on, Jack could not feel comfortable in a pair of cowboy boots. The high heel made him lean forward as he stood, and the pointed toes just looked silly to him. Jack told himself that there was no way Wyatt Earp ever hiked a mile in something like these boots. Jack was a hiker. He had taken to wearing Nike hiking boots and swore by them. His cowboy days were going to be spent in those hiking boots. He didn't care if he looked the part or not.

The shuttle van that picked him up for the ride out of the city to the ranch had been late. Jack was the last pickup, so there was only one seat open. That ride had been the longest two hours of Jack's life. He was seated between a thirteen year old girl and her eight year old brother. They must have been bickering for quite a while already, and the open seat between them meant to be a demilitarized zone. The arguments continued, with Jack fulfilling the ineffectual role of the UN peacekeeper. They argued about who started the argument, who ALWAYS came into the other one's room without permission, who ALWAYS bugged the other when they were on the phone. They would lean forward, lob a verbal artillery shell across No Man's Land (Jack's lap), then bounce back upright in their seat. Most annoying was the ad nauseum, "You're stupid; no, you're stupider; no I'm not; yes you are..." Jack was trying to choose between hanging or carbon monoxide when the girl declared, "I'm not going to talk to you anymore," and started tapping into her cell phone.

"The United Nations declares JustinBieberLand the victor and is eternally grateful for the peace and stability to the region," Jack mused.

"Who wants to talk to a stupid girl, anyway?" the boy said.

"I am NOT stupid! Mom, he's calling me names again!"

"So much for unilateral disarmament," Jack thought as he closed his eyes and worked through how to tie the noose.

He usually tried to make a mental map of places that he went, but he was so distracted by the siblings' border war that he was surprised when the van came to a stop in front of a beautifully restored, or at least a model of, an Old West ranch house. He jumped out of the van as fast as he could. The rusted, bent metal sign hanging over the front porch told him he had arrived at the 'Bar None Ranch'. That was when the boots got noticed. He hadn't even gotten inside the front door before the snide comments began:

"Hey Preppie."

"I guess you're why they call it a 'dude' ranch."

"Mister, them ain't cowboy boots."

What business it was to the bunch of drugstore cowboys hanging out on the porch, Jack couldn't figure out. He was looking forward to watching them all bandaging up the blisters they were going to have on day two and three of wearing their new, 'authentic' cowboy boots.

At the front desk, Jack was greeted by a cute college-aged girl with his keys and an itinerary.

"Go on up and drop your stuff in your room. There's no time to put it in dressers and get settled in. Your trail ride starts in thirty minutes. Remember, technology is a no-no. No computers, no cell phones, no tablets, no day planners here. Don't even think about bringing that stuff with you.

There is no Wi-Fi, and you probably can't get a cell phone signal anyway. Just relax for a week off of the grid."

No technology---a week off the grid, she had said. That was a hard thing to tell a guy who worked in the electronics industry. He perused the gear he had spread out on his bed as soon as he got to his room; book reader, laptop, cell phone, GPS, camera. It was amazing that he could carry all of that stuff in one bag. He wasn't sure why he had brought all of it, anyway. Most of the items did eighty percent of the same things the others did. He looked them all over, then decided that he could live without everything. Everything but the cell phone. No way was he going to be completely without some type of communication device. What if a girl called?

Then there had been Diablo. Seriously. A horse named Diablo. At a dude ranch. That huge beast was black as coal, with eyes that bulged out of their sockets. Eyes that spoke. Those eyes said 'I am every bit the Devil my name implies. Please, just try to put your city slicker butt in that saddle. Just try it.' Everyone else preparing for the afternoon trail ride was feeding apples and carrots to their Shetland ponies, with names like Cupcake and Butterscotch. Jack was afraid that if Diablo wanted a snack, it would be his arm up to the elbow. He looked for the exit, wondering if this really wasn't someone's effort to rub him out.

The ride started out calmly enough. Diablo was deceitfully compliant about the whole ride idea while the ranch staff was watching. They filed out of the corral and onto the trail single file. Diablo was almost manageable, for a while. Even though they proceeded along the trail with the group, Jack never really felt like he was driving. Mostly, Jack was a passenger in a single seat taxi cab. Jack had just begun to relax when his taxi driver, Diablo, started weaving in and out of the traffic lane to get around the other cars...or riders. Jack had been on a cab ride or two like that before. All it took was a short comment to the driver about throttling back a little and he would back down and go with the flow of traffic. Only with Diablo driving, not so much. Diablo clearly possessed more testosterone than Cupcake, Butterscotch and the other horses, because he insisted on making his way to the front and leading this troop. Darrell, the college kid trail boss charged with escorting the troop today, kept offering helpful suggestions to Jack on how to keep Diablo in line.

"Hey Buddy, what's your hurry?"

"Just pull back a little on those reins and he'll do what you want him to." Jack thought it would be nice if Darrell would make the suggestions directly to Diablo, since the horse was not heeding any inputs from Jack.

Darrell was mostly interested in the pretty blonde riding near the front of the line. Jack had flirted with Meghan some in the stable before the ride started, but the thought of hooking up quickly left his mind as his Devil horse was presented to him. While Darrell would occasionally ride up and back down the line of riders, he spent most of the time riding shotgun next to Meghan, impressing her with his extensive trail boss skills of riding a horse and spitting tobacco. The closer Diablo got to the front of the line, the more his machismo took over. The quick spurt of line jumping changed to a lope past two or three riders at a time. Jack nearly lost his head to a low branch as Diablo focused only on getting in front of the lesser animals. Darrell noticed the commotion and took the opportunity to impress Meghan.

"Hey now. We are all going to same place. You don't have to be in front," he shouted. To Meghan he added, "Don't you just hate drivers that have to weave in and out of traffic?" Darrell pulled up on his reins and wheeled around to take charge of the situation. Making a big deal of cutting off Jack and grabbing his reins, and looking back to make certain Meghan was duly impressed, Darrell started leading Diablo and Jack to the back of the procession.

"Back of the line for you two. Now take charge of your horse and stay in line. Ya gotta show the horse who's boss, ya know." With that, Darrell spun his horse around like The Lone Ranger and easily loped back up to the front of the line. Jack thought he could see Darrell suck in his gut and

41

straighten up in the saddle as he rode past Meghan. She glowed. "How could she be buying into this act," Jack had fumed. There would be no blonde for dessert, at least not for Jack. He sunk down into his saddle and hoped for a quiet ending to this dreadful ride.

Apparently, Diablo didn't take to being shamed any more than Jack did. As they came to a bend in the trail, Diablo picked up his pace again and resumed the same passing maneuvers as before. This time, however, the horse in front of Diablo also did not like being the last in line and lunged forward. This spooked the next horse and caused a chain reaction of mass confusion at the tail of the line. Diablo chose this moment to veer off in an entirely different direction. Jack tried to turn Diablo by pulling on either rein but got no response. He tried a few short 'Whoa's'. He tried to yank back hard on the reins, but mostly he fought to stay on the horse as they careened in and out of the underbrush, around solid tree trunks and under low branches. It took a while for Jack to decide his pride was expendable and he needed to call for help from Darrell. When he did try to yell, he couldn't squeeze much volume out of his lungs as Diablo bounced him in and out of the saddle. Jack was frantically searching for a soft spot for a self-imposed ejection when the decision was made for him. As he looked up from surveying the ground for a suitable place to jump, a large branch filled his vision like an oncoming train. The blow knocked Jack back in a somersault over Diablo's tail and onto the ground, where Jack spent the next several minutes counting the stars in his blurry universe.

8

The day of searching for his idiot ranch hands had taken a toll on Bart. They had ridden all over the countryside and had not come across any sign of those Bowe brothers and Davey. They had stopped at a few ranches, pushed around some homesteaders, caught sight of a few wandering Indian braves riding horses, but they'd not had even a sniff of those idiots. Bart wasn't sure what was more important to him---finding his cowhands or getting the whiskey they were carrying back to him. He was tired and wanted that drink, a feeling he'd had more and more often lately. At least the next stop on the trail held some promise. That Hope Sugar was fine. He had seen many women in his time in this man's country...spindly, weathered, Bible thumping prairie dogs mostly. Hope was a pleasure to look at. More than that, though, she had personality. Sure, Bart got what he needed from the whores. There were always plenty of whores in the West. What Bart wanted was a woman with a brain. That was Hope. He knew it from the first time he had ridden by her ranch to tell her he was going to buy it. It was a shame, a pretty widow like that living all by herself. He would have to make a big deal of those Indians they had seen earlier. A little fear might help prod her in his direction. He had thought many times about going over there in the night and just taking what he wanted. But he knew he would never be able to win her like that. He was interested in the long-term gain. A smart, attractive woman like that at his side would be very helpful in the political world. No, she would come around. He was already the richest man around, and with all of his political dealings he was moving up the powerful list. Persistence would win this race. The competition was laughable; smelly cowhands and dirt poor farmers. A town full of cowardly shopkeepers. She would come to him if he just played his cards right.

Bart and his men rode up to the front of Hope's ranch house. He instructed his men to take the horses down to the stream, or what looked like a new pond, and water them. He wanted them as far away from his prize as possible. There was no need to take unnecessary chances. Bart hopped down off of his horse hoping to be invited in. Hope came out of the doorway looking radiant as usual. Bart's face lit up. He was halfway through the tipping of his hat and a "Good day, Mrs. Sugar" when his expression sagged. Jack had followed Hope out of the door way, and was now leaning up against the porch post like he owned the place.

"Good day, Mr. Decker. You are a long way from home?"

Bart was too far off balance to answer her immediately. He tried to size up Jack without taking his eyes off of Hope. He couldn't seem to form the words that he wanted his mouth to say.

"Well, yes...um...we are... a long way from home." was all that he could get out.

Seconds passed---Bart's eyes flicked from Hope to Jack, then back. He recovered a little.

"Yes, we sure are. We're out here looking for a few of my boys. They didn't come home last night, like they were planning to."

"I see some of your men over there watering your horses. Now which boys didn't make it home to their warm beds to get tucked in last night? It wouldn't be those rotten Bowe brothers and their fool acquaintance, Davey, would it?

That was a second surprise for Bart. How had she known who was missing?

"It is them, in fact. Do you know anything of their whereabouts?"

"After the ruckus they started in town last night, I don't think anyone in Dawson's Creek would miss them if they disappeared from God's Green Earth."

So his boys stirred up some trouble. That wouldn't be the first time, nor the last.

"Well now Mrs. Sugar I don't know about any trouble in town last night. I'm just looking for some of my boys that should have come home. Have you any idea where they might be?"

"No, Mr. Decker, I do not make it a habit to keep track of your ranch hands."

Seeing that he wasn't going to get anything from Hope, Bart changed tack.

"I'm sorry, Mrs. Sugar. I don't believe I've had the pleasure of meeting your gentleman friend."

"The name's Banyan. Jack Banyan," Jack answered for her.

Bart instantly disliked Jack. Who was this stranger? What was a strange man doing at her place all alone? Where did this new competition come from?

"Got them all watered, Mr. Decker." Bart's men had come up from the stream. Bart heard but did not acknowledge.

"So you're new around here, Mr. Banyan?"

"That's right."

"Are you planning to stay long?"

"I don't rightly know."

"Where are you coming from?"

"Oh I've been all over," answered Jack. "Most recently from Denver."

"What exactly do you do, Mr. Banyan? I can always use another hand at the Decker Ranch if you're any good with a horse."

That brought a snicker to Hope's face and an outright laugh from Jack.

"No, Mr. Decker. I don't believe horse riding is my strongest quality. But thank you for your offer."

Bart's face distorted into one of disdain. There was something familiar about this stranger, but Bart was certain they had never met. He was used to getting a lot more respect from people around here, especially in front of his men and a lady. There would come a time when Jack would learn that. He was going to enjoy teaching Jack Banyan that lesson. Tired of asking questions and getting not much in response, he turned his attention back to Hope.

"Mrs. Sugar, you should keep an eye out. We passed by an Indian raiding party earlier today. We saw 3 or 4 of those devils, and you never know how many were there that you didn't see." He paused to let the words sink in.

"Have you given any further consideration to the generous offer I've made for the purchase of your land?"

"I don't need to give it further consideration, Mr. Decker. I'm not selling my ranch. As I told you the last time you asked, this is my home."

"Yes, I understand, Mrs. Sugar. Perhaps, then, you've reconsidered my offer to join me for dinner at my home."

"Thank you kindly, Mr. Decker, for your offer. I will have to decline again."

While Bart was expecting that answer, it wasn't easy to hear it. Biting his tongue, Bart bid her good day and mounted his horse. He and his men rode off in the direction of Dawson's Creek, with Hope's dog Biscuit barking after them. Jack and Hope got a good laugh as Biscuit was giving one of the riders all he could handle in keeping his horse under control. Once the riders were clear of her territory, Biscuit fell back, having completed her protective duties for the day.

9

Bart had been in a fiery mood before the stop at Hope's ranch. He was tired, thirsty, and upset with the fool Bowe brothers. Being rebuffed by Hope, again, would have been enough to stoke those flames of anger. But seeing her with her new best friend Jack was too much. Somebody was going to have to pay.

"Those cowhands better turn up soon or it will be more than a day's pay they'll suffer," he grumbled to his men. He led the group towards town, thinking maybe he could get some information, and at least a drink.

It was getting on toward nightfall when they reached the dirty little town. A quiet hush came over the street as the six riders made their way toward the saloon. Maybe it was the scowl on Bart's leathery face that caused people to back into their doorways or quietly shuffle out of the way as he rode down the middle of the street. Bart didn't like coming to this place much. He usually sent somebody to do his bidding here.

It was already quiet in the saloon when they entered. Bart leaned up against the bar and growled an order for a bottle of whiskey.

"Quincy, have you seen those fool Bowe brothers?"

"Not since last night, Mr. Decker," the bartender answered with a little shaking in his voice.

"Which way did they head out of here?"

"They left in the direction of Decker Ranch at about 7:30. They had been drinking, but they were sober enough to make it home."

Bart considered the possibility of their getting waylaid on the way to the ranch. It wouldn't have been the first time a traveler had not made it to his destination in these parts. Maybe those Indians they'd seen had something to do with it. He heard a rider pull up to the front of the saloon. Mike, Bart's ranch foreman, came through the door.

47

"Mr. Decker, them boys came in on foot this afternoon. They claim they were ambushed by forty Indians." The silence in the room was broken by a few gasps from the bar girls. Nobody liked the thought of Indian trouble, especially not on the scale of forty marauding braves.

"Any of them have arrows sticking out of them?" Bart asked scornfully.

"No sir. None of them was injured at all. They came walking in without their horses, their guns or your whiskey."

"Forty Indians, huh? That's an interesting story. More likely those boys drank my whiskey and fell off their horses onto their drunken asses!" There wasn't much standing between Bart and a full on rage now. He knocked back his first whiskey and poured himself another. Several shots went down before Bart slowed down the pace. Quincy had slipped down the length of the bar, wisely putting some distance between Bart and himself. Bart waived him back over.

"I heard there was a commotion in town last night. What happened?"

"A commotion? I ... I don't know nothing about no commotion last night," Quincy said, and started to wipe down the bar, slowly moving in the direction of the stock room.

"Is that so?" Bart muttered as he poured himself another. Bart took his bottle of whiskey over to a table. He looked over at one of the saloon girls and asked her the same question.

"Bart, Honey," she said as she walked over to stand close behind him. She pressed her bosom into the back of his head, and rubbed her hands across his chest and shoulders. "If it's a commotion you want, come on upstairs, and I'll give you a commotion."

Bart softly caressed her hand.

"I thought you didn't want to play my games anymore?"

"As long as we're here I'm sure it'll be ... safe." she answered.

He locked his fingers around her wrist in an iron grip and pulled her down close. "Scarlet, Honey," he growled into her ear, with special emphasis on the 'Honey'. "Just tell me what went on here last night."

A scared Scarlet gave Bart the quick version of the Bowe brothers harassing some stranger that Doc brought in.

Bart laughed and released her.

"So Doc's trying to bring in another lawman is he? Maybe this one will kill himself with a gun instead of a knife."

Bart's men all laughed. The rest of the bar nervously joined in.

"Yeah boss, the newspaper will say 'New Sheriff Commits Suicide by Shooting Himself Seven Times with a Six Gun!'"

There was another round of laughs.

It occurred to Bart that he'd already met the stranger.

"Tall fella, dark hair, fancy shirt?"

Scarlet nodded.

"Damn it!" Bart cursed. "That was Doc's new lawman? I should've shot him right then." Bart picked up the half empty bottle of whiskey by the neck and heaved it at the bartender. It crashed into the wall behind Quincy.

"The next time I ask you a question, you better have a much better memory then you did just now. Now bring me those three bottles of whiskey that those Indians supposedly stole from my boys. You can get your payment from the Indians. Or the Bowes, I don't care which."

Quincy did as he was told. Mike picked up the bottles as Bart and his men kicked over a few tables and chairs on their way out of the saloon.

10

Zeke, Elijah and Davey had taken a long time in getting back to Decker Ranch on foot. They were not in a tremendous hurry to explain what had happened to them, and to Bart's whiskey. They had arrived late in the day, well after Bart and the others went out searching for them. Since it had been late when Bart returned to the ranch, drunk and angry about the wasted day and the appearance of Jack, he hadn't wanted to bother with hearing their excuses. In the morning, Bart sent his foreman Mike to bring Zeke, Elijah and Davey up to the ranch house to tell their story.

When the three cowhands arrived, they could see that Bart was still hung over from last night's drunk and plenty mad about searching after them all day.

"Well, boys," Bart started out in a low tone, "what in Hell have you done with my whiskey? Drank it all, I'll bet."

As the leader of the motley crew, Zeke answered. "Boss, we had your whiskey, and we was making right for home with it, when out of nowhere we was waylaid by a maraudin' band of injuns. They done set a trap for us, and they had the drop on us. It was them that drunk your whiskey, not us, Boss."

Elijah decided to help further the story. "Yeah Boss, there was forty of them, all painted up for war. We're lucky to still have our scalps."

"Is that so?" asked Bart. "Forty of them, huh? Then you boys must have shot 36 of them of them raiders dead, since the only Indian raiding party we saw while we were riding all over the territory looking for your sorry asses was a tiny little group of four Indians trailing three spare horses."

"No sir, Boss. We didn't kill no 36 injuns," Zeke cut in. "Maybe the bigger group split off."

"Hmmm," thought Bart, out loud. "Either you were too drunk from drinking my whiskey to defend yourselves, or you're just a bunch of idiots that walked into a trap set by a couple of old Indians and their squaws. Which is it?"

Elijah didn't know when to hold himself back, especially when it was a multiple choice question.

"We didn't drink that whiskey. We're just plain idiots boss; just plain idiots."

"That is the first believable thing you've said today. What took you boys so long in getting out of town with that whiskey in the first place?"

Zeke decided to take back control of the conversation from his plain idiot brother. "Boss, we were having some fun with a greenhorn we ain't ever seen before."

"Having some fun? With the new lawman Doc brought in?"

"Lawman?" Zeke asked, incredulous. "That greenhorn ain't no lawman. He was a dude for sure."

Elijah started to cut in. "He was dancing in them..."

Zeke cut him off with a stare and finished Elijah's sentence for him. "Dancing a jig in the street for us, Boss."

Zeke didn't want to be embarrassed by the story of losing his boots to the Indians. Besides, he figured on getting those boots back some day. He wasn't sure how he was going to do it, but there was no way he wanted Bart to get his hands on them before he did.

Bart seemed more interested in the trouble they'd caused in town.

"I told you boys, no trouble, unless I tell you. You'll get your chance to have some fun, but you'll do it when I say, or you can pack up your gear and hightail it out of here. You idiots will not mess up the plans I have for this town. Is that understood?"

"Yes, sir, Boss. No trouble unless you say," they all agreed.

"Mike there will set you boys up with new horses and rigs. We'll be docking your pay until it's paid for. I want you boys to ride into town and find out all you can about this stranger."

Mike broke in at that point.

"Boss, we have that break in the fence on the west side that the herd is just walking through. We need to patch the fence and round up about twenty head before they are long gone or on some Indian's plate for supper."

"Damn it, Mike. Put somebody else on it." Running the cattle ranch was one of Bart's least favorite things to do.

"You sent everyone else out already this morning to 'convince' the last bunch of ranchers to sell. I was counting on these three to do some work around here."

"Alright. They can earn some of those new rigs back by hauling fence rails and roping those strays." It frustrated Bart that he had to do all the thinking in this outfit, and still issue specific directions when he wanted something done. Couldn't anyone take orders around here? Bart turned to the three dejected cowhands. "But you better get that done and get me that information I want. We made it very clear to those people that we were not going to put up with another hired tin star. If he is a new lawman, I expect you boys'll teach him a little respect."

With that, the three cowhands filed out of the room. After a short period of murmuring voices outside the door, there followed a quiet knock.

"Yes," Bart growled.

Zeke cracked the door open and slipped just his head inside. "Say, Boss, we just wanted to be clear. If that stranger does turn out to be a new lawman...?"

Bart finished his sentence for him. "I'm saying, you can have some fun."

As the door closed, Bart could hear Zeke interpreting for Elijah. "I told you that's what he meant, Lij. You are such an idiot!"

11

The ride back to town was almost pleasant. Not that his horse was taking Jack's directions or behaving obediently. Jack still couldn't get that animal to do a thing he wanted. When he tried to lead Charley off of the trail and behind some bushes to relieve himself, Jack couldn't get Charley to stop. Jack was sure Charley would take off without him if he dismounted. Charley was heading home, and if Jack needed to go, he was going to have to do it standing in the saddle. OJ had let Jack in on a little secret: leaving the stable was the hard part, he had said. But coming back, you could let go of the reins and go to sleep and that horse would get you back home all by himself. Jack decided a little bladder pain was worth not fighting the dumb animal all the way back. It was kind of nice to not have to clutch the saddle horn just to stay on. Jack sat back and watched the stars while he tried to make some sense of this adventure.

What sort of group training was this? He could appreciate team building. There was probably some value to establishing how hard working individually could be, before coming together as a team, but that lesson had been learned by now. Working on his own had him imitating Michael Jackson in the street. But spending all day at Hope's ranch? How was that going to help TechTran Corp?

Not that he was complaining about his day with Hope. That was perfect. He had the feeling at first that she didn't really want him there, that he was wasting her time...and his. But there was no disguising the look of admiration on her face when he moved that boulder. That was a moment that he could dwell in over and over again. The way she made him feel like he was the only man in the world, capable of anything, with just that look--- and she had invited him back tomorrow. So whatever lesson he was supposed to be learning for TechTran, it would have to come by Hope's ranch tomorrow to find him.

Jack rode into town just a short while after Bart and his men left. Of course, his horse took him straight to the stable, where one of Adolf's sons was ready to take the horse to his stall and brush him down, which was fortunate, as Jack made a flying dismount and dashed awkwardly toward the outhouse.

With a deep sigh of contented relief, and a bit of a swagger for his new found mastery of horse riding, Jack felt like stepping over to the saloon to catch up on what was going on. Pulling the dollar out of his pocket that Doc had spotted him last night, Jack asked the bartender, "How much for a rum and cola?"

"Just what you see on the counter, Mister," Quincy shot back.

What Jack saw was whiskey. Just whiskey. There were two different brands, but whiskey was definitely the only option on the menu. No cola. Maybe that was water in the pitcher on the counter. Maybe it was just more whiskey. Neither was good for Jack. He had never developed a taste for hard liquor straight out of the bottle. To be more exact, many late nights in college spent doubled over the toilet had convinced Jack that hard liquor straight was not his drink of choice.

"Whiskey, then, I guess," he replied with a sheepish smile on his face, "on the rocks, please."

Quincy's face screwed up into an exasperated expression of disgust.

"Mister, I just gave away four bottles of whiskey to that damned Bart Decker. I'd rather give it all away before I'd watch you put rocks in it!"

"Now I'm gonna pour you a whiskey. It'll cost you 25 cents. If you want to ruin it with some rocks, you go outside to do it. Comprende?"

Jack took his whiskey and sat down at a table near some men playing cards. He heard from them and Scarlet about Bart and his threats. So the lesson must be that he was vulnerable alone. Maybe tomorrow he would join up with his coworkers and start to take on some challenges. Building a log bridge or taking a zip line would have to be easier than getting shot at by Bart and his men. Jack laughed to himself. It would have felt a lot funnier if he hadn't had that nagging thought in the back of his head all day - why were those Bowe brothers using real bullets?

Jack awoke the next morning with a terrible pain in his neck. Sleeping on straw may have looked fun on Hee Haw, but the real thing was uncomfortable as Hell. Maybe he needed one of those Hill Billy Honeys in the straw with him for comfort. Maybe he just needed a bed. This 'roughing it' crap was starting to wear on him. Realism was great, and all, but even camping out got a tent and sleeping bag, and maybe an air mattress. Jack ate breakfast with Adolf and his family, and told them of his plans to visit Hope again today. They were quiet, giving Jack a sense of disapproval. Maybe that wasn't in the story line. Jack thanked them for breakfast, then made his way over to the stable. Adolf's son helped Jack put on the bridle and saddle. Jack mounted Charley with a new found confidence after his quiet ride home yesterday evening. As he climbed into the saddle, Jack patted Charley on the neck.
"Well, ole boy, I guess this is a new day. You and I are gonna get along great, as long as you..."
Whatever it was that Jack was going to say was swallowed, along with his tongue, as Charley bolted out of the stall with Jack barely able to stay in the saddle.
"Whoa! Whoa! Hold on Charley!" was all that Jack could manage as Charley sped through Dawson's Creek, past the shops and offices just opening their doors and windows. People up and down the street laughed heartily as they watched Jack bound from front to back and side to side, all as Charley weaved in whatever pattern crossed his horse brain as he left the town behind in a cloud of dust. Ben Riley doubled over in a laughing, coughing fit as the horse and rider disappeared into the brush with a fading yell.
"God Damn You, Chaaarrllleeeyy!"
Jack had no idea how long they went on like that, Hell bent for destruction. He was thankful for two things. One, there

were no low branches so far. His head still smarted from the last one. Two, somehow Charley was headed in the general direction of Hope's. If he could just hold on long enough, maybe he could bail out as he passed near her ranch. If he chose a nice soft bush or patch of grass he might not break anything. About then Charley veered off away from Hope's, a situation that required immediate action. In a moment of perfect horse riding clarity, Jack thought maybe he had been applying the reins incorrectly. Instead of a constant pull, maybe he needed a more forceful, immediate wrenching back on the reins. As he did this, Jack shouted in his most commanding voice, "I told you to stop, Horse!"

For his part, Jack was right on the money about controlling his horse. Strong, forceful control was just what was called for. And a strong, forceful stop was just what Jack got. Charley felt the bit pull into his jaw, forcing his head back. His immediate response was to stop. Charley did this by thrusting his front two legs in front of him and locking them into two straight shafts of stopping power. Charley left skid marks as his feet dug into the Earth, coming to a quick and complete stop of all forward motion. For Jack, forward motion was going to continue for a while. Quite a while. Jack flew gracefully head first over 15 feet before executing a belly first touch down landing that Navy carrier pilots would be proud of. That was the end of anything graceful. His body tumbled across another twenty feet of dirt and brush, arms and legs splaying about wildly. Nobody could have been proud of that part of the maneuver. Jack laid there on the ground, staring into the sky while he assessed the many pain signals coming into his brain from the remote regions of his body.

"I have got to get me a wagon."

Jack stood up and dusted himself off. His chin stung a little. He laughed. His whole body stung a little! There wasn't actually any part of his body that didn't hurt in some way. He looked over at Charley, quietly munching on some grass about forty feet away. Clearly marked in the dirt and grass along the distance between the two was Jack's landing, no, crash zone.

"Well horse, I guess you made your point. I'll walk from here, thank you very much." Jack started walking over to Charley to collect the reins and lead him on to Hope's. When Jack got within ten feet, Charley popped his head up, trotted off about forty feet, and stopped to graze again. Jack had no idea how to catch a horse on foot. Charley, on the other hand, had plenty of ideas on how not to get caught. Jack tried offering some grass in his hand. Charley trotted away. Jack tried sneaking around and coming up from behind. Charley let him get close, then trotted away. They kept at this game for most of an hour. Finally Jack gave up.

"Screw it!" He would have to find a way to buy Doc a new horse. Then he would own Charley. He could come pick him up in a helicopter. Yeah. And their first stop would be the glue factory.

He shouted over to Charley, "Hear that, Charley? It's the Glue Factory for you, Pal!"

If Charley could understand the threat, he made no reaction, other than to amble away from Jack. Jack kicked the dirt and started off walking in the direction he thought was toward Hope's ranch.

With the cool morning breeze in his face, and loosening up from the exercise, most of the pains from his crash landing subsided. He was walking along at a good pace when what he saw in front of him stopped him in his tracks. Lying on the ground were four sleeping Indians. Not the brilliant software programmer kind of Indians he knew from work. These were no kidding, full war paint Apaches. Or Cherokees. Or whatever. Jack never was any good at history. Now he was living it. What were Indians doing on his dude ranch leadership exercise? As bizarre as these last days had been, never in his life did Jack expect to see four real, live Indians sleeping around a campfire, hugging their rifles, with a bunch of liquor bottles laying around...and a pair of Nike boots just sitting there.

"My Boots!" he cried out loud. Then, a little more wisely, Jack whispered quietly, "Those are my boots." He looked down at the ratty-ass pair of Zeke's cast offs he had been wearing. They sucked. He wanted his boots back.

The decision was made. The only thing standing in his way were four Indians. Correction. Lying in his way. Their snoring sounded like the sawmill in town, and Jack could see that those liquor bottles were mostly empty. He figured quickly that they were most likely drunk off their asses from the booze they drank all night. Most likely. They all seemed to have rifles cradled in their arms while they slept. Jack could see their horses tied up a few hundred feet beyond the camp fire. He needed to find a way to sneak into the camp, grab his boots, get to the horses, spook them to create a diversion and get away. No problem.

He took off Zeke's boots and crept over to where the Indians lay. Very quietly, he traded the old boots for his Nikes. He grabbed all of the ammunition belts lying on the ground, since trying to pry the rifles out of the Indians' grasp didn't seem wise. He turned and picked up a smoldering branch from the fire and two of the liquor bottles. He quickly made his way over near the horses. He stopped behind a bush and used his pocket multitool to separate the bullets and drain several of the cartridges' gun powder into the empty bottle. His plan was to spook the horses away to the south and hightail it to the north under the cover of the brush. He felt certain the Indians would chase after their horses. He would be long gone toward Hope's before they would be back to deal with him. He could use the gun powder and whiskey bottles as grenades if they decided to chase him. He was pretty certain he could pull it all off, without accidentally hurting anyone. Maybe a few flying glass injuries from the bottles was all. He was disconcerted to find that these Indians also had real bullets. This game was getting way too serious if everyone was going to go around shooting hot lead. Jack slowly crept up on the horses, fearing that they would wake the Indians and his game would be over before it started. He worked his way around to the other side of the tree to which they were tied. He untied the rope, pointed them south, and swatted them on the haunch. The horses all bolted, kicking up a dust cloud and a rumble of noise. Jack crouched low and started walking backwards, expecting the Indians to jump awake and start shooting. There was little more than a rollover from the intoxicated Indians. Jack continued to creep backwards, keeping his eyes on the threat as he increased the distance. He walked backwards about a quarter mile before he bumped smack into ... Charley? Charley nuzzled Jack in what had to be the closest thing a horse could do to say "I'm sorry." Seeing the need to put more distance between him and the Indians, Jack passed the reins up over Charley's head. Making sure he had Charley pointed in the direction that he wanted to go, he cautiously mounted. To Jack's surprise, Charley started off at a nice trot and gave Jack no trouble for the ride to Hope's ranch.

As he rode, Jack tried to make sense of it all. Sure, he'd managed to slip away with the boots without causing any real harm, but somebody could have gotten seriously hurt. There seemed to be no rules to this game. He could not believe the authenticity of all the equipment, people, places, and bullets. He was perplexed at the effort that was expended to create this environment. If he didn't know any better, Jack could really start to believe he was actually in the Old West.

12

Hope had invited Jack back for several reasons. It was good to have a man around. Jack had been right about the need for an extra pair of hands around there. He had proven very useful around the ranch. No, he wasn't much of a horseman, but that contraption he built yesterday was unbelievable. Where did a person learn things like that? He had done for her in one afternoon something that she had been trying to do for years. He wasn't just useful, though. When Bart rode up with his men yesterday, none of the interaction was any different than before. But having Jack standing there with her gave Hope all the confidence in the world. She had not realized how deeply afraid she really was living out here on the ranch all by herself. Having Jack around today would be reassuring all over again, what with Bart's news of an Indian raiding party on the prowl. Of course, she had no way of knowing if Bart wasn't just trying to scare her into seeking his protection, but it wouldn't hurt to take some precaution. She knew there was one reason that she wanted Jack back today that she wasn't admitting to herself. Not out loud anyway. It had been three long years since she had felt that tingling down there. The sight and smell of Jack sweating so close to her had made her feel sexual again. She had forgotten just how wonderful that feeling could be. Yes, there were lots of good reasons to invite Jack back. As the morning wore on, she jumped up to the window more and more often to peek out and see if he was coming down the trail. Once or twice she chided herself for acting like a school girl, but that didn't stop her from jumping up again at the next bark of the dog.

When she did see Jack coming up the trail, it wasn't as she had expected to see him. Where yesterday he was walking ahead of his horse, today he sat confidently in the saddle. She stepped back from the window and waited for him. It was all she could do to hold herself down in the chair and not rush outside to greet him. She waited until she couldn't stand it any more.

"Oh, what does it matter anyway?"

She hopped up and bounded across the room to the door. As she opened it to go outside, Jack was just dismounting. The first thing she noticed were those magnificent boots. He had somehow gotten them back. His stock was going way up!

"Well, I do declare, Mr. Banyan. It looks like you have gotten your boots back. I guess we will be dancing in the streets of town together."

Jack beamed at her excitement to see him.

"Yes I have, and they feel wonderful. I look forward to our dance."

"So tell me, how did you get Zeke to part with them?" She hoped it had been at the end of a gun. That darn Zeke deserved it. Until Bart came along and took an interest in her, Hope had been Zeke's favorite quarry. She could not imagine doing any of the things with Zeke that she had been thinking about doing with Jack. Jack told her the quick version of his morning adventure, including the turnabout in Charley, and asked Hope for a brush. He unbelted the saddle and removed the bridle from Charley as she fetched the brush. When she returned and gave it to him, Jack proceeded to brush Charley as Hope asked questions about Jack's adventure.

"Are you sure you aren't hurt from the fall? Your chin looks cut. I can wash that off for you."

"Ok, but give me a minute to take care of Charley here. I think we may have come to some sort of understanding. He'll let me ride as long I don't get to thinking it is my right. Isn't that so, Charley?" Jack asked as he patted Charley's neck. A snort was Charley's response in the affirmative.

"You can let him graze in the pasture with my horses," Hope told him.

The two spent the morning working and talking. Jack filled in all the details of his regaining his boots, and his fights with Charley. Hope laughed and laughed at Jack's description of his morning ride out of town. She wondered how long ago it had been since she had laughed so hard, so He was as interesting a person as she had ever known. But just what did she know about Jack? Not enough to fill a thimble.

Jack relayed Scarlet's information about Bart making threats last night in the saloon.

"He apparently left here and went straight into town and stirred up trouble." Jack didn't realize the impact of what he'd said.

"Oh my!" worried Hope. "I am afraid my resistance to that man's advances may be causing those poor people in town harm."

"Even if that were so, Hope, what else could you do about it?" Jack asked as he clipped off a piece of fencing wire for the chicken coop.

"You can't concede to selling your ranch, or having dinner with the man, just because he throws a tantrum."

"No, I suppose you are right. But I do wish he could just take no for an answer."

"What is it that he plans to do with all the land he is buying up, anyway?" Jack asked.

"I've often wondered that myself. He already has the largest spread for miles, stretching from almost Denver up to the Wyoming border. You'd think he had a mind to own all the land between Cheyenne and Denver so that he could walk from one place to the other without having to step off of his own property."

"Well it would be a long, lonely walk," Jack answered a little suggestively. "If it isn't too forward of me to say so, I am most interested in the land between Dawson's Creek and here."

"Oh, so you are interested in becoming a land baron? I suppose you mean to charge me a toll every time I wish to go to town?" she teased. The thought of Jack being her neighbor definitely pleased her, though.

Hope finished tacking down the last section of wire while Jack held tension on it, pulling on it using the pliers of his multitool.

"I don't believe I've ever seen a tool quite like that," Hope said. "What are all those attachments?"

Jack held out his multitool. "Oh, it really is a great tool. It has fifteen different attachments and a flashlight." Jack flipped out all of the attachment tools and twisted on the flashlight. He hadn't thought of this being against the 'no technology' rule the desk clerk had emphasized. He never went anywhere without it.

"Isn't that hot?" Hope asked of the flashlight. Jack was holding it right at the twist cap end.

"No, it's an LED." Hope's quizzical expression didn't get any less quizzical.

"It's a cool bulb," Jack said. He was beginning to feel a little uncomfortable and thought maybe this was too far out of storyline. "It's really more of a portable lantern." With that he turned the light off, folded the tool and put it back in his pocket.

"Looks like we are done with this chicken coop," he suggested.

Hope had been looking forward to this point all morning.

"Time for some lunch," she said, a little too excitedly. "Are you hungry?"

Of course Jack was famished. Up at the crack of Cockledoodledoo, a short breakfast and a long walk, followed by ranch work til the sun was high overhead. He was definitely hungry. Hope had fed him yesterday. They'd had beans and cornbread with some milk. It tasted wonderful, but Hope apologized several times for not having a finer meal prepared, and that given enough warning she would have provided much better for Jack.

"Come on, let's wash up." They went over to the creek and washed away the morning's sweat and dirt. Twice Hope caught Jack's eyes darting away from watching her pour the cool water over her shoulders and arms. She was almost sorry to see him wash away his manly scent. The tingling had returned as they worked so close together.

"You wait here and I'll be right back." Jack obliged by taking a seat in the shade.

Hope ran to the house and was lost inside for a while. She came out carrying a huge basket with both arms, and a blanket draped over her shoulder.

"I thought we might picnic up on that little hill there. It has a wonderful view of the entire valley."

Jack grabbed the basket, and they started up the hill. Hope whistled and Biscuit followed.

When they reached the crest, Hope spread the contents of the basket onto the blanket.

Jack was impressed. There was enough food for a feast laid out in front of him; roast beef, green beans, cabbage, fresh bread, butter and jam. And tea to wash it all down.

"Wow!" he exclaimed. "I'm impressed. How long did it take to prepare all of this?"

"Oh, not long," Hope lied. She had spent all of yesterday evening and most of the night cooking and baking. Of course she wanted to treat company to a nice meal. Yesterday she had been unprepared for Jack staying for dinner. She took great pride in her hospitality, and was ashamed to only be able to offer beans and cornbread to Jack. What's more, after taking a liking to him, she really wanted to impress Jack with her cooking. She could tell by the way he was devouring it that she had hit her mark. Jack was eating as if he had not had a well cooked meal in quite some time.

"I have never had a meal that tasted so good," he declared between bites. "Everything seems to taste better here."

Hope's face lit with pride. She was excited to be cooking for a man again. There had been too many nights of meals for one, eaten alone or with the dog. That was not how life was meant to be lived. Life was meant, like a good meal, to be shared.

Jack's accolades were meant for Hope's cooking, for sure, but he was actually reflecting on all that he had eaten since arriving in Dawson's Creek. Everything was bursting with flavor. From the first time he had tasted the fresh milk in the stable, Jack had noticed the vivid tastes and smells of life here. Maybe the dulling of his mental senses from all the bumps and bruises he had suffered since he got here had shaken up the rest of his senses. This was Jack's only explanation for the heightened sensation. Right now, enjoying this meal with Hope, it was a tradeoff that he was willing to make.

Hope sat up straight and pointed out over the horizon to the west. Jack could see the familiar site of the Rocky Mountains cutting a jagged line across the sky.

"I come up here most afternoons to reflect, and in the evenings to watch the sunset," Hope said. "I just love the colors that light up the sky. They are spectacular."

Jack had shifted his gaze from the mountains back to Hope as she stared off into the skyline. He was lost in spectacular, but it had nothing to do with the sky. Hope was downright beautiful. She didn't have a bit of makeup on, and Jack couldn't see how it would have helped. Her green eyes were all the color he ever wanted to see. That beautiful long blonde hair brushed back behind her ears. Her cat shaped eyes and high cheekbones gave her the look of a mountain lion, with all of the beauty and power that animal exudes.

"Don't you get lonely out here all by yourself?"

"Sometimes I do. But I prefer being on my own. I have the ranch to keep me busy, and the animals for company. Still, I never thought I would spend my life alone. Even after James died, I assumed that at some point I would find a man to share my life. I think everyone gets a special person to go through life with. I thought James would be mine. Maybe you only get one chance with that one special person?"

"Now Bart does present an opportunity for a fiiiiiiine life full of fiiiiiiine things," she said with a wink in her eye. "But I would rather spend the rest of my life here, alone, than waste it with someone like that."

Talking about herself and her desires came hard. It had been a long, lonely three years out here on the ranch. What she really wanted was to know more about Jack.

"How about you, Jack? You're on your own. Aren't you lonely?"

"I haven't had much of a chance to be lonely since I got here in Dawson's Creek. Everyone has been terrific to me, especially you. I've really enjoyed the time we've spent together."

"How about before that?" she probed. "You've only been here a couple days. I don't know anything about the rest of your life. Do you have a family? Have you ever been married? Is there someone special in your life?" The questions started rolling off her tongue in an avalanche. She forced herself to stop and slow down, lest she should seem an inquisitor.

Jack took a second to collect his answers. He was not sure how much he should reveal and how much of this would matter in the storyline.

"So the answers to your questions are: one; yes, parents and a brother; two; no, but almost once; and three; no one more special than present company."

"Almost?" she asked.

"I was engaged once a long time ago, but we went our separate ways, before the wedding."

"Oh," Hope said, a little too happily. "And where is your family? Where are you from?"

"You don't seem to be able to ask one question at a time, now do you?" Jack asked jokingly. "I am from Silicon Valley in California where my parents and brother live now."

"California!" Hope jumped at the mention. "I don't know of 'Silicon Valley'... where is that?"

Oops, Jack caught himself. Modern-day reference. She was very good at staying in character.

"Near San Francisco."

"I've heard California is wonderful. Why would you ever leave?"

"I left to take a job with a telecom ... a company in Denver," Jack corrected himself.

She could see that Jack was shaping his answers for her. Why was he so cautious in his responses? She asked several more questions and got the same sort of measured response each time. He had to be concealing something. And what on earth was a telecom?

Jack appeared more and more uncomfortable talking about himself. She didn't get a chance to continue the questioning, as Jack stood and brushed crumbs off of his lap. "Don't you think it's time we got back to work?"

They cleaned up the picnic, mostly in silence. There was a battle raging in Hope's head between how much she wanted to be with Jack and her innate sense of self protection. Who knew how long Jack would be here? He hadn't given any indication that he planned to stay. And why was he so mysterious?

Jack, on the other hand, was trying to balance how much to play along with the storyline, with how much he wanted Hope. What if he could combine the two outcomes? That was vintage Jack... maximizing every opportunity, especially when it came to women.

13

Jack had plenty of time for thinking while he rode back to town. He was trying to make sense of his relationship with Hope. Why had she pulled back from that kiss? They had been mending the rails in the stable fence. It was hard work and the sun was warm. They were both glistening with sweat. When they had stumbled and fallen to the ground with Hope landing on top of him, there had been that moment. That moment that always comes in the movies, when the hero and heroine get that first kiss. Their faces were inches apart, close enough to feel her warm breath. They both wanted it. It was right. It was perfect. Only as he moved closer to her lips, she rolled away and stood up. It had been awkward for a while after that. Their parting that afternoon had seemed hollow, so different than their meeting this morning. He knew that she wanted him. He could read all the signs. Where Jack had lost it he couldn't figure out. What was stopping her? Cameras? Was this whole thing being videotaped for a debrief at the end of the week? Maybe it was all fake, her enthusiasm just a part of the storyline. Maybe she was an actress with three kids and a husband at home. He felt a little nauseous at that thought, being new to the exposed emotions game, and he mentally dodged to a different subject. Where was everyone else in this leadership exercise? Three days were down and there was not much team building to show for it. If he were designing this program he would surely get the exercise started faster. Not that he minded too much. His days at Hope's were great. He certainly hoped that her enthusiasm wasn't acting, because he felt an intense attraction to her. She had an independence and strength that he had never seen in a woman before. She was as unique as she was beautiful, unlike in every way the women he knew. Jack blamed his general uneasiness and underlying confusion on his infatuation with her. He knew that there was something going on here that he should be focusing his brainpower on.

It was just much more pleasant to let his mind drift back to the warmth of her company.

As Jack was riding and thinking, he saw in front of him a wagon buried in the stream bed. Ben Riley was close by, sitting on a rock with his head in his hands. The water was running over the back of the wagon. Jack could see a few items floating away, and some lining the banks a little further downstream. It appeared that the wagon itself might wash down the stream at any moment.

"What happened to your horses?" Jack asked as he got off of Charley.

"I was just about to cross this stream when some Indians relieved me of my team, and some of my supplies."

"Then they pushed your wagon into the water?"

"Nope, they just took the horses and supplies and rode off."

"Then how did your wagon end up in the stream? Don't tell me you tried to push it across by yourself?"

"Nope, that ain't it either. Not ten minutes after those braves took my horses, five of those Decker Ranch ne'er-do-wells rode up. I told them what had happened and asked if they could help me out. They talked it over a minute, then one of them said, 'I guess today just ain't your lucky day'. Then they had a great time laughing and making fun of my predicament while they pushed my wagon into the stream and busted up what was left of my supplies. They have pushed me to my limit."

"Tie that rope onto the wagon and the saddle here, and let's see if Charley can pull it out of there." Charley gave it a mighty effort, but the wagon went nowhere. Jack could see that the wagon's weight plus the force of the water was driving the wheels down into the mud. He needed some lifting force to counteract the drag. He got one of the boards out of Ben's supplies that had washed ashore and used his multitool file to cut a notch into each end. Then he tied a length of rope to the back end of the wagon and looped it over a sturdy tree branch that reached out over the stream. He fastened the other end of the rope to the wagon right next to the point that he tied the first end.

"Jack, I don't think that you are going to be strong enough to pull that end of the wagon up, and there is no way we can both get out on that limb," Ben said doubtfully.

"You're right about that, Ben. That's why I brought a screw jack along with me." He wedged the board between the ropes, forming a diamond shape over the wagon. He climbed out onto the branch and began twisting the board in a clockwise circle. Near the points where it was tied to the wagon and the branch, the rope began twisting together and decreasing the length between the branch and the wagon. This lifting force pulled the wagon up six inches out of the muddy bottom. Several loud cracks in the tree branch gave Jack an indication that he had gone about as far as was prudent. He motioned Ben forward with Charley, and the wagon slid smoothly out of the water. After they dismantled the screw jack and collected what remained of the supplies, they walked alongside as Charley pulled the wagon back into town.

When they arrived back in Dawson's Creek Ben insisted on buying Jack a drink in the saloon. There were already several people having dinner, playing cards or just drinking. Ben regaled Jack's exploits in creating the screw jack and getting his wagon back to town. Everyone in the saloon was impressed. They also noticed Jacks boots were back with their rightful owner and wanted to know the story. Jack told them of his wild ride, the beginning of which was already comedy legend in the town, and graceless dismount, which brought on more laughter. He described approaching the Indians from the opposite side of the horses. One of the card players commented on how wise it was to come at them upwind to prevent the horses from alerting the Indians. The alcohol in Jack and the praise from the folks in the saloon prevented him from admitting that his approach direction was pure luck, and that there was little chance that the drunken Indians were going to smell or hear anything. He described slipping into the camp and retrieving his boots. Jack didn't mention the loud snoring and the alcoholic stupor that his adversaries were in. He did remark that he was so concerned about them waking when he scattered their horses that he walked a quarter mile backwards to the road.

"Well, I'll be," said someone with Army experience fighting Indians. "You musta knowed those Indians would have a Hell of a time tracking your footprints backwards!"

"Yes, sir. Our Jack is one Hell of a tactician," yelled one of the saloon folk. There were cheers of agreement throughout the room. Maybe it was the whiskey and maybe it was the accolades, but Jack started to feel a warmth for these people that he hadn't felt before. It was new and exciting to be the center of attention and it fed his self-importance and sense of belonging all at the same time. Jack was beginning to like this place.

Jack downed his whiskey, had dinner and a few more laughs in the saloon and made his way outside to walk the streets and clear his mind. He looked up into the crisp Rocky Mountain sky and thought maybe this wasn't a team building exercise after all. Maybe it was a personal confidence course. He knew his confidence was booming. In three days, he had gone from a street dancing, shoeless greenhorn with no friends, to a hero with people slapping him on the back. He had learned to ride a horse, earned his boots back and was developing a promising romance. He was going to enjoy the next four days.

14

Jack made it all the way to the far end of town on his walk, then proceeded off into the low bushes to relieve himself. This was why he didn't see Bart's men ride into town. Zeke, Elijah and Davey pushed through the saloon door like they owned the place. Mike had driven them hard all day, fixing the fence and rounding up strays. They had earned a drink and a little fun at that greenhorn's expense. Davey headed over to an empty seat at a card table while Zeke and Elijah headed straight for the bar. As usual, questions for the bartender were volleyed back by Quincy without actually giving out much information. Quincy found this easy going when dealing with Zeke's intellect, or lack thereof.

Zeke surveyed the room looking for an information source, stopping his scan on a young cowhand eating dinner at a table by himself. Zeke picked up his whiskey and Elijah followed him over to the table where they stood next to the cowhand. Zeke took a friendly tack.

"Harvey's your name, ain't it?" Zeke asked. "Mind if we join you?"

"Harvey is right. Suit yourself if you want to." Harvey continued to casually eat his dinner. Harvey knew he was big enough that Zeke wasn't going to take him on. Not that Zeke would be afraid to scuffle with him if it came to that, but Harvey had seen enough of Zeke to know that he didn't like to get his nose pushed in if he didn't have to.

"So Harvey, what do you know about this new lawman in town?" Zeke didn't take any time getting to the point.

"Don't know nothing about no lawman," Harvey answered truthfully.

"Ah, come on, Harvey. You know something about him. You saw us having a little fun with him in the street the other night."

"Oh that feller. Jake or Jack or something."

"Yeah, that's the one. What do you know about him?"

"Nothing, except he's the big hero round here now."

"Hero, huh?" asked Zeke. "What made that fancy dancin' dude a hero round here? Fetchin' a pussy cat out of a big ole tree?"

"I don't know for sure. Something about how he helped old Ben Riley get his wagon out of the stream with some genius contraption."

Zeke was quick to scornfully observe, "I don't see as that makes a man much of a hero, gettin' a wagon out of a stream."

Everyone in the bar could hear the conversation. Walt, one of the card players, having had a little too much luck with the cards and a lot too much to drink, boldly decided to push Zeke's buttons.

"Say Zeke," he said, "That's a scrappy pair of boots you're wearing. What happened to them nice new boots you got the other night?"

"Mind your own business Walt or I'll start using these boots to whoop your ass."

"Okay, Zeke, I was just wondering why you weren't wearing them and that Jack fella was in here not twenty minutes ago wearing those same boots?"

The funny thing about Zeke was the way his face screwed up when he got angry. Or ridiculed. Or beaten. He looked like a five-year-old that had just had his candy taken away. Elijah knew that look well and knew when to steer clear of it. Walt was about to learn that lesson.

Zeke's pistol was out in a flash. Walt found himself staring into the barrel.

"Why don't you tell me how that lawman got my boots?"

Self-preservation mode kicked Walt's alcohol induced swagger to the curb.

"He...," he answered shakily, "He stole them back from some Indians. It was...It was just him against four of them."

"Where is he now?"

"I don't know Zeke. He left out of here twenty minutes ago."

Davey stood up from the table and asked Walt where Jack was staying.

Walt responded without moving his eyes from their gaze down Zeke's gun barrel.

"I think he sleeps down in the stable."

"Okay, Zeke," Davey said in a calming voice. "Why don't you put that cannon away and let's go have us a talk with our lawman?"

It took a few seconds for the blood to stop pounding through the bulging veins on Zeke's forehead. As quick as it started, Zeke's rage was under control. He slipped his gun back into his holster and smiled at Walt.

With a slight slap across Walt's cheek, Zeke told him "That's a good boy." Then he looked at the cards in Walt's hand and announced, "He's bluffing. He's got nothing but a queen in that hand." As the gang left the saloon, Walt threw his cards down on the table and the other players all quickly removed their money from the spoiled pot.

From far down the street, Jack saw the three men spill out of the saloon like gasoline out of a ruptured tanker truck, just as ready to explode.

Elijah asked Zeke what he planned to do when he got hold of Jack.

"If he don't hold still, I'll cut 'em off of him!"

That worried Elijah.

"Won't that ruin them fancy boots?"

"I ain't gonna cut the boots, Lij. I'll cut his legs off at the knees if I have to. Now why don't you run into that hardware store and get me an axe?" That made even Davey worry.

Jack moved closer to the saloon, staying in the shadows as he tried to see where the men were headed.

Elijah stopped as they went by the hardware store. He broke the window on the front door and reached down to unlock the handle from the inside. He was a little embarrassed to see that there wasn't even a lock on the door knob as he hurried into the store to get the ax. Jack stealthily made his way back down the street. He could see the three men rushing toward the stable. Adolf's son Werner had the misfortune of greeting them at the entrance. Zeke grabbed him by the shirt collar and shoved him up against the stable wall.

"Where is that lawman with my boots?" Zeke growled as he shook the boy. Werner was confused, and scared. He had not even seen Jack since his return and did not know that he had recovered the boots.

Jack witnessed this in an increasing state of shock. He had no idea what lawman Zeke was shouting about, but it was pretty clear that Zeke wanted whoever was wearing the boots. It was one thing for these guys to play rough with him, but that sure didn't look like acting with that boy pinned up against the wall. Jack decided that he could play rough, too.

He slipped into the next door he came across, looking for something to get Werner out of Zeke's grasp.

"A bakery? What the Hell am I gonna use in a bakery?" Jack looked around behind the counter frantically. His eyes settled on the supply shelves. He grabbed a big bottle of vinegar, then large can of baking soda. He threw them into a burlap sack, along with some mason jars. He took the sack and slipped out the back door, then sprinted up the alley until he reached the general store across the street from the stable. He used some barrels behind the building to scramble up onto the rooftop. He could see that Adolf had come out to defend his son, and was now being worked over by Davey and Elijah.

Jack mixed the vinegar and baking soda into the mason jars, and started violently shaking one of them. He aimed for a spot far enough away from Davey and Elijah that they shouldn't be at much risk from the glass. The blood coming from Adolph's mouth bolstered Jack's confidence that this was all more than an act, but he still didn't want to risk seriously hurting someone. He aimed close enough behind them to get their attention, using their bodies to protect Adolf from the blast. The second that his hand released the jar he knew there was trouble. Having never thrown a mason jar full of volatile chemicals, and with his adrenaline spiking, he missed his aim point by six feet. The reaction between vinegar and baking soda gives off heat, and more importantly, pressure. Contained until the impact with the ground, the instantaneous pressure release had the effect of a small stick of dynamite. Dynamite that spewed razor sharp bits of broken glass up and down the backsides of those in its path. Davey and Elijah jumped, or were blown, forward.

"Son of a bitch!" Their pistols were out, but they had no idea where the grenade had come from.

"Who the Hell done throwed that bomb at me?" Elijah yelled. His pistol was waving back and forth from building to building, but he could not see the bomber in the dark shadows. Davey was twisting around trying to find the source of the dozens of stinging pains in his back and butt. Little red dots began to appear on Elijah's white shirt back.

"Lij, you're shot." Zeke dropped Werner and joined his brother in the middle of the street.

"Come out here and fight like a man!" Zeke shouted into the darkness.

Jack, hidden behind the thick wooden facade and sign on the General Store roof, answered.

"Is that how men fight, beating up little boys and ganging up on one man, and shooting real bullets?"

Jack immediately wished he had just kept quiet, as seven or eight bullets ripped into the facade and roof around him.

"Damn it! If those peckers are playing for real, then so am I!" He let go of the next grenade in a beautiful Kareem Abdul Jabar sky hook. It arced high in the air, tumbling end over end as it fell. All three of the men in the street stood transfixed, staring at the jar as it arced gracefully down toward them out of the black night sky. Jack had adjusted his fire perfectly, as the jar was falling to a spot equidistant between the three. Before it hit the ground, Jack had launched another. Zeke, Elijah and Davey all dove away from the impact point, but they were too late in getting their jump. This blast was larger than the first, and all three were peppered across the backside again with glass. They were up and running before the next jar hit the ground. Zeke stopped to get a few shots off. He screamed in a maniacal tone.

"Those are my boots, lawman. I took them from you fair and square. I want em back!" Elijah and Davey each grabbed an arm as they ran by and pulled Zeke along to his horse.

"Come on, Zeke. We got no time for them boots now. We're gonna get our heads blown off. We'll get em later."

Jack answered Zeke's demands with one last grenade, and the three cowboys wheeled their horses around and sped out of town.

Like a community of prairie dogs, people poked their heads out of doors and windows as the brothers galloped away. Jack lowered himself down off the roof, and crossed the street to check on Werner. The prairie dogs grew bolder and converged on the stable, patting Jack on the back and congratulating him. Mrs. Coors was going back and forth attending to her two injured men. The boy was shaken, but okay. There were scrapes and bruises forming where Zeke had manhandled him. Adolf was bleeding from the mouth and had some loose teeth.

"I'm sorry for that," Jack told them. "What were they after?"

"They were after you," Werner answered in a raspy voice. "I didn't tell 'em nothing, though."

"I know you didn't. You did a great job, Werner. You are very brave, and I owe you one." His mother took him inside to clean him up. The crowd was positively charged and the accolades for Jack were continuous. There was a universal sense of elation and growing confidence in Jack. He hoped that they would realize that they could stand up for themselves and fight back. Somehow the team building exercise had turned around on the players. They were the ones who seemed to have grown from the whole experience. Someone in the crowd shouted that Jack ought to be the sheriff. Ben Riley offered him the job, then offered him double what the last guy got. Jack felt proud that they would all rally behind him, but certainly didn't think that he was going to be there long enough to take on that level of responsibility. He tried to tell them they didn't need a sheriff, they just needed to stick together.

"Those boys won't be causing trouble around here again anytime soon," he told them.

Doc had made it out of his office and through the crowd. He was having a look at Werner and Adolf. Adolf was telling Doc about the few small pieces of glass in his leg from the first explosion.

"Jack, where did you get dynamite?"

"Wasn't dynamite, Doc. Just a few things I found in the bakery. Sorry about the glass, Adolf."

"No, tank you for what you did. I tink maybe you save my boy's life. You really scared those men off. They are lucky you only meant to scare them."

"You know," Jack said loudly, addressing the entire crowd. "Adolf makes a good point there." Once the adrenaline rush of combat had dissipated, Jack had a nagging thought. He had created explosives and thrown them at people. They were most likely seeking medical treatment for glass injuries, and possibly ruptured ear drums. Could he be liable? Guilty of assault? If this really was only a scripted exercise of some kind, he might be in sincere trouble. But Adolf's injuries looked real enough, and he had been convinced that Werner was in danger. What were the Colorado laws about deadly force in self-defense? Still, everyone here was treating him like a hero. They were sincerely thankful, relieved even, that he had taken those three thugs down.

"If there is something going on here, something that I should know about before someone gets seriously hurt, then somebody needs to speak up now." Jack passed his eyes over the crowd. He got nothing but blank stares and silence. Jack looked directly at Doc, his stare demanding an answer.

"I don't know what else to tell you, Jack. We've told you what we are up against. Those men work for a terrible man. If anyone is likely to get hurt, it will be at his bidding, if not by his hand."

"You don't know those men like we do," one of the ladies said. "They will be back."

Another piped in, "And Bart is going to be beside himself angry." Jack watched their fragile unity start to crack. These people had taken him into their homes. He owed them, at least while he remained in...whatever this place was.

"All right. I don't know how long I will be here, but I'll be your temporary sheriff and do what I can."

A young man pushed forward through the crowd, carrying Jack's hat.

"Looks like you might need a new hat, Jack," he said as he handed it over to Jack. Jack poked his finger through the bullet hole that went through the crown.

"Real bullets," he whispered as he put it on his head.

15

As soon as Zeke and the boys returned to the ranch, they reported in to Bart. They were a mess. Zeke was mostly uninjured, as Davey and Elijah had taken that first blast up close. All three had blood stains across their backs, and riding on butts full of glass slivers had been pure Hell. All of their wounds were superficial, though, and they worried that Bart would be angry that one man had driven them away. Their description of Jack's glass grenades sounded as though they had been ambushed by a cannon. Their ears were still ringing from the explosions. Bart asked if anyone had been seriously hurt.

"What?" they all shouted back in unison. Bart had to tell them to quit shouting.

He raised his voice.

"Was anyone hurt?"

Zeke laughed a little.

"Maybe that stable rat has a sore throat from where I lifted him up by his neck and pinned him against the wall."

Bart was furious with himself for sending them on the assignment in the first place. What had he been thinking, sending these idiots in to do an important job by themselves. He was going to have to find smarter idiots to do his work for him.

"You fools were supposed to get information and report back."

"But Boss, you said we could make a little trouble, have a little fun, if they brought in a new lawman."

"You idiots!" Bart yelled. "All I wanted was for you to rough up one man a little, not get the entire town agitated and turned against me. I need those people to impress the high rollers coming in on Tuesday. Which will be quite difficult if they think I send my men in to rough up little boys. Now you three have messed things up royally."

"Maybe," he postulated, as he pulled his .45 out of his holster and pointed it right at Zeke's nose, "I should shoot you now and end my misery?"

"Hold on, Boss." Zeke didn't care much for being on this end of the barrel. "There ain't no reason to go shooting anybody. We was only doing what you told us to do. We didn't know he had a bunch of dynamite. We didn't know it was gonna turn out the way it did."

"No, you didn't, but I should have known," Bart emphasized the 'I'.

"I need something to remind me so that I don't make that same mistake again."

With that, Bart lowered his pistol toward the floor, and Zeke could breathe again. He never could tell when Bart was just making a point, or when he was serious. He thanked God that this time was not the serious one. The sound of Bart's gun going off, and a massive force pinning his foot to the floor, registered in Zeke's mind at the same time. A long slow moan came out of his mouth as he looked down to see the hole in his boot, and blood start to seep out from underneath his sole.

"Now get out of here before you bleed all over my floor," Bart commanded.

Davey and Elijah helped Zeke out of the door. Elijah tried to soothe his brother.

"That hole goes clear through, Zeke. Good thing you weren't wearing those fancy boots. We're gonna get you those boots back, and teach that lawman a lesson."

Zeke was in pain, feeling nauseous, and angry, and it was all Jack's fault.

"I am going to kill that son of a bitch!" The pitch of his voice was higher than normal, making the statement both a whine and a threat.

Bart sat at his desk and poured himself a whiskey. To his surprise, he had actually developed a taste for whiskey straight out of the bottle. When he had first come to this place, he had been a beer man. The whiskey helped him deal with the morons surrounding him.

"Now what to do about those people in town?" He found himself talking out his thoughts a lot lately. It helped him keep some of the most evil demons in his head at bay. They were voicing their opinions more and more often, though. He had spread the news last week that he would be showing some dignitaries around Tuesday, that he was hopeful that they would all leave with a good impression. Like the sheep they were, they had accepted it without so much as asking who and what for. Now that Zeke had spooked the herd, some damage control was necessary.

"How to do that best?" he pondered. It was so important that this town appear to be his stable base of operations and support. Not that he imagined that the town would approve of anything he was doing, let alone provide its support. He just needed the appearance of stability and support, what with the railroad people coming Monday and the Party people coming Tuesday. He needed these people for just a little while longer. So he would have to go smooth things out some. Maybe he needed a little inspiration from the church.

Once he had the gears in motion, his need for these people would diminish rapidly. Then Zeke could rough up all the little boys he wanted.

"Hmmm, that sounds kind of fun. Maybe we'll join him," he laughed as though someone else in the room had said something humorous.

Sunday morning arrived on Dawson's Creek with a rich red sunrise and a beautiful clear sky. By 8AM, the Baptist church was a standing room only crowd, which wasn't saying much for the small building and twelve pews. Still, almost all of the town's Protestants were in attendance, ready for the sermon from Pastor Will.

Jack and Hope stood together along the wall in the back of the room. Jack was taking it all in, asking questions about who this was, what did he do, where was the rest of the town? Hope explained that nearly everyone in the town attended one of the two churches, Protestant or Catholic.

Not that there was any animosity, but the two groups generally stuck to their own circles. There was the occasional spat over who had the better bake sale, or which congregation sang the prettiest, but it was nothing serious. Jack couldn't help but remember the nightly news he had seen growing up of the Irish Protestants and Catholics blowing each other up. He assumed that their argument was over something more than bake sale brownies. Pastor Will led everyone through a rousing rendition of 'We Shall Overcome,' and proceeded to open his Bible to begin the sermon. Before he could start, a man in the back pew with his hat down low over his eyes began a slow, purposeful clap. Bart removed his hat and stood up.

"Well ladies and gentlemen of the Baptist congregation, that was as nice a version of that hymn as I believe I have ever heard. I am certain that the Angels are rejoicing at the sound." Bart made his way to the preacher's podium.

"Pardon me, Pastor, but I just need a moment with the flock and I'll be on my way." Bart tried hard but couldn't say the word 'flock' without a scornful tone.

"Folks, please pardon me for interrupting your morning worship service. I just felt that we were having a little communication problem lately. Now, I thought that I had made it clear that our town was not in need of the services of a law enforcement officer. I believe I mentioned that quite clearly at the funeral of the last one... Um, God rest his soul." There were murmurs and a few gasps of disbelief from the crowd. "We all share the same interest in a peaceful, stable place to live and work."

"Then why don't you keep those young cowhands of yours off the streets? Keep them from shooting up the town and burning down buildings," someone shouted from the back of the room. A round of 'Amens' rang out.

"I understand your concerns about some of the indiscretions of our more youthful town citizens. I can assure you that I have taken it upon myself to restrain the activities of any person in my employ."

"It isn't anyone else's boys causing problems. It's those boys from your outfit," shouted a protective mother of three young boys.

"Now, ladies, please." Bart seemed to be getting out of his comfort zone. He had come here to offer a truce and had been put on the defensive. He tried to think of the words that would bring everyone together and the speech just popped into his mind. He was fairly new at giving speeches, and didn't even realize he was plagiarizing.

"People, I have a dream. A dream that someday your boys and my boys will live together, work together and play together." He knew there was something else about being 'free at last', but didn't think it really fit in this case.

Jack could hardly keep a straight face. He had actually started to believe that he had somehow been transported into the Wild West. The reality of last night's conflict had all but convinced him. Now, finally, somebody had slipped out of character, and blown the story line. It had been four days since he had seen or heard anything of the modern world. These people had been perfect, right up until now.

Bart continued.

"Now if having a town sheriff makes you feel better, then I suppose that I can support that. In fact I would be happy to contribute to his wages, to pay my fair share." Bart was staring at Jack as he spoke. Jack couldn't tell if Bart's eyes were saying "I can buy and sell you," or if they were saying "you'll never live to collect your first paycheck." Neither option seemed very appealing.

Bart returned to the reason he came to town. "I have some prominent gentlemen from Denver coming to visit in the next few days. It is very important to me that they leave with a good impression of our wonderful town. To that end, I would like to throw a party Tuesday night. There will be plenty of food, music and dancing. You all are invited. Consider it my way of apologizing for any inconveniences that my boys may have caused you fine people. Now if you don't mind I need to head over to the Catholic church and let those folks in on the party plans. Of course I knew that the Baptists would be up before the Catholics so I came to speak to you fine folks here first." Bart smiled like a politician as he left the podium and walked out the door.

Jack was still smiling from the thought of Bart's hack job on Martin Luther King's speech. It was pretty good for off the cuff plagiarizing. Jack wasn't sure he could quote it correctly, either. Hope was not as amused.

"Did you hear that?" she asked, as she proceeded out the door to see where Bart was going. Jack followed.

"Yeah, not bad, as far as speeches go. Maybe he's coming around," Jack said hopefully.

"Throwing money at us? A party is supposed to make it all better?" Her mind was racing and the questions kept coming. "Why now? No Jack, he needs something from this town. I don't know what he's planning, but it can't be good. Did you hear that part about paying you? Last week, he threatened to kill the next person who came into town wearing a badge. He's ALREADY killed men wearing a badge. Somehow, your being here suits his purpose. Our being a good little town suits his purpose. Just who are these men coming into town, and why does he need to impress them so? And we still haven't figured out what he plans to do with all the land. We need some answers, Jack." Without waiting for a response, she started off down the boardwalk at a determined pace. "Let's go see what Doc has to say."

Bart delivered his speech for the Catholics. It was much the same speech, including the Martin Luther King plagiarism. Bart was learning to play to his audience. On his way off the podium, Bart winked as he told them, "I am counting on you folks to make this a lively party. I think we know the Baptists will be quite... reserved." There were laughs and even some clapping as Bart left the podium. Bart had learned the first rule in politics; nothing wins a crowd over better than free food and free drinks.

16

Hope marched over to Doc's at a pace that said she was on a mission. Jack's long gait helped, but even then he struggled to keep up.

"Hope, slow down. What's your rush?" Jack's sense of urgency had waned from the moment he heard Bart slip out of character. He was relieved to push those crazy thoughts out of his head, and get back on solid ground. It was only a game.

"There is something odd about this whole thing. That man is up to something, Jack. Something bad for this town, and bad for us."

They made it to Doc's office in record time. Hope knocked, then went straight in. Doc had been sleeping on the operating table, wearing only his long johns.

"Morning Hope. Morning Jack." Doc smelled like he had just returned from a party of his own. Hope grabbed his pants off of the shelf and tossed them to him.

"Put these on," she directed. As he dressed, she went into the oddities of the speech and Bart's actions, including trying again to get her to part with her land. She told Doc also that there had been news from the Schindler family that they had agreed to sell, helped in their decision by a burning barn.

"Doc, what do you think that scoundrel is up to?"

"I don't know, Hope. Maybe he just likes to collect things. He is collecting land like trophies. He wouldn't be the first cattle baron to want a larger empire." Doc dunked his head in the wash basin.

"But he doesn't run that many cattle. You don't really think that is all there is to it, do you?"

"No, you are probably right. But what is it that we can make a decision from. Like I said, he hasn't done anything with the land he's bought. So far he hasn't really hurt anybody. Nothing that can be pinned on him, anyway. If you'll recall, I argued until I was blue in the face over the court's determination that Sheriff Kent had committed suicide by stabbing himself. Logic and reason don't account for much against a judge sitting on a stack of Bart's money."

"Besides, what are you going to do to stop him? If it makes you feel any better, I gave him a bottle of what he thinks are ordinary sleeping pills last week. I tripled the dose, though he doesn't know it. I figured any time he spent sleeping he couldn't be stirring up trouble. Until he does something rash, or you can get some more information on what his plans are, you are powerless to stop him."

"Bad move, Doc," thought Jack. Of all the words Doc could have used with Hope, 'powerless' seemed the least likely to cause her to stop. 'Powerless' to Hope was a dare, an insult. This Jack knew after only a few days with her. Doc should know better.

"Maybe Doc is right." Jack tried to bring her back to reality. "Why don't we wait and see what his next move is. I mean, we can't exactly just go right up to Bart and ask him what he plans on doing with all that land, who these people are, and why are they important. No, ---"

"We can't, can't we? Certainly we can," she interrupted Jack. Dropping her chin and raising her eyebrows, she pointed a finger at Doc.

"Don't ever tell me I'm powerless." With that, she strutted out the door.

"Powerless? Really, Doc. You should stop and choose words that you know won't rile her up like this," Jack scolded.

"I know, I know. Sometimes I speak before I think. So Jack, how are you feeling? Let me see how that bump on your head is healing," he asked as he leaned over to look at Jack.

"I'm alright. I had a headache for a day or so, and I am still feeling a bit confused. Everything else seems to be ok."

"No nausea, blurred vision, dizziness? No dulling of the senses? Trouble figuring out where you are?"

"No, unless you count the five minutes or so after I fell off that horse of yours," Jack laughed. "I had all of those for a while. Really, though, a few days of good work and good food has me feeling great. In fact, my senses are in high gear. My lungs feel incredibly clear breathing in this fresh country air. My sense of smell and taste has come alive lately."

Jack thought, "Not entirely truthful, but who is when a doctor is questioning them?" He had no clue where he was or what he was supposed to be doing. And there was that constant sense of discomfort, unease, that kept nagging at the back of his mind. Good thing the Doc hadn't asked about paranoia.

"Your taste buds will perk up as you eat new foods," Doc replied.

"That's not what I'm saying, Doc. Things that I have eaten a million times before seem to burst with flavor. There are smells that I seem to have always known were there, flowers and trees and grass and animals, but I sense them much more acutely now."

"Well, nothing harmful about that. Do you mind if I ask what your plans are?"

"I don't exactly know how to answer that one. This is the fourth day that I have been here, and I've only got the three left. I haven't really planned what I'll be doing with those."

"Hmmmm," Doc said, which Jack knew was doctor language for "I'm not saying anything but you are a goner."

"Only three days left? You're not going to turn into a pumpkin after three days, are you Jack?"

Jack was in a quandary. He wanted to stay in character, for whatever this game was, but the events of the last 24 hours had put serious doubts in his mind about any theories he might have had for where he was and why.

"No, I suppose not. I've just given myself a week to figure out what it is I want to do." He turned to leave. "I'll probably keep helping Hope out for the time being," he said as he walked out of the office.

It was no trouble finding Hope once Jack got outside. She was just down the street, laughing and talking to someone in front of the general store. Jack stood and watched for a moment. He could see Hope's face, bright and shining as she carried on her conversation. Jack was fascinated just looking at her. Seeing her talking to a man made him realize how much he wanted Hope. Jack couldn't help thinking that all men must want her like this. Then thousands of years of instinct propelled Jack into motion. His face warmed a little. He needed to claim his object of desire before that other male animal could claim her. He saw that she noticed him coming across the street. As Jack got within earshot of the two, he had trouble comprehending what he heard.

In her most perfect imitation of Scarlet O'Hara, Jack heard Hope almost sing, "Why thank you kindly, Bart. I would love to join you for dinner this evening."

Hope started walking past Bart, reaching up and just touching his arm as she breezed by. Jack was shocked. Stunned. Jealous? He opened his mouth to speak as she approached, but his lips failed him as he met Bart's gaze. That little crooked smile of Bart's spoke silently across those thousands of years of biological history. "She wants me, because I am a better male than you are." Now came the nausea that Doc had asked about. Jack did manage to squeeze out "What the ..." before Hope turned him by the arm and led him back down the street. Jack looked back over his shoulder, and thought he saw Bart thump his chest as he entered the store.

Jack's cheeks were on fire now. Why on Earth had she jumped tracks so quickly? He thought that they had become close. He thought Bart was the enemy. Sure he was rich and powerful, but that didn't make him a better male. Jack was a good male. He knew he was.

"Has he gone inside yet?" Hope asked. Jack's response belied his feelings of hurt and confusion.

"Yes, he has, beating his chest like a gorilla."

"Good. We have plans to make."

"Plans?" Jack asked in a higher pitched voice than normal. "Only thing it looks like there is left to do is figure out what pretty dress you are going to wear to dinner at Bart's tonight!"

"That is the easy part," answered Hope. "Something low cut." Jack's heart writhed in the pain of being crushed in a vise. Breathing was out of the question.

She continued, "We'll need to find someone who has been in Bart's home before. We need to know the layout."

It took a second, a very long second, but Hope's plan finally came onto Jack like a ton of bricks. Wow! Had he been stupid! 'Little head thinking for the big head' was the first thought that came across his mind.

"So you are only going to dinner with Bart to get information?"

"Yes, and..."

"To get inside his house?"

"Yes, of course. What did you think? That I had taken a sudden liking to that barbarian?"

"So you think that there is some information on what his plans are somewhere in his house?" Jack asked, ignoring the "I am an idiot" confession that he knew she was looking for... and maybe deserved.

"There has to be something there that will help us figure out what he is up to."

Brilliant. She really was smart. And gutsy.

"So how do you plan to get a look at his private files? You can't stay there until he falls asleep, and you can't really drink him under the table. It could be dangerous being all alone with a drunk Bart. You're not planning on whacking him over the head with something, are you? He would be on to you as soon as he came to."

"No, he can't know that we are onto his plans," Hope said coyly.

"So I can't see how you are going to turn his attention away long enough for you to sneak off?"

"I'm not. I am going to be so funny and so alluring that his attention is sure to be fixated on me... "

She emphasized the word 'me' unnaturally, in such a way that the last brick of her plan finally fell onto Jacks head.

"You want ME to sneak into Bart's house? Are you crazy? Bart is fourth or fifth on the list of people that want to kill me at Decker Ranch!"

"It's the only way, Jack. You said so yourself. I can keep Bart distracted, and the cowhands will all be in the bunkhouse. Bart wants a private dinner. I'm betting that after he shows off how many servants he has to make dinner, he shoos them away, also."

"So I am supposed to slip into his house, find the information that blows the lid off of his plans, which we know is bad for everyone in town, and then sneak out unnoticed? In the meantime, you are having dinner alone, with that barbarian... Alone. The longer you are alone with him, the more danger you are in. You won't be able to fend him off all night. As soon as you stop pretending to be interested and have to get out of there, Bart is likely to figure out something is going on. Which means I am in trouble."

"That's why you will have to hurry."

"Hurry? I don't even know what it is I am looking for."

Jack was beginning to regret that whole smart and gutsy side of her.

17

How long had it been? Was he sure that he hadn't seen any or were they right there all the time, and as usual he just didn't take note of them? Jack thought back hard, trying to remember when he had last heard or seen an airplane or its contrail. He had worked outside for two days with Hope. They had spent time on the hill top, staring off into the sky. Of course he was distracted, looking at Hope most of the time, but he had looked at the sky and noticed how clear and colorful it was several times. He could not remember seeing or hearing a plane since he got here. It was easy enough to confirm, though. He stepped out from under the porch and looked up. The clouds were broken, and there were large gaps of sky exposed, but not enough to confirm his theory. Jack made a mental note to keep checking. What to make of it if there were no contrails was another story. Not since the weeks after 9-11 had the skies over the US been clear of aircraft and their contrails. Jack's mind drifted to a random thought...What was the movie where the guy goes back in time and they have to push the DeLorean with a train to get it up to 87 MPH?

"Hey, where's my DeLorean?" he laughed.

Jack realized by now that he was not going to build any bridges nor do a zip line with his coworkers. The Leadership Exercise theory was out. He would have seen someone he knew by now. Personal growth, then? Maybe this was part of the management track. See how a prospective leader makes decisions when the pressure is on. Jack couldn't imagine his manager making a decision while getting shot at with real bullets, no matter how much he trusted the actor's marksmanship. Those pants would need some heavy laundering. Fantasy Island, then? He hadn't seen Ricardo Montalbon anywhere, and definitely not Tattle?... Tattoo?... the short guy with the grainy voice. Jack had a lot of questions, but there didn't seem to be many answers. None that made sense, anyway.

Jack could also make no sense out of what he wanted from Hope. Well, long term wanted. He had no problem figuring out what he wanted right away. He could see that she was interested in him, but wasn't sure if that was real or part of this acting job. He knew what he wanted that answer to be. Each time he looked at her she was more beautiful than the last. With each word she spoke she became more interesting, smart, and funny. He stopped himself. What the heck was the matter with him? Nobody was perfect. She probably just had good writers for her part of the story. His week would pass and he would be gone and she would be studying lines for the next guy to get a free dude ranch adventure in the mail. It was getting harder for him to stick to the story line with all of Hope's questions about his presence in town, and about his intentions.

Hope was even more worried and confused. Jack had no idea just how hard she was falling for him. If he was more enamored with every look, every word of hers, she was already gone. Jack kept surprising her with his resilience, his strength, and his ingenuity. Getting Zeke off of that little boy and running those Bowe brothers out of town had been one courageous feat. And he had done it without a gun. Who knows how to do all of that stuff? Where did he learn it? She had asked him, but he just shrugged it off. She was ready to commit fully to Jack, although she knew next to nothing about him. She knew that whoever he turned out to be wouldn't matter, since her heart was already his.

They were headed to the saloon to have a talk with Scarlet. It was no secret that Scarlet had been one of Bart's favorites when he first came to town. The frequency of their business transactions had slowed to almost nothing since, as Bart's interests turned to younger, wilder girls. Scarlet would know the layout of Bart's ranch, and would have no problem helping them out. Hope probed Jack as they walked.

"So Jack, what is California like?"

"It's wonderful. A lot like here, but the trees are magnificent. Some of them are as big around as a house, and several times as tall. The weather is milder."

"What is your family like? Are they close? Do you miss them?"

"Sure I miss them. I don't talk with them often enough. My brother says I never call. But we are close, as family goes these days."

"You make the trip all the way out there and don't call on your brother? Shame on you."

"No, I mean I don't call him on the ---" Jack stopped himself. Break character or not. It would be nice to just be himself, to relieve some of this confusion. He wondered if she would help him do that, if only for a moment. "Telephone" Jack said, and looked at her face to gauge her response.

"Hmmm," was all he got, with an unreadable facial expression.

"It probably costs quite a bit to correspond with telegraphs." She had assumed telephone was some new term for the familiar telegraph. "I should think that you wouldn't do that very often."

"How about your mother and father? Do you correspond? They must miss you terribly." Hope had only her own experience to go by. She wrote monthly to her mother in Philadelphia, more out of protocol than a desire to communicate. They had stopped communicating years ago, when Hope refused to be the buttoned down, quiet, unassuming socialite wife in waiting. Her father had been the one to encourage her independent thinking. He taught her to question everything, and the value of being aggressive. She might have stayed in Philadelphia if he were still alive. After his death, her relationship with her mother grew steadily more strained. Hope had been a bird in a cage, stifled by Philadelphia society and the bleak promise of trading her mother's cage for some suitor's. She had run away with James at their first opportunity. She had not regretted her decision even once since then.

"No," Jack said, "I haven't gotten a letter from them since I left California. I don't think I have ever gotten a letter from them, now that I think about it. Of course, it isn't all that surprising, since I have never sent them one, either. Unless you count email." He looked for the shock. Would she break character?

"What is that," she asked? "Email?"

Nothing shook her. "Oh, just a fancy word for telegrams." She was either very good, or very authentic. Jack was back to being as confused as ever.

"Why don't you keep in touch with your family? Are you sure there isn't some conflict there?" She was pushing a little harder to get below the surface now. Jack had a wall around his entire life.

"No, there really isn't anything wrong. Families just don't communicate that much anymore."

Hope took her last shot. What about his work?

"Well what exactly do you do for that company in Denver that you left California, and your family, for? Technical Transients, or something?"

"I am an Electrical Engineer for TechTronics," answered Jack. "What I do for them is---"

She stopped him with a wave of the hand. She may not be overly sophisticated, a prairie ranching woman, but she grew up and went to school in Philadelphia.

"Never mind, Jack. I am having trouble keeping up with all of your complicated words for everyday things. I suppose you will tell me that 'Electrical Engineer" is just another name for someone driving those big new trains for the railroads that keep popping up everywhere. You clearly don't want to tell me about yourself, so I won't ask anymore."

Jack hoped that last part was true, but had a feeling he would hear about it again. He didn't really have anything to hide from Hope. He just didn't know what to think of the situation he was in, and how much to convey to Hope. He surely didn't want the end-of-exercise debriefers laughing at him.

"Hey Darla, get a load of this. He actually thought he traveled back in time! That he really was going to score with Hope. Perfect!" If she had given him some kind of recognition for his modern day references, he might have tried to be more open with her. What if this actually was some bizarre time travel adventure? He could not imagine her response to a complete expose on whom he was and where he was from. Didn't the ladies always faint in the old movies? As it was, he was just sticking with the story line. Maybe he could redirect the questioning, and soften a little of the aggravation he had heard in her voice.

"How about you? Do you stay in contact with your family? Sisters? Brothers? Parents?" He could string together five questions at a time, too.

Normally Hope would have been happy to pour out her life story to Jack. She could have kept him going for quite a while with that one topic. But not now, not after he was so protective. She wanted to open up to him, but it was going to have to be a two way street. Her heart may have been an easy target, but selling her head on the relationship was going to take a lot more than that, Mr. Banyan. Besides, they had reached the saloon.

Scarlet proved to be a wealth of knowledge of Bart's place. When they were done talking to Scarlet, they were sure that they had a complete layout of Bart's ranch. Before they could leave, she stopped Hope will a firm grasp on her arm.

"You'd better think twice before you go out there by yourself, Sweet Pea. Bart ain't exactly what you might call a 'gentleman' in private. I've seen my share of ---unique requests. Bart ain't looking to have fun. At least nothing that anyone else might consider fun. I was glad to get out of there at all, and I'm not ever going back."

The grim look in Scarlet's eyes and the still firm hold she had on Hope's arm confirmed their fears of what Bart had in store for them and their town.

18

Jack was jealous. There was no other way to describe it. Hope looked like a hundred dollars. She had not taken all that long to get ready for the dinner, but she was positively radiant. While that was good for Jack, it was also bad for him. She was looking radiant for that other male animal, the one with the smirk. That stung. They rode together in her wagon on the trail toward Bart's. What had started out that morning as a colorful sunrise had turned into a cloud filled sky that threatened to open up at any time. As they rolled along, they went over the plan again.

"So I'll jump out of the wagon before we get to Bart's and you'll keep on driving?"

"Yes."

"I'll walk the last couple of hundred yards while you ride up in the wagon?"

"Yes."

"I'll avoid the vicious dogs, slip past the servants' quarters and the crazed cowboys in the bunk house, then sneak in the back door while you two are in the parlor having cocktails?"

"Yes."

One word, and that little smile of hers, where she just turned up the corners of her mouth, and Jack's concentration was gone. He fought to keep his mind on the mission.

"So while you two are in the dining room having dinner, I'll be digging, very quietly, through all of Bart's files and drawers and records, trying to find something that exposes his evil plans for world domination?"

"Yes." Her reply was accompanied by a quizzical, slightly confused look.

"Sorry," Jack said. "Are you sure you don't want to trade places? You can look for whatever it is I'm supposed to find. I don't think I will even recognize it when I see it. I might enjoy the cocktails and the dinner part of the plan. Do you think Bart would be disappointed?"

She giggled. His confidence reassured her that she had placed her trust correctly. Just days ago Zeke had her and everyone else in town convinced that Jack was inconsequential. Her opinion of Jack had risen immensely.

"And then you will leave and I will go out the same way I came in, and we will meet back where I got off in the first place?"

"Yes."

"Piece of cake," Jack boasted with false bravado. "What could go wrong?"

"I don't know if Bart will serve cake," Hope responded dryly. "There are the dogs, Zeke and the gang, Bart will be drunk, someone might hear you, we don't find anything... there's plenty that could go wrong, can't you see?" Her voice was filled with disbelief. How could they be this far along and Jack not see all that could go wrong?

If this thing was going anywhere, they were going to have to work on this girl's ability to recognize sarcasm.

"Of course, you're right, Hope. Let's go ahead and add 'rain' to your list," as the sprinkle became more steady.

"A little rain should make my evening stroll that much more enjoyable." he added under his breath.

Hope popped open her umbrella and held it over the two of them as she drove the wagon. She stopped the wagon when they were near Bart's ranch.

"It's just beyond the next rise. You'd better hop out now. We don't want them to see two people in the wagon."

Jack hopped over the side and landed softly.

"Good thing I've got these fancy boots," Jack bragged as he flashed a cocky smile at Hope.

"Seriously, Jack, do be careful in there. There are a lot of dangerous people here and you said it yourself. They all want to kill you."

"Thanks for pointing that out. I seem to have that effect on people around here." Jack started jogging toward the rise. He called back over his shoulder, "You be careful, too. As soon as you feel uncomfortable, promise me you'll get out of there."

"I promise I will, Jack."

The rise in front of them was mostly barren of trees. If he crested the hill in the open Jack would be silhouetted against the late afternoon horizon, so he bore to his left where the tree line provided some cover. At the top of the hill, Jack realized Hope's concept of distances was different than his own. As it turned out, 'Just beyond the next rise' was actually a two-mile hike. Fortunately, the rain was still light. Jack could see the wagon approach the ranch house as he was still quite a distance away himself. He worried about Hope alone inside with Bart. She had proven that she could take care of herself, but she was no match physically for Bart. Jack only agreed to the plan because it allowed him to be in the house with her. He picked up his pace. With about a quarter mile to go, Jack came across some wooden fencing at the tree line. There were only a few cattle on the far side of the corral, so Jack thought nothing of slipping between the boards and taking the shortcut. Through the increasingly dense rainfall he could still make out a barn that he could use as a base to plan the rest of his approach. He tried to stay low and unnoticed as he moved forward, keeping the ranch buildings in front of him while stepping over and around the cow pies beneath him. If Jack had an extra set of eyes, or a better sense of priorities, he might have noticed that one of the cattle had taken notice of him and was heading in his direction. Jack's entire knowledge of the term bullpen came from watching baseball. His awareness was instantly expanded as the movement to his right caught his eye. He now realized that he was in the middle of an actual bullpen, occupied by an actual bull. A bull that was closing the distance between them at an alarming pace. Jack kicked his feet into high gear, while his brain started computing likely outcomes. His initial estimate of his speed and the closing rate of the bull afforded him ample time to exit the pen. About halfway there, a quick look over his shoulder forced a recalculation. It was going to be close. Very close. The bull seemed to be picking up speed, swinging the odds securely in the bull's favor. Jack's mind flashed to seeing the running of the bulls in Pamplona on TV. He had laughed at the panicked mass of people darting out of the bulls' path. Now he could appreciate that panic. He realized he was not going to make it and wondered what sort of bodily damage resulted from being gored by a bull. Jack did gain back a crucial half-step as the bull slowed as they neared the fence, whereas Jack took it in one bound. Half a step was something, but it wasn't enough. In the middle of his jump, Jack was propelled up and over the rail by the bull. The height of the jump actually scared Jack, but his recent experience with landings proved useful, as he managed to land in a roll in some straw. He was winded and shocked, but not hurt. Jack brushed himself off and turned to face his adversary. Holding out one hand with his thumb and index finger slightly held apart, he taunted the snorting bull. "Missed me by that much." The bull didn't appear to have any misconception about who possessed the disputed territory...that would be Jack's last stroll through the bullpen.

Jack turned back to the problem at hand. Between him and the ranch house remained the servants' quarters, the bunkhouse, and some dogs. Piece of cake?...that sounded even less funny now. Which way around the servant's quarters? The bunkhouse lay to his left, and the right looked like a lot of open ground to cover.

He chose to keep as much distance between him and any possible encounter with Zeke. He kept low and moved quickly around the side of the servants' quarters. He got only two steps out into the open before two large black dogs spotted him. They bounded toward him, sounding the alarm with vicious barking and growling. Jack retreated to a spot under the porch of the servants' quarters. The dogs took up position in front of Jack and continued barking. An Asian man came out of the front door waving a broom and shouting at the dogs in a language that Jack hoped the dogs understood. They backed off a little, but maintained the barking alarm. Jack looked for a way out from under the porch, but was blocked from exiting any other way than he had come in. Great. He hadn't even made it into the house before everyone knew he was there.

Hope's evening with Bart had begun splendidly. She kept him entertained and in the front of the house with some chit chat, a little laughing and some wine. She was surprised at how charming Bart could be when he tried. He was certainly trying. She could also see that he was drinking. The wine bottle was empty and she was still on her first glass. "Small sips, Locked hips," her mother used to say. That was wise advice here. It was apparent that Bart had started before she got there. Not that it was all that unusual for men to knock back one or two during the day, but she started to worry about Jack's warning of just what a drunken Bart might try and how she was going to extricate herself from the situation should it arise. She had not heard nor seen Jack, which she told herself must be a good thing. That was when she and Bart heard the dogs barking outside. Bart walked over to the window. Hope hoped that it wasn't Jack that they were barking at. Surely Jack was already inside, wasn't he?

"The rain is really coming down now," she said. "It's not fit for even a dog outside." Bart looked at her for a moment, then shrugged his shoulders.

"If you say so." He pulled open the door and called the dogs. "Zeus! Apollo! Come!" The barking stopped and two dogs came running through the door and off into the kitchen. Hope convinced herself that would make Jack's escape less difficult. He was probably well through his search by now. Hopefully he had found what they needed. She wondered how much longer she would have to keep her charade going. Bart was getting less and less charming as the minutes passed. He summoned the kitchen staff for another bottle of wine and then dismissed them for the evening.

"Drink up. We're just getting started." His words were slurred and he spilled some of the wine as he poured.

"Zeus! Apollo! Come!" Jack had been looking for something to throw at the dogs when they heard the command, turned and ran around to the front of the ranch house. He watched through a gap in the porch floor as the servant turned and went back into the house. Just like that, Jack was alone again with only the sound of the rain falling even harder now. He darted across the open space and up onto the back porch of the main quarters. He took a quick look around to see that he was unnoticed, then tried the knob on the back door. Unlocked. He started to enter, then froze. His boots were caked with mud. There was no way he could pass through the house without leaving a muddy calling card. He took off the boots and set them down just outside the door, then stepped softly into the dark room. He was in a store room that led to a long hallway. There was music playing through a side opening about twenty feet down the hall. As he tiptoed toward the opening, Jack laughed at Bart's attempt at mood music. It certainly wasn't John Coltrain, or even Colby Caillet. Bart's music selection seemed less pathetic as Jack neared the opening and heard Hope laughing and giggling. He tried to keep himself focused by repeating, "It is all an act...It is all an act." Jack peeked around the corner and saw Hope facing him. Bart was paying attention to Hope. Close attention. Her eyes widened and her eyebrows lifted slightly when she saw him. Jack shook his head to indicate that he was just getting started. She showed the slightest frown, then laughed at something Bart was saying as he poured more wine. Was Bart slurring his words? Could he already be drunk? She gave a quick head jerk, motioning him down the hall, then returned her attention to Bart. As Jack slipped past the opening, he saw that the dogs had come back into the dining room. One of the dogs must have seen the blur of motion as Jack whisked past the hallway entrance, and let out a loud bark. The other chose that time to do a shake, splattering water all over Bart. Bart scolded the dogs and sent them into the back of the house. Hope could think of nothing fast enough to stop them as the dogs lowered their heads and cowered into the hallway behind Jack.

Jack had just slipped into the first of several doors in the hallway. He had the good sense to close the door behind him. He was in Bart's bedroom. The first things he noticed were two glasses and a bottle of wine next to some cheese on the bedside table. Getting a little ahead of yourself, aren't you, Bart? Knowing what Bart thought was going to happen tonight got his blood boiling, but he focused himself on searching the bedroom thoroughly. There was nothing there that shed light on Bart's plans.

"Must have trouble sleeping" he said quietly, as he read the label on a bottle of pills on the dresser. He started out of the room for the next door, but spotted the two dogs lying down in the hallway back by the dining room entrance. Not again! He closed the door quickly and started pacing back and forth in the bedroom. He eased the stopper off of the wine bottle, took a long swig, and reached for some cheese while he thought. His eyes lit when he realized his escape was in his hands.

He grabbed the bottle of pills from the dresser, rolled the cheese into small balls and stuffed a few pills into each. He pulled the door open to toss the cheese balls down the hall, only to be greeted by the snarling teeth of both dogs standing in the doorway. "WHOA!" he let out under his breath and swung the door back closed. He could hear the two dogs growling menacingly and sniffing at the doorway. Jack slid the cheese balls under the door, nearly losing a finger as the dogs snapped them up. Jack had no idea how fast the medicine would work. He sat on the bed and waited.

Hope had been going through stall tactics, asking about the Chinese gong that was against the wall, and what that painting was over the fireplace, and where had Bart gotten it. It was a picture of a man, dressed as a Greek warrior, sitting on a throne, being fed wine and grapes by a group of adoring women as the gods looked on approvingly. Bart went on and on about it, describing its meaning and extolling its subtle story of power and stature. Hope had never seen a painting so garrulous and demeaning. There was nothing subtle about it. All she could manage was "Oh, yes, I see," as she tried to keep that little bit of vomit down in her throat.

"And how about that vase?" Everybody liked to talk about their taste in art, she had learned in Philadelphia. Bart was no exception. She had also learned that every man's interests changed in direct proportion to how intoxicated he was, and Bart was showing ever increasing signs of intoxication, and ever increasing interest in being near her, touching her. "Hurry it up, Jack!"

Jack peeked under the door and saw nothing. He eased the door open and looked around the corner. The two dogs were curled up together like a couple of puppies with bellies full of warm milk. He slipped out of the bedroom and into the next doorway. Bingo! The room had a large desk, cabinets and bookcases in it. Jack took out his little multitool flashlight. He dove into the desk drawers first, then the file cabinets and shelves. Mundane receipts and records for running a ranch was all that he could find. He wasn't sure what it was that he was looking for, but he knew that he hadn't found it. Once he had gone through everything he could see, he sat down in the desk chair to think. This had to be the room. He switched off his flashlight and let his eyes get accustomed to the dark. He felt like he had seen something while he was looking through the room that should have been different. Something out of place. Or out of time! He opened the bottom desk drawer again. There it was. A wristwatch. He could see on the face the little luminescent dashes marking each hour, and the glowing hands showing it was almost eight o'clock. Luminescent watch dials in 1870? A wristwatch? He didn't think so, but he wasn't sure. He re-examined the drawer. From the outside it appeared to be much deeper than it was. He flipped out the knife on his multitool and pried the drawer bottom up. It was the old false-bottom-drawer trick he had seen many times in movies over the years.

There were several letters, logbooks and a map in the hidden chamber. The map covered the local area all the way from Cheyenne to Denver. Bart had drawn all over it, marking the land he had bought or intended to buy and the present owners. The highlighted areas surrounded a rail line printed on the map. There was a large section of the map highlighted with the name Sugar in the corner. The letters were from Democratic Party officials in Denver discussing political strategies, prominent contributors and likely roadblocks, and their fees for facilitating one common thread---supporting Bart as a candidate for Territorial Governor! One of the letters outlined a potential strategy elevating Bart to the top of the Democratic Party and being nominated for President. There was a ledger book on the bottom of the drawer. Inside Jack found notes on who took money from Bart, how much and when. Favors promised and crimes committed were recorded like a daily journal. The last entry was a bribe to a Judge Thaddeus Stevens in Denver of three hundred dollars for 'future considerations.' Bart was so confident that he even recorded the things he had done to force the landowners into selling their ranches to him.

"Yeah, this is what we're looking for." He stuffed some of the most damaging letters in his pockets and put the rest of the items back into the secret drawer. He stopped as he was placing the rolled up map back into the drawer. It was laminated with clear plastic. The light shone on the small legend in the corner of the map. His eye was attracted to a number that couldn't be. The print date on the map was 2008! He had stopped wondering whether he had travelled back in time, but now the confusion came flooding back. He sat for a second switching the LED light on and off. If he was in 1870, then how to explain the map date? Light on, light off. If he was still in his own time, then why all the bullets and abuse? Light on, light off. When the answer formed in his mind, it ushered in a fire hose of realization and more questions all at the same time. Mostly, it scared the Hell out of him. He closed the drawer and raced down the hallway. He had to get Hope out of there, and he didn't care if he had to go through Bart to do it!

Hope had run out of stalling tactics. The alcohol had released Bart's inner nature, which meant his hands were all around Hope like a tornado. Hope was trying to remain pleasant, but Bart was more and more insistent, and strong as an ox.

"Come on, Honey. Just a little kiss to start us off right. You haven't been held by a man in a long time, I'm guessing. That's why you came over here tonight. You want a real man with power and money. Listen, I see that Jack fella with you and I just get sick. I know you do, too. You don't have to settle for a greenhorn like him. I'm a real man, Baby and I'm right here."

Bart had her by the waist in an iron grip. He reeked of alcohol, desperation and...depravity. That was the sensation that was sickening her. She was doing her best to writhe away when he slipped his hands down to her butt and pulled her up tight against his pelvis.

"I'll even bet I can make you forget that first man you married, the one that brought a beautiful high class filly like you out here to scratch yourself a living out of the dirt."

Sober Bart was almost charming. Drunk Bart was an ass. She didn't even realize her hand was moving until she heard the crack of the slap on Bart's cheek.

"Enough," she declared. It worked. He let go of Hope and stood back one step. Then his nasty little smirk came out, and his arms were back locked around her waist in the iron grip.

"Standard procedure with you whores," he hissed. "Pretend to be offended. You want it rough? I can play it that way."

Bart pinned her up against the fireplace as he started to kiss and bite her neck. It seemed as if he had eight hands, he was violating her in so many places. She heard him slur out the words, "You know you want..." before she brought the Chinese vase down on his head. The impact broke the vase into a thousand pieces. His skull was thick, but not thick enough to withstand that. He fell to the floor, knocking over the fireplace tools with a crash.

Jack had just cleared the office and leapt over the sleeping dogs in the hallway. The crash in the dining room brought several horrible conclusions to the front of his mind about how the night was going for Hope. She must be in trouble. He came around the corner and stopped in his tracks as he surveyed the situation. He could see that Hope was definitely able to take care of herself. She shuddered once or twice, as she released in low tones, "Don't you ever talk about my men or touch me again, you bastard." She looked up to see Jack, who gave her the thumbs up as he said "I got what we wanted." She looked at Jack, then down at Bart in a crumpled heap on the floor.

"So did I." The kitchen door opened and the Chinese cook rushed in. Jack slid back into the hallway shadows as the woman focused on the unconscious Bart. Jack was expecting the woman to be shocked at the scene of Hope standing over her boss, visibly shaken and holding the remnants of an expensive vase. The cook just shook her head back and forth as she made the "Tsk Tsk" sound.

"You okay?" the cook asked Hope. Of course she was, but knowing Jack had the goods, Hope upped her performance.

"I can't believe the things he said, the things he did!"

"I'm very sorry, Miss Hope. This is not the first time he force himself on girl."

She pressed a cloth onto the cut on the top of Bart's head to stop the flow of blood. The woman chuckled a little.

"This," the cook pointed to the unconscious Bart sprawled out bleeding on the floor. "This is a first. You not like the other women come here for dinner."

"I should hope not," Hope declared.

"No, I like you, Miss. Take my advice. You don't want to be with this man. You much better off if you stay long way from him."

"Thanks. I intend to," Hope said as she gathered her things and strutted out the door.

Jack turned down the hallway to slip out the way he came in. The hallway was a mess of muddy paw prints that Jack tried to avoid. He had a long hike ahead of him and he wanted to keep his feet nice and dry. He could have left his boots on had he known Zeus and Apollo were going to make such a mess of the place. He slipped out the back door and onto the porch. He needed to get those boots on fast and get out of there. When he looked down to where his boots should have been, there was nothing but some mud, and... what looked like a telephone book? Jack picked it up and could see in the dim light that it was a mail order catalog, with about half the pages torn out. He read that Durable Men's Pants were available for $1.25. Jack looked around the porch to make sure he had come out the same place he went in. The surreal nature of this night seemed to have no end. Those boots should be right here. He found foot prints in the mud leading up to, and away from this spot on the porch. The tracks led to the bunk house. One of those cowhands had his boots.

"Damn it, I want my boots back." He could see light and hear voices emanating from the bunkhouse, and he wondered how many cowhands were in there. Then he pictured the very real blood flowing from Bart's head, and the real bullets that had been in every gun he had seen since he got here. Maybe he could wait until they were asleep. That had worked once already. But he couldn't let Hope sit in the rain waiting for him all night, wondering if he had been caught. It burned inside as he admitted he would have to leave his boots. He steeled his jaw and stepped off of the porch. It was sloppy going while he was still in the area of the buildings, mostly mud with a little grass. His feet were soaked and his socks were nothing more than mud collectors. He skirted his way around the bull pen, but this took him along the tree line with its sticks and roots. Jack grew to appreciate the term 'tenderfoot' fully as he tried to gingerly tiptoe his way over the distance back to the meeting place.

In between Ows, Shits, and Ouches, Jack tried to make some sense of what was going on. He had pretty much disproved the team building exercise possibility, and given up on the Personal Development theory. While he still wanted to fit this whole thing into some Fantasy Island sort of adventure, he kept coming back to the craziest idea of them all.

"Outstanding, Jack." There wasn't any risk of being overheard out here in the rain. "Simply outstanding. Not only did you manage to fall through some crazy-ass time portal and land in 1870, fighting a running battle with Indians and a gang of cutthroat cowboys who would kill you for your boots. No, that's not enough. You have to fall in love with the girl that just happens to be the last thing standing in the way of the meanest dude around. Only he isn't from around here, is he? Nope!"

"Ouch!" He tripped over a tree root. "Well give the man a cigar for figuring out he's not the only Future-Boy around. You're fighting someone with just as much knowledge as you have. Maybe more. And he has all the resources he needs to do whatever he wants. Wonderful!" Jack nearly went down as his foot slipped in the mud. He stopped, breathing hard and squinting through the rain. How on Earth was he going to get any of this across to Hope?

When she saw Jack come trudging up through the mud, Hope bounced up and down in the seat, clapping and cheering. His spirit changed the second he saw her exuberance. He bounded the last twenty yards and leapt up onto the wagon. They clasped hands high overhead and shouted for a moment in the rain. When their eyes met, they locked together in a bond that lasted the best part of a minute. He lowered their still clasped hands to their sides as he closed the distance between them. When their lips met in that first kiss, they each knew that this was the person they had waited their whole lives for. Neither of them spoke as they stood kissing in the rain, their lips and their bodies locked tightly together. The horse's growing impatience with standing in the rain, rocking the wagon back and forth, brought them out of their shared trance. There was an awkward, embarrassed moment, then they sat down on the bench seat and started off toward home. Fortunately for all of them, the horse knew the way. Jack and Hope just sat staring at each other, smiling and laughing in the rain.

19

As they rode back to Hope's in the glow of that first kiss, with the rain falling down around them, the couple was not paying much attention to the usual dangers of the West. They rolled right upon the band of Indians that they both knew were in the area. Jack recognized them as the former, very temporary owners of his boots. Now he was also just a former, temporary owner.

"Damn it, I want those boots back!'" he cursed. Then his mind returned to the reality before him. The four braves were pointing rifles and lances at them. Hope had no choice but to stop the wagon. As the Indians approached, to Jack's great surprise, Hope began to speak to them in what he could only suspect was their own Indian language. Hope and the lead brave spoke, then argued back and forth. At least Jack thought it was arguing. Hand gestures were flying. The Indian seemed to be very interested in Hope's possessions. The brave kept pointing at the horses and wagon, and at Jack. What little he could guess about the conversation left Jack with the suspicious feeling that he was just another one of the livestock being bantered and bargained. Hope was pointing off in the distance, and touching her hand to her chest. Finally, she turned to Jack.

"His name is Tonkawa. I don't know him, but he has heard of me and he knows that I am a friend of his chief, so he says no harm will come to me."

"Whew. Thank God!" Jack let out the breath he had been holding since they had first come upon the Indians. He smiled and laughed at the other braves as Hope and Tonkawa continued talking. One of the braves, the one holding the lance with feathers draped on it, gave Jack a big smile back. Jack was disturbed to see several gaps where there should have been teeth. He considered asking Hope to find out how they'd gotten the boots from Zeke. He reconsidered as he realized that he might have to explain how he knew about the boots. That could be problematic, although he was beginning to think that these Indians were likable enough. These three seemed friendly, and they were smiling. He looked back at Hope and tried to make some sense of the conversation. The Tonkawa fellow didn't appear to be as amicable as the others.

That Indian language sure sounded hostile, even after they had all figured out they were friends. Tonkawa was still pointing at the horses and Jack. If anything, the volume and animated hand gestures had increased.

The conversation seemed to reach a conclusion.

"Finally," Jack said. "Can we all get out of the rain now?" Hope looked concerned, and the toothless Indian started laughing and poking at Jack with his lance.

Hope turned to Jack and said, "Tonkawa says I have the respect of the chief, but you and the horses do not, so they will be taking you all."

Jack's heart sank down into his cold, stockinged feet. Tonkawa came around to Jack's side of the wagon and saw Jack's mud-caked socks. He pointed and laughingly said in Indian what could only have translated to "nice shoes," and all the Indians got in another round of laughs. Jack felt the heat of anger and embarrassment well up inside of him. He was getting tired of being laughed at around here, and he was already angry about the boots. He pointed down at Zeke's boots on Tonkawa.

"Nice boots yourself." The other three Indians burst out laughing. Even Tonkawa had to laugh at that.

Jack added, "If you want those nice boots back, you'll find them a couple miles back down this road at the big ranch." He pointed back towards Bart's ranch, though he had no idea how much of that Tonkawa understood. He motioned for Hope to translate. Hope did so without understanding what was so funny about all that.

Hope started to talk to Tonkawa again, and the arguing and pointing at Jack began anew. Her tone seemed to change to the bravado of a salesman. Her hand gestures and voice were filled with grandeur and hype. Without interrupting her own presentation, she put an elbow into Jack's side.

"Take out your portable lantern and shine it at them." Hoping to save his skin with some fancy bartering, Jack took out the multitool and made a grand display of turning on the flashlight. As expected, he got a chorus of "Oohs" and "Ahhs." What he didn't expect was the Indians' response when he tried to point it first at Tonkawa, then at Toothless and the other two. Try as he might, he couldn't catch an Indian in its ray for more than a second before he would spring out of its way. There was genuine fear in their eyes as they darted to and fro to get out of the beam. The Indians were so light on their feet, frantically dodging the beam, that Jack felt like he was playing the laser pointer game with cats. It seemed as if the ray of light was causing terrible pain as it landed on the Indians. Tonkawa bolted for his horse, and the others followed. The four Indians leapt onto their mounts, riding off in a gallop and leaving Hope and Jack untouched. Hope started a slow laugh that increased to the point of doubling her over. It was all she could do to start the wagon rolling back toward her ranch.

"Okay, I'll bite. What did you tell them?" asked Jack.

When she'd caught her breath, Hope told Jack, "I told them that you were a great medicine man from over the mountains. That you had strong medicine, and that they should respect you. If they didn't respect you, you would make the light in your hands. The light of their great God Manitou, and if you caught them in this light they would be trapped. You would own their souls and they would never enter the afterlife. It looks like they believed it." Jack had his own laugh for a while at that. Jack the Medicine Man. He was sure happy he hadn't run the batteries down back in Bart's office.

20

Hope drove the team along in the pouring rain back to her ranch. Jack held the umbrella almost exclusively over Hope's head. His natural instincts to protect her were in full force. Jack explained to Hope what he had seen in Bart's office. He described the letters to the powerful businessmen and the comprehensive logbook showing all of the bribes that Bart had given to build his power. He told her of the map showing all of the land that Bart had purchased and of his intention to sell it to the railroad company. He didn't mention the production date on the map. She could see that Bart was going to be a very rich man. He had already built quite a war chest. What she hadn't guessed was his aspiration for political office.

"He's got it all laid out already," Jack said. "These men coming into town on Tuesday are from the Democratic Party in Denver. Bart intends to demonstrate to them that he is the man that they should put forward as the next governor. He needs to use the town to demonstrate that he has a base to build his candidacy from. He will be in full charming mode for this party coming up. Some free food and drinks, and most of the people in town will be singing his praises. Anyone that might wish to disagree with the new image of Bart will have one or two of those cowhands whispering in their ear. They are capable of burning more than outhouses and barns."

"Oh, that is despicable!" Hope agreed.

"This territory will be a state soon. As soon as he can, Bart intends to jump from the governor's office to the Senate, and maybe even on to the presidency."

"How can that be?" Hope exclaimed. "Surely those men would have to see through someone like Bart. They couldn't let a man like that hold high office."

"They will do anything for money. It doesn't matter to them from where it comes, or whom, as long as it spends. They'll have no qualms at all about putting Bart in office. The one thing they won't do is gamble on a loser." Even as Jack was saying it, he was contemplating how to prevent it. He could not allow the people of the state to suffer that travesty. More importantly, he could not allow history to be altered on that scale.

"All of us will suffer," he thought. Was he part of the suffering group? What he saw in Bart's office was convincing enough. This was 1870. He had no explanation for how he'd arrived at this point; who had initiated it, nor what mechanism carried him through time. Worst of all, he had no clue how he was going to get back. No freaking clue! His stay at the Bar None was only supposed to be for a week, not a century! Although he knew he had to find his way back, he had a job to do first. One look at Hope provided all the convincing he needed.

Hope was still talking about those fools that would put a man like Bart in power.

"They put people like that in power all the time, Hope. They think that they can control him once they put him there."

"He is a snake," she said. "He will turn on them and bite them as soon as he can." She felt the bite mark that Bart had left on her neck that was already swollen and sore.

"Well, we will just have to stop him. So how are we going to go about doing that?" he asked.

"We know of his plan to buy up all of the land between here and Cheyenne so that he can profit from the railroads. Let's find a way to prevent him from getting that land." She hoped it would be as easy as that.

"The easiest part of that is your ranch," Jack though out loud. "It occupies all of the land between Dawson's Creek and the bluffs to the west. Bridges cost money and time, the two things the railroads don't have. They are in a rush to lay track and get a return on their huge capital investments. Bart needs your land to connect the North and South strips that he owns. Without it, the railroad would just shift to the east of the creek and Bart would be without a paddle."

Jack knew the minute he used the colloquial term that he was going to have to explain it.

"I don't understand. A paddle boat?" she asked.

"No, I'm sorry. He would be out of options. No land, no railroad, no money. With no money, there is no Democratic Party support, and no governorship."

"Well, then, it's that easy. I just won't sell. I never intended to sell it to him, anyway."

Jack knew it was a good plan to start with, but he had seen the map. That railroad would be built, he knew. Right down the middle of Hope's ranch land. Could they stop something that did, in fact, happen? Would his efforts to protect history from Bart alter it in some other way? Would that way be better? Or was history locked down, and nothing he did would change the eventual outcome?

"Jesus," he thought, "Why did I skip all of those philosophy bullshit sessions in college?" This problem was too big to fit inside his wet, soaked head. Too big for tonight, anyway. He looked back over at Hope. Even wet, she was beautiful. Maybe even more beautiful wet than dry. Water was dripping off of her lips. She ran just the tip of her tongue over her lips to lick up the drops. He wanted to taste those lips again. If he was going to change history, he wanted it to be with her.

She felt him looking at her, and glanced back at him.

"What?" she asked, batting her eyes and giving him the slightest smile. She might be just a prairie girl, but she knew exactly what she was doing to Jack. And exactly what she wanted to be doing with Jack.

Jack searched for an excuse for why he was staring at her, but none came.

"I was just thinking how beautiful you look."

"Soaked to the bone? I don't believe it for a second. I am sure I look just as much the drenched cat as you do," she bantered.

"Only because you're hogging the umbrella!" he said as he pulled it from over her head, letting the rain drench her even more.

"Oh, you...!" she screamed. Jack reached his arm around her to hold her close while they talked and laughed throughout the long, wet ride back to Hope's ranch.

21

"I sure would like to buy me some of this fine gear," Elijah wished. He paged through the mail order catalog while seated in the outhouse. Even with the candle burning, the place smelled something awful. The rain made it worse, and it sure was a pain to trudge through the mud to get there. He gave it three shakes like he always did, never more, ever since that time Zeke told him more than three was playing with himself. Happy to get out of the stench, he stepped out the door and headed back to the bunkhouse.

"I wonder if that cook has anything left over from Bart's fancy dinner." Some nights he could pop his head in after supper, and she would have something special saved for him. He had really grown to love that China food Bart had her cooking up for him all the time. He had never heard of food like that before, and it was wonderful. And Cook, she seemed to like mothering him. She said he reminded her of her second son. Elijah made a beeline for the back porch so that he could stay under the awning as he walked around to the kitchen side of the house. He hadn't even put his foot down on the porch when he saw them sitting there. They appeared right there in front of him, like they were a gift from the angels. The fancy boots! He had wanted those boots since they'd taken them from that greenhorn. He wanted them something awful. But Zeke took them first. Like always.

"Served Zeke right to have to give them to those Injuns," he'd thought.

Now the angels were giving them to him. He picked them up and caressed them as though they were kittens. Elijah tried to take off his boots standing up, but they were swollen tight from the rain. He plopped his catalog down on the porch and sat on it. He managed to wrench off his old boots and slipped the new ones on with ease. Too much ease. They were several sizes too big. Elijah was swimming in those boots.

"No No No!" he cried silently. He pulled them back off and pulled the catalog out from under him. He frantically started tearing pages out, crumbling them up and stuffing them into the toes of the boots. When he put them back on, he smiled. He could walk in them, but he had to lean forward and clench his toes up to stay in them.

"Fits me perfect," he said gleefully as he sloshed his way back to the bunkhouse. He nearly lost a boot every time he tried to pull his foot up out of the mud, but he managed to waddle his way to the back door.

"I got me some fancy boots," he whispered as he wiped them dry and hid them under the dirty cloths. He would be the first one up in the morning to make sure that nobody stole his gift from the angels.

22

When they arrived at Hope's, they were in a warm mood despite the wet night ride. Jack helped her down out of the wagon, and together they put the horses away. Once in the house, Hope started a fire.

"We need to get out of these wet clothes. I still have some of James' clothes back here. I could never seem to get rid of them." She stepped into the back room for a moment, and emerged with a shirt, pants and boots. "I hope these old boots of his will fit you. They have holes in them, but at least the tops of your feet will be dry," she teased. "I will just be a second." She disappeared again into the back room of the little two room house, closing the door behind her this time. Jack put on the dry clothes, but all he could think about was the woman on the other side of that door. He wondered if he should just open it and walk in. Was it done that way in 1870? Would she be glad if he took her into his arms, or would he get a swift slap in the face? He stared at the fire for a while, weighing his options. When he could stand the tension no more, he stood and tiptoed over to the door. The floorboards creaked and moaned with every step. "If you're gonna make a mistake, it might as well be the one with the biggest upside," he whispered to himself as he reached for the knob. Just then Hope called out from the other side of the door.

"Okay, here I come." Jack jumped back and tried to comb his hair out, or at least straighten it with his fingers, and look nonchalant while doing it. The door opened to reveal a beautiful Hope wearing a long green evening robe. The satin material clung to her curves in a perfectly provocative way. Jack had never seen anyone so beautiful. He was close to getting what he wanted, and he had never wanted it more. So why was he frozen in his tracks? Why couldn't he open his mouth, tell her how beautiful she looked? He was transfixed, for sure, but that wasn't it. "Oh my God," he thought. "This is what it's like to have a conscience!" He couldn't move because he knew he didn't deserve what he was about to take from this beautiful woman. How could he one-night-stand her completely trusting nature? It would crush her. It wouldn't be right. At the end of the week he would be gone, and she would be left here, used, taken advantage of. He couldn't do that to her.

She stepped into the warm glow of the fire light and asked, "What's the matter, don't you like it?" in the sweetest voice he had ever heard.

"Oh Hell, I love it!" he thought. The gown shimmered in the flickering light as it flowed down over her hourglass figure. She swayed her hips back and forth, costing him what little breath he still had. All he could manage was a faint "Yes, you look great." She floated over to the cabinet and pulled out a whiskey bottle and two glasses. "Wait a minute!" Jack thought. "Is SHE seducing ME?" For a second, he was winning the debate in his mind about whether that made it okay. How could he be to blame if she initiated it? His newly acquired conscience found its footing, though, and he admitted that it would still be wrong.

Think fast, Jackie boy..."So how do we go about exposing Bart?" Jack hoped to steer the conversation back to solid, platonic ground.

"Oh, we'll just take those letters you grabbed into town in the morning and show them to everyone. Whiskey?"

Jack felt the need to turn the steering wheel a little harder. He was aching for this woman, and his conscience was the only thing stopping him. Whiskey would put a killer wrestling move on his conscience and that battle would be lost.

"What makes you so sure that will do the trick? What if they don't see the importance of stopping him?" Jack tried again.

"Well, if those letters show the bribes and treachery that you say they do, people will put an end to Bart and his plans." Her brow furrowed. "They do clearly show all that?"

"Yes, of course they do." Jack was glad to be back on platonic ground, but he felt a little shaky from her concerned tone.

"Maybe we should have a look at those letters, Jack," Hope demanded more than asked.

"It's all here," Jack assured her as he walked over to the pile of drenched clothes. He bent down and retrieved the rolled up letters from his pockets, seeing for the first time how soggy the paper was. He took them over to the table and slid the candle closer to provide more light. He had a tough time peeling the pages of the letters apart from each other.

"This is tougher going than I thought. I didn't realize they were getting this soaked."

As he peeled the pages back, Hope let out a shriek. There were runny blobs of ink where the words were supposed to be.

"Jack, that was supposed to be our evidence! Tell me you have more. Why didn't you keep them dry?" she begged.

"Not one inch of me is dry. I didn't know it would run like this!" His heart sank.

"You didn't know? How could you not know? Of course ink runs when it gets soaked. Why didn't you wrap it in something?" Her voice had risen in pitch and volume, so that Jack became completely defensive.

"How was I supposed to know? Besides, I was in a bit of a rush, don't you think? It's not like there was a lovely map case laying there to carry these in." Jack could remember plenty of times finding paper in his pants pockets out of the washer that had survived just fine. How was he supposed to know ink ran in 1870? How was he supposed to know anything about 1870, damn it?

"How does any man that can read and write not know that?" Hope asked angrily. "Our whole plan was to get in there and get evidence. Now what have we got besides some soggy paper, Jack?"

There was way too much emphasis on the 'Jack' in that last sentence. Like it was all 'Jack's' fault. And how could 'Jack' screw up the plan so badly. She was being unfair and it was really getting under his skin. His volume went up, also.

"I didn't let the ink run on purpose. Look, we know what Bart wants to do and how he plans to go about doing it. We had some letters, but we still know what was in them. We can still get the town to back us up."

Hope was on fire. She had come up with a way to stop Bart and protect her ranch. And they had gotten the evidence they needed. All Jack had to do was wrap them up. Keep them dry. It was a simple thing.

"No, we don't have any evidence. We needed those letters. It isn't like we can just go get more. Even if there were more, how would we get back into the house?" She paused for a moment, then asked, "Are there any more?"

"I told you. There is a map and a log book. But those are things he would miss, and that army of his would be on us before we could do anything with them. Besides, you said it yourself, how could we get back in there?"

"I could tell him I was sorry for whacking him on the head. That things were going too fast. You could sneak back in..." She didn't get the rest of her thought out before Jack interrupted.

"No way. You got out of there tonight because he wasn't expecting the vase over his head. You would never get another shot at him before he was all over you."

"I can take care of myself. We must have that evidence to make up for the letters that you let get ruined."

"I didn't 'let' them get ruined!" Jack fired back. "Going back is out of the question. It's too dangerous. We will just have to go to the people with what we know."

Hope hadn't been told what to do since Philadelphia. She didn't like it then, and she certainly wasn't going to put up with it now.

"Too dangerous?" she asked. "For who, Jack? I walked out of there just fine. The most danger you were in was from stepping on a thorn after you lost your shoes!"

In arguments, sometimes words escape that should never get past the thought stage. Hope had gone too far with that last comment. Jack wasn't afraid to go back in for himself. It was foolhardy to try to get back in there, and especially dangerous for Hope. And bringing up the boots only stoked the fire. Jack was already mad at himself for losing what was his a second time.

Jack picked up his things and made his way to the door.

"Where are you going?" Hope demanded.

"Back to the stables. Hopefully I won't step on any thorns. I am going to get this information to the townspeople tomorrow," he said. "I've only got a few more days in this place to make a difference anyway."

"Fine!" Hope shouted. "See how many of them rush out to Bart's with you when you show them your ink blobs." She tossed the ruined letters in his direction, then opened her bedroom door, went in, and slammed the door behind her.

"A few more days?" he had said. And then what? Gone? For good? It couldn't be. He had said he was going to stay. Hadn't he? She was sure that he had said that. Or was she just thinking wishfully for the last couple of days. Why had she let her heart get exposed? She had not felt this kind of pain for years, but she felt it just as keenly now. The intensity of the hurt in her heart demonstrated to her just how much stock she had been putting into Jack in these few fast days. He had been wonderful; all that she had hoped for. On the surface of it, she had seen herself being happy again with Jack. Subconsciously, though, she knew now that she had completely fallen in love with him, committed to him in a way that she didn't think she was capable of again. "A few more days," she whispered. Then she would be back to the hardened, solitary existence that she hadn't realized she despised so much. It had to be better than this feeling of rejection and loss++. How had she read him so wrongly? Thoughts like these passed in and around her head for what seemed like hours before she finally drifted off to sleep.

Jack felt physically sick. If he thought vomiting would have helped, he would have gladly wretched the emotion up from his soul. He had created that whole argument. He knew he had to do it, but that didn't make it suck any less. Was this how Rachel had felt when he called off the wedding? Was this how all those women felt after he had grown tired of their relationship? 'Relationship' was too generous a description for most of the women Jack had casually dismissed. This was payback in spades. At least the rain was cathartic, washing away some of his guilt. He had seen the look on Hope's face when he told her he was only going to be here for a few days. Of course, it was nothing he had any control over. That is how it always happened in those time travel movies. Just before the nuclear powered aircraft carrier was going to change Pearl Harbor history, whoosh! Plug your ears, its back into the vortex. Christopher Reeve finds the penny in his pocket, and Jane Seymour is left all alone for the next sixty years. Jack couldn't do that to Hope. He had to protect her, by leaving her.

"This sucks! How could doing the right thing screw everything up this badly?" he yelled at the top of his voice. Charley barely seemed to notice as he plowed on toward the stable.

23

At the morning's first rooster crow, Elijah was up and in those boots. He had actually dreamt of the boots. He was a famous gunfighter, known all over the territory. He gunned down three men in the streets of town, all at once. He was so quick on his feet in the boots that their bullets couldn't touch him. Pretty girls were throwing themselves at his feet, and all the men were slapping his back and wishing they were 'El Pistolero' with the fancy boots. He was just about to get a kiss from the most beautiful girl he had ever seen when that darned rooster blasted Elijah back into the waking world.

Elijah managed to keep his feet under the table while he ate breakfast. He hadn't yet figured out how he was going to keep Zeke from taking the boots. Zeke always took what he wanted. It just wasn't fair that Zeke was bigger and older. It wasn't the first time that painful thought had run through his mind. If Elijah had been the biggest, and Zeke had found these boots, Elijah knew he would let Zeke keep them, because he was a better man than Zeke. He wouldn't go shoving anybody's head into the horse's water trough. He wouldn't go putting horse pies down anybody's shirt. Or any of the other things Zeke did to him to get the other guys to laugh, just because he was bigger. No, he was just going to have to figure out a way to get Zeke to let him keep the boots. He started to think it might be better to hide them for a while until he had a plan. A shocked cry from Zeke relieved him of the need for any planning.

"God Damn it, Lij! You're wearing my boots!" Zeke had been staring down at the hole in his boot and thinking how awful the pain was, and how painful it was going to be to have to work again all day on it, when he'd caught sight of the boots under the table. "How did you get my boots?"

Elijah had pushed back from the table and stood up, backing slowly away toward his bunk.

"I don't see your name on 'em anywhere." He made a show of looking for a name on the boots. "Nope, doesn't say Ezekial anywhere on 'em." Elijah knew he could divert the argument if he used Zeke's hated full name.

"Don't think I'm gonna forget your wearing my boots just because you call me by my stupid name, you idiot." Zeke was much better focused than usual. "Now take off my boots and tell me how you got 'em."

Zeke limped forward as Elijah continued backing away.

"I ain't taking off MY boots. I found them on the porch last night. After you lost them... to only four Indians," Elijah added, hoping again to divert Zeke. The other cowhands had all backed away so that Elijah felt as alone as if there were only the two of them in the room. He desperately needed some support, but none was coming. Every man in the room had seen Zeke beat the tar out Elijah before, and none of them wanted any part of Zeke now.

"It was forty Indians, and it will take more than that to stop me from giving you the beating of your life if you don't get out of my boots!" Zeke's eyes took on a wild look as he grimaced in pain, stepping down too hard on his gunshot foot.

Elijah was backed up against his bedpost. Cornered and alone, his entire body sagged as the courage drained out of him. He had lost. Just like a thousand times before. Suppertime, Zeke got the biggest steak. Christmas, Zeke broke his own toys then took Elijah's. Girls, Zeke was always putting him down in front of them, hitting him, knocking off his hat. All to embarrass him and steal the girl. The list was endless, and now there was one more thing on it. The fancy boots. Elijah put his arm up to stop the oncoming ass-whooping, and bent over to take off the boots. Looking down at them, though, they seemed to wink at him with a little sparkle. A sparkle that grew into a surge of strength that rose up from the boots and filled Elijah's heart. No, not today. Not anymore. Not these boots. Without actually thinking about what he was doing, Elijah twisted to pull his revolver out of its holster hanging on the bedpost, took a quick aim, and pulled the trigger.

For the second time in two days, Zeke watched a gun pointed at him go off. He had the now familiar sensation of having his foot pinned to the floor, and again let out the moan of disbelief.

"Ow!... Ow Ow Ow! God Damn you Lij! You done shot your own brother!"

If Elijah heard the comment, no one knew. He had disappeared out the back door in a blur. The group of men in the room rushed to the door to watch in amazement as Elijah ran with the speed of a thoroughbred. Zeke, grabbing a pistol, managed to force his way through the crowd and hobble onto the porch. He started to fire at Elijah while yelling obscenities and threats. "I'll kill you, you son of a bitch! And Ma and Pa will thank me for it. They always liked me better than you."

Once he'd made it to the tree line, Elijah started weaving in and out of the trees as Zeke took shots at him. Davey, amazed at Elijah's new found speed and agility, commented to nobody in particular, "It's gotta be the shoes."

While gunfire was not unheard of on Decker Ranch, it was unallowable given the incredible pounding that was already pummeling Bart's head. He had managed to get up and rinse the blood out of his hair, and was standing on his porch getting some air when the shooting started. Bart looked around the corner to see Elijah hightailing it into the woods. He tried to shout at whoever was doing the shooting, but he couldn't be heard over the cussing and laughing. It only made his head hurt that much more. He walked through the mud over to the back door of the bunkhouse.

"Zeke, what are you doing? Put that gun away. And why in Hell are you bleeding from your other foot?"

There was still fire in his eyes and a gun in his hands, and for a moment no one in the room knew what Zeke was going to do. Hadn't Bart shot him in his other foot just yesterday? He was mad, and in pain, and he wanted to do something about it. But bullies like Zeke don't break years of taking orders from their masters easily. The gun went into his belt and his eyes returned to their usual, only mostly crazy look.

"That damn brother of mine shot me in my other foot," whined Zeke. "Now I've got holes in both my boots. I'll kill him when I catch him!" Zeke sat down on the porch and pulled off his boot. Davey gave him a cloth to stop the bleeding.

Bart offered a little advice. "Maybe he's getting tired of all the ass-whoopin's you give him. Maybe you're lucky he only shot you in the foot. Maybe we all ought to be a little more careful around Elijah from now on. The boy is starting to act like a man."

"Listen to me, Zeke. You aren't going to kill anybody, at least not someone that works for me. If you're smart, you'll forgive him and forget this ever happened. I think our little Elijah might just raise his aim a little the next time you come after him. If you're lucky, he'll just gut-shoot you and let you die. Or maybe he'll aim six inches lower, to make sure he is the only Bowe brother capable of producing a child. And then you'll wish you were dead every time you see a whore, or a pretty little gal in town that you might want to start a family with. No, I'd say your days of picking on Elijah are over."

The thought of losing his manhood brought Zeke back to reality. But he couldn't let Elijah just shoot him and run away with his boots. Not his fancy slipper boots.

"Boss, I at least got to get my fancy boots back from him. These ones got holes clear through. Besides, I took them from that greenhorn fair and square. They're my boots, Boss."

"Zeke, if you go trying to take some old boots from Elijah, you are likely to get them back with a bullet in your gut. No pair of boots is worth that. If you need boots, see Mike about a pair and we will take it out of your pay." Bart was starting to feel a little sorry for Zeke. One of those holey boots had been his own doing.

"Boss, these ain't no ordinary boots. When you put them on they are like wrapping baby blankets around your feet. They are real soft and light, and you can move like a cat in them.

We all seen Lij run like the devil in them. Maybe that's why they have that razor hook symbol on the sides of them. Maybe they're the Devil's own boots."

Bart was barely paying attention to what Zeke was whining about, right up to the point that Zeke had drawn that razor hook symbol with his finger in the air.

"What did you say that symbol looked like?" Bart asked with renewed interest. "Draw it for me."

In his own pool of blood, Zeke slowly scrawled a perfect Nike swoosh symbol. Bart felt the cold chill of the damp morning for the first time, and his head throbbed again. He had visitors. That explained a lot.

"If you took the boots from that lawman how come you're wearing two holey boots not fit for walking in?"

"Because those Indians took them from me with all my other gear."

"Then how did Elijah get them? Don't tell me he beat forty Indians and won those boots back."

"He said he found them outside the house last night. I don't know how they got there.'"

Bart walked slowly back to the house, putting together the pieces of the puzzle.

"So we have a visitor? Just what am I up against here?" He was talking to himself again. It wasn't Indians that left those boots by his house last night. Somehow Jack had regained them, and had snuck into his house. Of course! Hope had been a part of the little burglary. She was the diversion. That was why she changed her mind about having dinner with him. So she had meant to crack his skull the whole time, huh? For what? What was it they were after? She was the major holdup in his plans. Her land was the key. Now she and Jack were a greater threat than he had imagined. They were on to something, and they took a big risk coming here last night to get proof. He wanted to know how much they knew of his plans, and how much evidence they could have gotten last night.

"Only one way to find out," he thought. "I guess I'll have to invite them back over today and have a little talk with them."

While the talk sounded interesting to him, Bart was already planning what he was going to do after he had the information he needed. There was an order to these things. First, get the information so that he could clean up this little leak. Then, extract some respect from that Jack character. That would be entertaining enough, but his real interest was in the final scene. Getting from Hope all that he expected last night, and more. Oh, so much more.

24

Hope wasn't sure how long she had been sleeping or what brought her out of her restless slumber. It was unusual for her to sleep past dawn, but the still thick clouds had darkened the morning sky such that it was only a deep grey outside. She was having trouble registering why the dog was barking. She sat up in bed to let her brain catch up to her senses. When it did, she smiled the smile of someone rescued from a precipice.

"Thank God, he's come back!" Her heart had been right all along. He wasn't leaving. Not today. Not in a few days. Her Jack was coming back! She leapt out of bed and bounded into the front room. She stopped at the window to see if Jack was tying up Charley or putting him into the barn. She scanned the entire window view looking for Jack. Biscuit must have finally recognized Jack and Charley, for she had stopped barking. Still, there was no sign of him out front. Just as Hope was turning away, the window filled with the snarling face of Davey.

"Rrraraaggghhh!" he growled in an attempt to scare her for some fun. It worked better than he expected, as Hope jumped away from the window, screaming loud enough that Davey winced and covered his ears. Three of Bart's men burst through the front door with guns drawn. Davey followed close behind.

"Where's your gentleman friend?" Davey asked in a suggestive tone after he had surveyed the room. "Alright you lawman," he shouted. "Put your pants on and come on out of that bedroom. Slow, you got it?"

Having regained some of her senses and all of her pride, Hope defended her honor. "There is no one in there," she said in her most high society Philadelphia tone, forgetting that there just might have been if things had gone a little differently last night. She jerked to free herself from the two thugs that held her by the arms.

"I'll thank you to release me," she demanded. There was a short period of silence in the room before all the men started laughing.

"I don't think so, Miss Sugar." Davey said, as he looked cautiously into the back room. "Why don't you tell us where that lawman is hiding? Not very gentlemanly to duck out and let his woman do his fighting for him. Of course, he showed a pretty long yellow streak down his back when he was doing his little dance for us the other night," Davey chided, earning laughs from the other men. He had learned this role quite well watching Zeke over the years. "Now you'll tell me where that coward is, if you know what's good for you," he directed her. Hope let out a laugh of her own at that.

"Or what, Davey? Just what is it you're thinking of doing? Because I'm betting that your boss didn't send you here with that authority. No, I'm guessing he told you all, very clearly, that nobody better lay a hand on me, didn't he?" she asked confidently.

"Well, Miss Sugar, you are right about one thing. Ain't nobody gonna do no harm to you." Davey gave a little nod of his head, and the two thugs on Hope's arms each lifted at the same time. They started walking toward the door, spreading apart some as Hope began kicking and shouting.

"Put me down you, you, ---" she tried to finish the sentence, but all resistance quickly drained out of her. The only thing running through her brain now was the realization that Jack had not come back, that he really was gone, and that she was all on her own again. She quieted down, stopped kicking, and let them carry her out to her wagon, which they proceeded to hitch up to two horses. Davey tied his own horse to the wagon, then jumped into the driver's seat and snapped the reins. With a lurch the wagon started off, towards Decker Ranch, Hope guessed. She also guessed she would receive a much less hospitable welcome on her arrival this time.

Jack reflected on what was a completely wasted night. He'd ridden for an hour in the rain back to the stable after leaving Hope's. He slept fitfully in the hay, with his mind racing in several directions on what to do. Although the grey skies made it hard to tell what time it was, at some point after dawn his thoughts congealed into what he knew he had to do. This wasn't his battle, and Hope might be better off without him in the long run, but she needed him now. If she thought the only way to protect her ranch from Bart was to march up to his front door and confront him, then that was what he intended to do. She had been right about everything else up to this point, only his anger had obscured his judgment last night. She was very good at pushing his buttons. He smiled as he thought about how well she seemed to know him after only these few days, and how well he wanted to know her. "If this were only a different time," he thought. Then he laughed, a little bit insanely, when he realized that this really was a different time. How screwy was this whole thing? For all the things that had gone wrong on this train wreck of an adventure, Hope was the most right thing that had ever happened in his life. If she were in his world, he would never let her get away. Letting go of her now would be just as tragic. That was why he was back on Charley, and back on the road to Hope's. "Love," he laughed out loud, "will make you do some crazy shit."

The skies had lightened, allowing Jack to see the ranch up ahead. The image of the hero and heroine running into each other's arms was playing in his mind as he rode up to the porch and hopped off of Charley. Jack wondered where the dog was as he tied his horse to the rail. She was usually right on him as he came up the road. He had thought Biscuit and he were becoming friends over the last few days.

"Females... always sticking together," he said aloud. What he saw as he climbed the steps sent a chill down his back. There was a confused mess of muddy boot prints on the porch. Jack's heart leapt into his throat.

He called out to Hope as he burst through the door. As he feared, there was no answer. There were more muddy prints on the floor inside, making it all too obvious to Jack what had happened. Bart had her. That son of a bitch had kidnapped her, or sent his lackeys to do it. He bolted back out the door, intending to jump on Charley and ride straight to rescue her. Movement off to his right caught his eye. There was the dog, tied to a fence post and straining to free herself. Jack approached to find Biscuit struggling against the rope tied around her neck in such a way that it got tighter with each pull. Jack fought against Biscuit's natural instincts to struggle, finally working the rope over her head. Biscuit could only manage a low wheeze as she took in her first full breath in some time.

"I'll get those bastards for you, girl," Jack told Biscuit. "I'll get them for leaving you here to strangle yourself."

Helping Biscuit free herself had at least given Jack some time to rethink his frontal assault on Decker Ranch and its small army. He was going to need a few things. He ran back to the porch and jumped on Charley. On the ride back to town Jack formulated his rescue plan. He knew that riding up to the front door, guns a-blazing, was a suicide attack for him and for Hope. That was what Bart wanted. Bart must know that they had been through his house. He would surely assume that his intentions were uncovered. Did Bart suppose that they had learned enough to stop his plans? Bart was certainly worried enough to kidnap Hope. Jack also assumed that by now Bart had the Nike boots. Those boots were enough for Bart to place Jack in the house last night. And if he had the boots, Bart was certain to know Jack's little secret. So in Bart's eyes, Jack and Hope were a dual problem. Hope would be safe as long as Bart didn't have Jack. Or as long as Jack didn't kill himself in a blazing rush of gunfire riding into the teeth of Bart's army. He couldn't take the town out there with him, either. The appearance of a mob would force Bart into doing something drastic with the mob or with Hope, and Jack couldn't count on Bart's imagination if he was forced to make a hurried choice. One man slipping in alone was the only safe approach. It was crazy to think that he could get into the house and free Hope, but that was the one thing Jack had going for him. It was the last thing that Bart would expect him to do.

25

Jack made it back to town in record time. Charley seemed to sense the importance of his role on this team. Jack rode straight to the hardware store, rushed in and explained to Edgar, the owner, what he needed. Edgar led Jack through the store picking out the items Jack required. A quick stop by the newspaper office netted Jack some photo flash powder. Jack rushed over to Doc's office. Jack had knocked the dogs out once using that sleeping medicine; it might come in handy again. Doc was on the porch.

"Howdy, Jack. Everything all right? You're a bit flushed."

"No time to chat, Doc. Bart has Hope, and I am going after her. I need a few things from you, if you don't mind helping."

"What exactly does that mean, 'Bart has Hope'? They seemed to be right friendly with each other just yesterday morning."

"He's kidnapped her, Doc. We slipped into his place last night. Well, I slipped into his place. She was having dinner with him, but not like 'having dinner'. She was just doing it to give me some cover. I drugged his dogs so I could get in to where he had the map, and now he's got Hope." Jack hadn't realized how pumped up he was, and trying to explain to Doc just seemed like time wasted. He had made his way into Doc's office, and Doc followed him inside and closed the door.

"Jack, I'm sure that all makes sense to someone who was there, but for those of us who weren't, could you slow down and fill in some of the holes, please?"

Jack sat down in Doc's office and took the time to fill Doc in completely. It took a while, but it helped settle Jack down to a level that he could speak, and think, coherently. Doc seemed to understand the biggest part of it all by the time Jack had finished. Jack knew that he was leaving a small hole in the story. That little part about Bart knowing things that were going to happen, and how Jack knew that Bart was from the future, and that Jack knew that was possible because he too was from the future. A 'small' hole in the story. But Doc was nodding his head up and down, pouring them some coffee and asking some very pointed questions.

"So why does Bart have Hope? What does he want from her? And what do you think he will do to get it? The bottom line, Jack; is she in danger?" Dealing with the here and now. Jack liked that about Doc. He didn't seem to get bogged down in the 'what if's' and the long term issues. Must be the medical training. He realized that made Doc the one person in this town that might be able to accept, maybe not understand, but at least accept the whole time travel theory. When this was all over, Jack decided to confide in Doc to see if he could help figure some of it out.

"Bart kidnapped Hope because she is a threat. I don't know how much he thinks that she knows, or what he plans to do about it. But he knows that she and I were at his place last night, snooping around. He knows she was bold enough to con him into having dinner with him, so that he would be distracted. He also knows she is a very capable woman. She split his head open with a vase last night. That is a lesson he won't soon forget."

"Good for her. So tell me what it is that you found that is so threatening to Bart."

"We know his plans are to amass a huge holding of the land between Cheyenne and Denver. Now that the transcontinental railroad has decided to go through Cheyenne, Denver must have a trunk line in place soon or it will dry up and become irrelevant. There are rich men in Denver that can't let that happen, so they will pay anything to someone that can fix that problem for them. Bart has been buying land, bribing officials, and lining up support from businessmen and politicians. He has the plan, the money and the resources to make a fortune. But that is only the first part of the problem. Bart has built a power base that will launch his campaign for Governor of this territory, and then Senator once Colorado becomes a state. He is laying a foundation to spring into the Presidency."

"Good Lord!" exclaimed Doc. "That would be a nightmare!"

"He's got a significant part of the plan already in place," Jack told him. "The Party Officials are coming in on Tuesday. Bart has already lined their pockets with enough money to get their attention. If he can demonstrate that he is a viable candidate, they will put him on the ballot for governor. This party he is paying for Tuesday is intended to demonstrate that he is electable. He will be able to buy support from some, and they will coerce it from the rest."

Jack continued, "I have seen a map showing all of the land that Bart has purchased and of his intention to sell it to the railroad company. He is very near to achieving his goal."

"What is standing in his way?" Doc asked.

"A feisty little gal with about 500 acres of land between the bluffs and the creek. His plan hinges on getting hold of Hope's land, but she won't sell it to him. Without it, the railroad will be forced to go around to the East of the creek. Since that's Indian land, Bart can't get his hands on it without the Federal Government's help. I don't think that he has got that kind of reach. Not yet anyway. What we don't know is what he is willing to do to force Hope into selling. From what I gather, and from what I have seen of him, there is not a lot that Bart won't do to get his way."

"So you think that he has her back at his ranch. Didn't you say he is expecting some railroad people there today? Wouldn't that be risky? They wouldn't be too comfortable doing business with a kidnapper, I imagine. Bribes, graft and kickbacks are okay with those railroad tycoons, and they don't mind killing off a few thousand Indians, but they don't usually like to get their hands too dirty."

Jack hadn't put that piece of the puzzle into place just yet.

"It's a pretty big house. He could hold her in the back and entertain up front, no problem. And I can't imagine he would keep her anywhere else. They grabbed her under cover of rain and darkness, but I don't think even Bart could run around the country with Hope tied up without some interference. He is trying to establish his viability as a candidate. There are people that work for him that most likely don't know the depths of his depravity. I think his only option is to keep her close, under wraps."

"And the danger, Jack. Is she in danger?" Doc knew the general answer to the question was yes, but wanted to know how imminent the threat was.

"Bart won't do anything as long as I am still out here. He can't take the chance of doing her harm while I am still a loose end. I know he has her, and I know his plans. He will need to shut us both up, or he loses everything. She should be safe for now."

"Then let's go get us a posse," Doc said as he rose to head out the door and sound the alarm.

"No!" Jack stopped him. "We can't do that."

"I don't see how we can't, Jack. Hope is in danger. We don't have any time to lose."

"No posse, Doc. I have to go in there alone. If we go out there with a mob, Bart will know his plan is finished. He won't have to worry about keeping up the pretense of being a political candidate. What's worse, he will be forced to make a decision about what to do with Hope. He'll kill her for sure, then cut out of here and start his plan all over again somewhere else." Jack knew that was a real possibility. With his unfair advantage of knowing the outcome of events, Bart was going to be successful wherever he went.

"Then how do you propose we get her out of there?" Doc asked.

"WE aren't going to. I just told you I am going in alone, Doc. I appreciate your offer, but I can't take responsibility for you getting killed, or endangering Hope. You can help by providing a few of the supplies I'll need."

"I'll give you all the supplies you need, Jack, but you'll have to take me along. You can't get in there all by yourself, and getting out will be even harder than getting in. At least I can give you some cover fire for your escape. I can see you care deeply for Hope, but you aren't the only one around here that does. Whether you take me with you or I follow you there, I'm coming, so you might as well get used to the idea."

Jack could see that Doc wasn't going to be denied, and there was some sense to what he said about getting out being harder than getting in.

"Okay, Doc. You're a stubborn one. You know it will be dangerous. You know what's at stake." Jack stuck out his hand. "I'd be proud to have you along."

Doc shook Jack's hand with a firm grip. "You won't regret having some back up."

"I think you may be right, Doc." Jack listed the supplies that he thought Doc might have, and Doc did indeed have most of the items on his list. Doc suggested a few alternatives for the missing items, and before long the two had several bags full of equipment.

They spent the next hour or so building up some 'force multipliers'. If Jack was to have any chance of getting Hope off of Bart's ranch, he was going to need a few advantages. Surprise was essential, but difficult, since Bart had to know that Jack would be coming after Hope. He was going to need some 'shock and awe'. He had been able to scare the Bowe brothers out of town with a little vinegar and baking soda. This was going to take a little more firepower. There was plenty of lantern fuel oil around, so he showed Doc how to make a Molotov cocktail with the fuel oil, an empty bottle and some cotton material for a wick fuse. For the shock part of the equation, he poured some flash powder onto squares of newspaper, then tied them off around a fuse with some string. While it was dangerous to handle, rescuing Hope was worth any risk.

They saddled up three horses, throwing their attack kit onto one and mounting the other two. They rode in silence for a good part of the way. Doc could see that Jack was planning his attack strategy and left him alone to his thought. Finally, Jack broke the silence, but in a way completely unexpected to Doc.

"So, Doc. When did you get to Dawson's Creek?"

"I think I've told you that, Jack. About four years ago," Doc answered with a note of confusion in his voice.

"Yeah, you did tell me that. Only you never did mention where you came from?"

"Well, like most folks from back East. I left Atlanta without any real direction in mind and ended up putting down a stake right here."

"Is that right?" asked Jack. "You put a stake down right here, did you? You named the town, right?"

"Yeah, that's right. Named it after the creek." Doc didn't mind chitchat, but he didn't see how this conversation was going to help Hope.

A minute or two passed before Jack added, "And I guess I was pretty lucky you were Johnny on the Spot that day I got here. How did you come to find me?"

"I'm pretty sure I told you that one, also, Jack. Are you going somewhere with this conversation?"

The sun was shining and the wind had blown the clouds mostly from the sky. Jack surveyed the clear blue expanse.

"Look up at that sky. I was thinking that was about as clear a blue sky as I have ever seen." Jack pulled up on Charley's reins and stopped. He let Doc ride up next to him and looked him in the eyes.

"I can't remember the last time I saw an airplane or an airplane contrail."

Doc's expression was blank. After a few empty seconds, he said. "I'm not sure what you mean by air...?" He didn't finish his sentence. The grin on Jack's face was enough to tell Doc that his ruse was up. Doc smiled himself.

"How long have you known?"

Jack started riding forward again, laughing. "Like I said, you were Johnny on the Spot the day I got here. No questions about who I was, where I was from, where I was going. And I noticed that you are the only one who never found my way of talking to be strange, or needed an explanation. Just now I realized that you never flinched when I asked for aspirin for my headache that first night. You realize that wasn't even invented until about 1900? But I never put it all together, until I was in your office this morning and caught a peek at your medical license hanging on the wall. "This is to certify that the Hon. Marcus J. Welby has graduated with honors from the Paramount Medical College," Jack laughed again. "Marcus Welby, MD! Seriously?"

Between laughs Doc defended himself.

"It was the best Dr. name I could think of at the time. I wandered around for a couple of days when I got here. Mind you, I didn't have anyone to pick me up in a buckboard and carry me back to town and take care of me. I came upon a wagon train and a man that needed a broken arm set. I had been a corpsman in the Army and had no trouble setting the broken bone. After I figured out where I was, I decided I had always wanted to be a Dr. and there was no doubt I had more medical knowledge than anybody around here, so I drew myself up the certificate and began my medical career. And if I do say so myself, I have served this town quite well as their doctor."

"Okay, okay, Doc. We have a shared secret. After we get Hope out of there, you and I are going to have a long talk. There is a lot of this I just don't understand and hopefully you have some of those answers. By the way, Bart used the same travel agency we did," Jack told him.

"I'll be," Doc pondered. "I suppose that explains a lot. This is really starting to get interesting." After a short pause, Doc asked, "Alright then, we're in this thing together now. Don't you think it would be a good idea to tell me what it is that you are planning? How are we going to get in there and back out with Hope? We can't exactly go walking up to the front door and ask for her."

"I don't know about that, Doc, because that is just what we are going to do."

Doc's confidence in Jack's tactical planning ability plummeted. Jack could read Doc's concerns in his expression.

"Don't worry, Doc. I don't plan on getting anybody killed today. Here is what we're going to do." Jack detailed his plan of attack for Doc while they rode. If Doc's confidence ever returned, it wasn't evident to Jack. "It may be a long shot," Jack told him, "but it's the only shot we have."

26

Hope sat in the chair reflecting on what had gotten her into this mess. She knew Bart was serious about getting her ranch and making money, but she hadn't imagined he would be willing to kidnap her. Of course she knew he was capable of that, and a whole lot more, but somehow she had believed that she had some sort of preferential standing with Bart. Even if that had been true, the crack on his head last night would surely have changed things. It had felt good to let him have it, though. She wasn't sure it felt good enough to make being here now, as his prisoner, worth it. She could see no escape. She wasn't even certain where she was. Well, not exactly sure. Those mindless cowboys had put a blindfold on her once they got near Decker Ranch this morning, but any fool would have known where they were going by then. Now she sat with her hands tied to a chair and her eyes covered. Her Jack was gone. What did the rest of this matter? Sure, she could continue on, just as she had done for years, but for what? Why fight Bart? He was going to get his way in the end, most likely. People with money always seemed to win out over those that were just trying to do what was right. She had seen that play out many times in Philadelphia. The rich get richer at everyone else's expense. She could fight, probably alone, until they'd dammed up the creek to deny her water, run off her livestock, bribed the government to steal her deed, and whatever other underhanded tricks they had. For what? Those people in town didn't care about her and her ranch. They were all getting ready to have a party for Bart! A party for the man who'd kidnapped her. There was only so much one woman could stand. She needed to look out for herself now. Maybe she could actually get a good price for the ranch. That cut on Bart's head would probably cost her. If she had only known Jack was going to abandon her, last night could have been negotiation instead of confrontation. Now her bargaining strength was severely hampered. She resolved that when she got the chance to talk to Bart, she would ask him to make an offer. She took a deep breath and released it, feeling relieved of a great burden. Her life was upside down, but at least she no longer had to carry the weight of stopping Bart on her tired shoulders. She almost felt happy about finally getting to see California.

Hope didn't have to wait for long. She heard a heavy door slide open, and two or three sets of feet enter the room. She sensed that they stopped a few feet in front of her. There were a few seconds of awkward silence, then she heard Bart's voice.

"Well, if it isn't the little lady with the vase."

"Good," she thought. It was Bart. No time to waste. She opened her mouth to start the negotiations.

"Bart, I" was all she got out before the hot sting of a slap across her cheek stopped her mid-sentence.

"Don't open your mouth until I tell you to," he growled.

Hope was confused. Clearly he didn't know that he had won. This was going to go all wrong unless she could get that through to him.

"I just wanted to..."

Wham! This one was still a slap, but it knocked her head clean around to the side.

"You bastard!" It was all she could do to keep that inside, but the message to stay silent was clear. "What was I thinking? This bastard will never get my land!" again only to herself.

"That's better," Bart said. "I think I have your attention. Now I am going to let you talk. You are going to tell me where Jack is."

That was an easy one. "I don't know," she answered. But her emotion gave away more than she had meant to, and Bart was quick to pick up on it.

"Well, is there trouble in River City?" he asked.

She didn't know how to answer that, and she didn't want to risk another bone jarring smack. She sat silent.

"Too bad for your budding romance. It was never going to last, though. He would have gone back sooner or later. If he's smart, he will have already gone back."

"If you don't know where he is, then why don't you tell me what he was doing here last night? What was he looking for?"

"Bastard." she thought. She couldn't call him that name often enough. What does he know about Jack and me? Going back where? Denver? California? What Jack had probably done was gone back and warned everyone in town, which meant Bart's plans were already public knowledge. What better way to stab this bastard in the heart than to tell them his scheme was going to fail?

"He came here looking for a way to stop you, and he got what he needed. Right now he's in town putting a posse together to come after you."

Bart was silent for a moment.

"Hmmm... maybe that's true. Maybe not. They'd have been here by now if they were coming. And that doesn't explain why he left you all by yourself while he ran to town to ring the alarm. No, I don't think you got anything when you left here last night. I think this is all a big bluff. But I do thank you for telling me where Jack is."

"Mike, send three or four men into town to pick up the lawman." Several of the feet left the room. Hope sensed that only she and Bart remained. Bart leaned in close to Hope and spoke in a whisper.

"Even if Jack did get some information last night, nobody in that town will lift a finger to help him. No Darlin', I don't think anybody's going to be ruining my plans. I've worked hard and come a long way to get where I am today. No conniving woman and her two bit, pretend sheriff boyfriend are gonna stop me. What do you think of that?"

Hope despised his confidence as much as she despised the man. She wanted him to know that she knew.

"You are never going to get my land and you're never going to be Governor!"

Bart started to laugh. He removed her blindfold.

"What you don't know, Darlin', is that I already have your land. At least the part of it that I need. It turns out that eminent domain allows the railroad to claim an easement right down the middle of your property. I happen to know, or should I say 'own', a judge in Denver who will be ruling in favor of that motion very shortly. Of course you'll be paid some pittance for the use of your land, and you'll still own the two worthless strips on either side of the railroad. It's a pity I'll have to knock down that little house of yours." He paused long enough to let the images fill her mind. "So what were you saying about me not getting what I want?"

Hope strained against the ropes holding her back. If she could just get free to kill this bastard!

"You'll never get away with it! Jack will stop you. He is on his way right now." She said it, but she didn't believe it.

Bart could see that in her eyes. "You don't actually believe that, do you? Jack is long gone by now. He's gone back to where he's come from."

"No! No he hasn't. You don't know that!" Hope cried.

"I do, and I think you know it, too. Only I doubt you know where he's 'actually' come from." Bart put a strange emphasis on 'actually'.

"Do you, Hope? Do you know where Jack came from?"

"Of course I do. He's told me everything." Her answer started boldly, then trailed off weakly. She wished Bart would stop this questioning; just go away. He could have the ranch and the town and the whole state!

"You didn't understand me earlier when I said there was 'trouble in River City', did you? Don't bother denying it."

Hope remained silent.

"It's a phrase from a play called 'The Music Man'. I don't believe you've seen that play, so it's not surprising that you don't know the phrase. But there's another little secret that I know about that play. You see, 'The Music Man' won't be written for another 80 years." He paused to let that sink in. "Sometimes I say things that seem normal to me that the people around me don't quite understand. Have you noticed a similar issue with Jack speaking?"

Hope's surprise was noticeable. She had always thought that Bart spoke oddly, but she dismissed it as insignificant. Now that he pointed that out, she realized that Bart and Jack did have a similar manner of speaking. She thought back to the afternoon at the picnic and the many strange things Jack had said about his family and his job. She hoped that it meant only that Bart was also from California.

"So you have noticed. Then I will let you in on our little secret. Jack and I come from the same place. Only that's no place around here, and it certainly isn't Denver. At least not Denver as you would know it." Bart was enjoying conveying his story in a slow, confusing manner to Hope. He could see that while she understood his words she wasn't comprehending, didn't want to comprehend, the greater meaning of what he was telling her. She was a captive audience, though, so he continued.

"Jack and I are not from this time. We came through a time portal from the future; 140 years in the future. I was riding a horse in the hills when I came upon a cave. When I went into the cave I was somehow transported back in time. I wandered around dazed and confused. I sought help from some men that I came upon. They robbed me. I was nearly killed by Indians. When I finally got on my feet and figured out where I was I devised the perfect plan. I had always fantasized about living in the past but possessing the knowledge of the future. Now I could live that dream. I found my way back to the portal. I took a chance that it would work the same in reverse and return me to my time. It did so, but it took a greater physical toll on me than the first time through. I began studying in earnest financial history, stocks, railroads, land values. All of the things I would need to get money and power in this time. I came back through the portal and put my plan into place. The first part of that plan is nearly complete. Once I have the railroad deal, there will be no stopping me. Your Jack must have come through that same cave. It's too bad that you and Jack chose to be on the losing side. You might have been useful to me. As it is now, you're just in the way." He stopped to gauge her reaction. "Do you understand what I'm telling you?"

She did. Tears were welling in her eyes. She understood what he was saying, but couldn't grasp the reality of it. It was a lot of information to process. He was from the future.

Jack was from the future. She had already lost her ranch. Bart was going to win. Jack was gone. She had no trouble understanding the finality of it all.

"Stop, please! Why are you telling me all this?" she begged.

"Because I'm going to kill you, of course, and the villain always tells the kidnapped victim everything before he kills them."

A cold chill started down her spine. She looked at his eyes and knew he meant to do it. She had not contemplated the possibility that things had gotten so far out of hand that Bart would actually kill her.

"I'm trying to decide if I should wait until I have Jack or if I should just do it now." He reached over and stroked her hair. "I might like to have a little fun with you first."

Hope jerked her head away and stared at the ground. She heard the door open and Zeke's voice call out excitedly, "Hey Boss, there's a group of men riding this way."

Hope's heart leapt back up out of the depths of despair. Her rescuers were coming. Her Jack was...

"Ha Ha Ha! You think those sheep from town are coming to save you. Not on your life. That will be the railroad men I invited to lunch to finalize our business deal. The deal that will make me the richest man in this territory," he bragged. On his way out Hope heard Bart give instructions to Zeke. "Put the blindfold back on her. Stay here and watch her. And Zeke...," Bart said.

"Yeah, Boss?"

"Guess which part I shoot if you lay a hand on her?"

27

Jack and Doc rode together as close to Decker Ranch as they dared. It was likely that Bart would have posted a lookout somewhere along the road.

"Here we are, Doc. Time to split up and put operation Damsel in Distress into action. You ready for this?"

"Ready and willing," Doc replied.

Jack took off his hat and passed it over to Doc.

"Trade with me."

"So that was why you made me change into a white shirt before we left. You want them to think it is you riding up the front lawn for as long as possible?"

"Now you're thinking, Doc. We need to swing the odds a little in our favor every chance we get. They'll know it's you, but not until you are right up on them."

Jack prodded Charley and the extra horse off the road and into the trees of the forest behind Decker Ranch. He was farther out than last night when he and Hope split up, but this time he was riding Charley and the distance would go faster. Charley picked his way in and around the scrub trees and made excellent time. Jack was impressed with his own ability to slip through the woods with two horses silently, almost ghost-like. Soon the ranch was in sight. Jack found a nice patch of grass for the horses to graze on while they waited. He rigged a rope line between two trees and tethered the horses to it. He patted Charley's neck.

"Wait here for me, pal. It's gonna be a little noisy down there for a while, but don't you worry about that at all. I'll be back in no time with Hope."

He removed his satchel of supplies and slipped the strap over his shoulder. He crept forward, but an eerie sensation that he was being watched came over him. He checked his six several times, but saw nothing. Jack kept telling himself that he had been silent on the approach, so it was probably just his imagination...probably. If there was someone out there, they would have jumped him by now. Or just shot him in the back. He pictured himself stalking through the forest, and then a bullet between the shoulder blades knocking him face down in the dirt. It was almost enough to unnerve him. "Focus on what's ahead of you, Jack. Focus."

He had reached the edge of the forest near the ranch. He took one last look behind himself, ran his hand over the back of his neck to force down those little hairs standing up, and stepped out of the tree line.

Doc had ridden right on down the road, taking his time like Jack had told him. As he came around the bend where Jack had separated from Hope last night, he could see a lone rider at the top of the rise. Doc continued slowly up the road. The rider had waited for a moment, then turned and loped off down the back side of the rise and out of view.

"Okay," Doc thought, "the lookout has taken the bait. So far so good."

He slowed his horse even more in order to give Jack time to get into position. The first part of Jack's plan was really quite good, Doc admitted. Feed Bart's over-confidence as long as possible. As long as Bart thought Jack was playing into his hands, he would continue to underestimate the threat. Riding right up to the front door like a cow to the slaughter was just what Bart would expect of an emotionally driven greenhorn. While everyone was paying attention to the obvious out front, Jack would slip in the back. Swing the odds. Doc continued over the crest and down toward the ranch house. He could see the entire spread as he got closer. What he saw was disturbing. It was a ghost town. Except for five or six horses tied up at the front of the house, and a lone cowhand sitting in a chair petting two dogs on the porch, there was no activity at all. What if Hope was being held somewhere else? What if they were riding right into a trap? Doc pulled his hat down low over his eyes to keep up his impersonation of Jack as long as possible.

Jack skirted his way around the fence line of the bullpen. No need to repeat his mistake from last night. He had thought of that bull every time he sat down on his bruised backside that morning. He ran low across the open yard over to the raised porch of the bunkhouse. He tied a thin rope between the rails of the steps about 8 inches high, then made his way back over to the barn. The barn divided the pasture, with the bullpen on one side, and the horse corral on the other. Jack hung close to the wall of the barn as he crept over to the horse corral. He reached into his satchel and pulled out some sedative-laced sugar cubes for each horse.

"Sweet dreams, Fellas," Jack said. He slipped under the fence and entered the barn from the corral side. He looked around for a second before he saw what he needed. He threw a long coil of rope over his shoulder, then turned to look at several cows in the stalls of the barn. Jack stopped to survey the animals. He actually started to ask himself which of the cows was the most attractive. Having no idea what made one cow more attractive than another, and realizing that he was grossly over planning the situation, he grabbed the collar rope on the nearest cow.

"You'll have to do, Honey." Jack led the cow out of the barn and over to the gate of the bullpen. The bull didn't fail to notice and trotted over to see what Jack and his beautiful lady friend were up to. Jack let the two kids mingle while he tied his rope to the handle of the gate.

"You kids are moving way too fast," Jack chided as the animals nuzzled each other through the boards of the fence. He gave them a moment, then pulled the cow away with him over toward the back door of the ranch house. Jack let the rope uncoil as he walked in a crouch behind the cow. Although he was not sure what anyone would do if they saw a cow walking through the yard by herself, Jack felt it was at least better than someone seeing him walking nonchalantly toward the back door. He continued reeling out the rope as he walked. About 15 feet shy of the house, the rope came to an end. Jack shrugged his shoulders and dropped it in the dirt. He led the cow the rest of the way to the porch and tied her to the rail. He tied another trip line at the top of these steps, then slipped into the house through the back door.

He started to make his way down the hallway, then softly smacked himself on the forehead. He'd forgotten something. He softly pedaled back out the door. After stopping to check that the yard was clear, he darted out to the rope end that lay in the yard and gave it a tug. The gate to the bullpen opened wide and the bull rushed out. Jack sprinted back onto the porch and through the back door again. The eerie sensation was back, but he chalked it up to a sense of déjà vu. He had certainly been here before. He stood there in the store room amidst the shelves stocked with sacks and jars of supplies, gauging the situation. Unlike last night, Jack didn't know how many people were in the house or where they were. The dogs were as yet unseen. There were several men's voices coming from the dining room, with plenty of talk about railroads and money and land. Bart was thanking all the men for coming out and he was sure that this was the beginning of a wonderful business relationship ...blah, blah-blah, blah-blah. Jack could hardly stand to listen to Bart's voice. He wanted to walk in there and pop him in the jaw, but that would surely not get Hope out of there. His first obstacle was that open hallway entrance. It had been a simple thing for Hope to see him last night when she was facing the doorway. Surely several of the men in the dining room would be able to see him as he walked by. Jack looked around the pantry he was in. His eyes stopped on a bag marked 'Beans'. He grabbed several of the dried beans out of the sack, then reached into his satchel and pulled out a hollow tube about the size of a straw. He put a bean in his mouth, brought the tube to his lips and tiptoed his way over to peek into the dining room. He could see that there were indeed 8 to 10 men sitting around the table having drinks and hors d'oeuvres. Jack realized his good fortune. With these railroad men here, Bart would have to be a lot more hospitable should he catch them. At least he hoped that was the case. He looked across the dining room and took aim at his target. He puffed a strong gust of breath through the tube and blasted the bean into the large Chinese gong that Bart had so proudly shown Hope last night. Even Jack was startled as the gong rang loud enough to announce an Emperor. Every head in the room turned, and he scooted across the open space. Immediately following the gong the cook emerged through the kitchen door carrying a platter of food. All the men in the room clapped as if the gong had magically announced the coming of lunch.

When it became obvious that it was not Jack, but Doc approaching, the surprised sentry on the porch stood and called out, "Doc? What are you doing here?"

"I'm here to talk to Bart," Doc answered, as he dismounted and took his time tying his horse loosely to the rail. Doc climbed up the few steps to the porch and started pounding on the door. The man on the porch had all he could handle restraining the two dogs. He had each of them by the collar, but they were dragging him forward to get to Doc as if he represented their next meal.

"Bart!" Doc called out. "Bart, its Doc. I need to talk to you." Doc kept pounding on the door until it opened. Doc was staring at Mike, the ranch foreman.

"What do you want, Doc?"

"I need to talk to Bart." Doc stepped forward toward the slim opening between Mike and the entryway, but Mike shifted into the space to block him.

"Bart's busy. He's got guests. I'll give him a message for you." Mike's gruff tone made it clear that Doc wasn't getting an audience with Bart.

Doc spoke loudly so that anyone inside could hear.

"Tell Bart I need to talk to him. Hope Sugar has gone missing." Doc hoped that would bring Bart to the door.

Mike closed the space between him and Doc.

"I told you, Doc. I'll give him the message. Now get back on your horse and move out." While Mike was saying that last bit, Doc could see over his shoulder that he had gotten what he wanted. Bart appeared behind Mike and dismissed him.

"Mike, I told you to take care of it. Now go keep those fat wallets happy." Before Mike could respond, Bart turned to Doc.

"Doc, what are you making all this noise about? What is it you've got to say about Miss Sugar?"

"Only that she has gone missing, and I wanted to know if you had seen or heard anything?"

"Well if that doesn't beat everything," Bart protested. "Just what would I have seen or heard about Hope Sugar going missing? Maybe you should ask that new lawman friend of hers."

"In fact, I did just that, Bart. He said she was out here with you last night?" It was both a statement and a question.

"Hmmm. I'll bet he did," said Bart. "Sure, she had dinner with me, but she left around eight o'clock." He unconsciously rubbed the nasty cut across the top of his head. "We wouldn't want people to get the wrong idea and start talking. You understand, don't you, Doc?"

Zeus and Apollo were almost unmanageable. They had pulled their handler all the way over to Doc, and they were growling and nosing him hungrily.

"Down boys. Get Down!" the cowhand was yelling as he pulled at the dogs. Doc nervously petted the animals and let them sniff and lap at his palms while he continued talking.

"Sure, I understand, Bart. So she didn't say she was going anywhere today?"

"She didn't mention her plans for today, Doc. Anything else?" Bart raised his eyebrows to signal he was done with the conversation.

"I can see you've got a house full of people in there to get back to, but I just wanted to know if you knew anything that could help us find Hope." Doc was running out of conversation to keep Bart occupied.

"I told you, the last time I saw her she was driving her wagon away," Bart told a little white lie, since he had been unconscious and bleeding on the floor at that point. "Good luck finding her," he said as he closed the door in Doc's face.

Jack listened at the door of Bart's bedroom, but could hear nothing. He eased the door open slowly and saw an empty room. She must be further to the back of the house. He moved down the hall and stopped outside the office. Nothing heard; he again slowly opened the door and peeked into the room. Empty. He started to close the door, then stopped himself. He went into the office and straight to the drawer where Bart kept his map. Jack put the map and the log book into his satchel, then closed the drawer and crept back into the hallway. Several more rooms lay down the hallway. Which one, he wondered? He tried a couple of doors but they led only to empty bedrooms. At the end of the hallway, there were two doors left. One led out of the house toward the servants' quarters, and the other looked like another spare bedroom. Certain that this was the last place Hope could be, Jack's heart was racing as he slowly eased the door open and peeked inside. His heart sank to the floor as Jack found an empty library. He had been certain that Bart would keep Hope close until he had both of them. Frustrated, Jack pulled the door closed and reached for the back door handle. He could see between the curtains of the window in the door the servants' quarters and an outhouse. The door of the outhouse opened and Zeke emerged, coming straight for Jack's hallway. Jack was trapped. There was no way that Zeke could not see him standing there with the slightly open door in his hands. But Zeke was only looking down, trying to set his feet down in the softest manner he could to minimize the pain of each step. Not knowing why fortune had smiled upon him, Jack quietly backed into the hallway and gently closed the door. He slipped into the library and stood against the wall behind the door, assuming Zeke was headed for the dining room.

Jack set the heavy satchel on the floor and held his breath as he waited for Zeke to pass on down the hallway.

"And that is where Lady Luck abandoned me," Jack thought with exasperation when the door handle began to turn.

No Hope, and Zeke turns out to be a closet academic. Of all the people Jack thought he might run into in a library, Zeke was not on that list. Jack crouched and prepared for hand to hand combat with the much larger Zeke. He fully expected to have to fight dirty to win. Of course, the crashing of bodies flying into bookshelves... his body most likely... would bring the entire house of people into the room. But it was better to go down fighting. The library door arced toward him, blocking his view of Zeke. As it swung closed, Jack leaned into the open space and started a swing, hoping to land the first blow. He threw a complete air ball, nearly falling over as his blow never landed. Zeke had entered and flung the door closed behind him, never turning his body from the direction he entered the room. He was completely self-absorbed as he hobbled across the room, making pitiful whimpers with each painful step. Zeke reached the bookcase on the far wall and pulled one side of it out slowly. It pivoted like a doorway, which Zeke entered and pulled closed behind him.

"Damn it," Jack thought. "I could have put that son of a bitch out of action right then."

"Of course you could have, you idiot. Then you wouldn't have seen the secret passageway, where they no doubt have Hope hidden away." Jack had a lot of these internal conversations amongst the many personalities in his head. He figured he was alright as long as the logical Jack won the arguments... most of the time, anyway.

Jack crossed the room on his tiptoes and eased the bookcase away from the wall. Sure enough, there was flickering candle light coming up some stairs from a room below. Jack eased down the steps one by one. He could hear Zeke grumbling out loud, sometimes followed by a muffled sound that he assumed was Hope.

"Bart says watch you, but don't lay a hand on you. Don't know why we shouldn't have a little fun while we are stuck down here together," Zeke said. More muffled noises.

When he reached ceiling level, Jack crouched down to peer into the room. There was Zeke, sitting on a chair facing away from him. On a chair facing him was Hope. She was tied to the chair, with a gag in her mouth and a bandana tied around her head covering her eyes.

"See, I can touch you here," Zeke poked Hope in the shoulder. As much as she could while tied to the chair, Hope recoiled from his touch.

Jack eased into a sitting position and reached into his satchel.

"And I can touch you here," Zeke poked her in the navel. "Isn't this fun?"

She thrust her head forward in a wild attempt to head butt Zeke, but struck only air.

"Uh Uh Uh, Sugar Pie. Now don't you go getting all excited for ole Zeke. I know you want me. You don't have to try that hard."

Jack pulled out the hollow tube and a cloth from his bag and carefully unwrapped it.

"And you are really gonna like it when I touch you here," Zeke said, reaching out to Hope's breast.

The attempted head butt had missed, but it did move the blind up a little on her eyes, enough so that Hope could see a piece of Zeke to strike at. She could just get her prairie boot about six inches off the floor, and she brought it down heel first on the middle of Zeke's foot. She was aiming for the little hole in the top of his boot, which she had thought was a little odd to begin with. What good was a boot with a hole in it?

The sound that came from Zeke's mouth was bizarre in that it was barely audible, but revealed perfectly the excruciating pain that he was experiencing. So much pain that he almost didn't register the blow dart entering his neck. Zeke fell off the chair and began rolling on the floor, crying in pain. Jack put another dart in Zeke's arm, then bounded down the rest of the steps and ran to Hope. He had to dodge Hope's second attempt at a head butt before he could remove the blindfold and the gag.

"Hold on, Honey. It's me, Jack." He reached around to the back of the chair to untie her, bringing his face well within head butting range. Hope doubled the length of time that it took Jack to untie her as she alternated between kissing him and thanking him.

"Thank God it's you, Jack! I knew you would come." When her hands were finally free, she threw them around Jack. The room was strangely quiet. Hope looked down at Zeke. The sedative on the darts had been a blessing for him. He was curled up in the fetal position, drifting off into a warm sleep.

"And how did you like it when I touched you, Sugar Pie?" she directed at Zeke in a voice dripping with sarcasm.

Jack didn't have the heart to tell her about the poisoned dart. Instead, he told Hope how they were going to escape. "We have to make it into the woods behind the barn where our horses are."

"What is in our way?" asked Hope.

"Bart, some business men, Bart's army of cowhands, two dogs and a bull," Jack replied with a confident grin.

"Easy Peasy," Hope smiled back.

Jack took hold of her hand and they started up the stairs. When they got to the door leading to the hallway, Hope pulled up short.

"Is it true, Jack?"

"Is what true," Jack asked, as he started to turn the door handle.

"Bart says that both you and he are from the future. How can that be true, Jack? Is it?"

Jack paused for a moment, as all the possibilities of the explanation passed through his mind.

"I'll explain it all once we get out of here. Let's head out the back and make a sprint for the horses." They entered the hallway and turned right to head out the back door. Again through the window, Jack could see two men coming from the outhouse toward the door.

"Damn it! What is this, the expressway," he asked nobody in particular. "Come on," he said to Hope, and they turned around and headed toward the other exit down the hall.

"Time for Plan B. Here, you take these," he said as he pulled a box of matches out of his satchel. Then he pulled out a couple of flash grenades and a Molotov cocktail.

He stopped at the opening to the dining room. The lunch crowd was boisterous. Whatever business propositions and deals had been offered, everyone seemed happy with their prospects.

"Light me," he said to Hope. Hope could only guess that the term meant, "Please strike a match and touch its burning tip to the fuse." While she lit the fuses, Jack saw the back door open and Mike and another man enter the long hallway. Jack had intended to throw both explosives into the dining room, but adjusted to the new threat. He tossed the first explosive near the gong, which amplified the noise of the blast into something terrible. He tossed the second explosive down the hall a few feet in front of the two men coming up that way. The burning Molotov cocktail was still in his hand. The men in the dining room were scrambling everywhere. There was nothing like an explosion to really stir things up.

Doc had been stalling for time at the front of the house, petting the dogs and trying to engage the sentry in conversation. The sentry was becoming increasingly hostile, and Doc was beginning to think it was time for him to finish his part of the plan, whether he had received the signal from Jack or not. He was looking for the best way to do it when the signal finally came. The explosions shook the windows at the front of the house, and Doc could see through those windows the flash and smoke. The sentry was taken aback by the blasts. He was peering inside the window trying to grasp what had happened. He turned to run inside, but stopped cold when his vision was filled with the dark color of Docs coat material rushing toward his face. There was a sickening 'TANG' sound and a crunch as Doc's forearm smashed directly into the bridge of the sentry's nose. Everything went black for the man as he slumped to the ground. Doc smiled, pulled up his sleeve and gave a quick kiss to the iron pipe tied to his forearm, then reached into his pockets and pulled out two raw steaks. The dogs were wild with anticipation. Doc tossed the meat on the ground and dashed over to his horse. He turned and started to ride away, looking back over his shoulder to see a stream of angry, coughing men pouring out of the front door beneath a billowing cloud of smoke.

"Time to go," Jack said with a smile. Hope started to cross the open doorway toward the storeroom entrance, but Jack yanked her back hard.

"Not that way, Honey." He pulled her back toward Bart's bedroom. Once inside, he threw the Molotov cocktail down in the door way with enough force to shatter the glass and spread the kerosene. A wall of flames jumped up from the floor, filling the hallway.

"Out the window."

Hope climbed out much more easily than Jack had imagined a woman in a long dress could do. For his own part, Jack fairly leapt out the window himself. He reached back into the satchel and pulled out another Molotov. He held it out for Hope to light, then pulled her into a run straight across the wide open middle of the yard. Even in her adrenaline pumped state, Hope thought running out in the wide open was risky.

"Why are we running out in the open?" she panted. Jack stopped just long enough to point out Mike and the other man stumbling out of the back of the ranch house near the library, and then pointed to the storeroom door. Hope turned her head to look where Jack pointed while Jack lobbed the burning Molotov cocktail through the window of the bunkhouse.

Hope watched just long enough to see several men come running out the ranch house door, only to stop in their tracks as they were staring a thousand pound bull in the eyes. One more man came running out the door, knocking two of the men down the steps. This was interpreted by the bull as a direct challenge to his authority, and maybe even a move on his new girlfriend, which he dispatched with a couple of well-placed head butts. The bull knocked both men back up onto the porch, and all the men chose to scramble back into the burning house rather than face the raging bull. Hope and Jack were running again. Off to her right, she could see the bunkhouse was on fire. Three men scrambled out the front door, and each went sprawling on top of the other in a heap as they tripped over the rope Jack had placed across the stairs. Once they had escaped out the far side of the barn, Jack stopped and held a Molotov out for Hope to light.

Sudden realization hit Bart once the fire started. Doc had been a feint, meant to draw his attention away from the actual attack. This was the real threat. He hadn't realized there was anything like a concussion grenade available in 1870. Bart shouted for the businessmen to go out the front, and sent his men out the back after Jack. Bart left the capture of Jack up to his men while he followed the businessmen out front, knowing that he needed to do some damage control. How hard could it be for ten men to capture a man and a woman escaping on foot? Bart emerged from the house to see Doc riding away. It was a long way off, but it looked like Doc was looking back over his shoulder and laughing at him.

"Big mistake, Doc. Huge. No one laughs at me."

Bart made a mental note that Doc had just elevated himself onto his 'enemies' list, and people on his enemies didn't last long. Bart turned his attention to the six businessmen that were already mounting their horses.

"Gentlemen, please, don't leave. We have the situation under control." Bart said. Just then the Bunkhouse burst into flames.

One of the mounted men replied, "Wishful thinking on your part, Mr. Decker."

Another moved his hand over to his pistol and said, "I'm not entirely sure that dynamite wasn't your attempt to kill us, sir. Should I discover that was indeed your intention, you will not have heard the end of this."

Five of the six men turned and rode off. The one remaining man removed some papers from his pocket and tossed them at Bart's feet.

"Our offer is rescinded, Mr. Decker."

Bart picked up the papers in a rage.

"Mr. Jameson, I have paid you good money to ensure this transaction is completed! You will go back to Cheyenne and do what I paid you to do! I have complete records of all our dealings, above board and below."

"Mr. Decker, the unraveling of this agreement was your doing, not mine. I did all that I had promised in your service, sir. Would those records of yours be somewhere inside that inferno?" He nodded toward the burning ranch house. "In any case, should you decide to present yourself at our offices in Cheyenne and make that case, you will most certainly find yourself being escorted away by our fine sheriff, who happens to be my brother-in-law. Good day, sir." Mr. Jameson turned his horse and galloped to catch up with the others.

Hope started to strike the match, then realized that the only thing left to burn was the barn.

"Jack, no. The animals," she begged.

Jack had gone into battle mode, and was completely caught up in his anger at Bart. He didn't just want to get away; he wanted to destroy everything Bart had. Hope's voice calmed his anger, and he stuffed the Molotov back into the bag. They sprinted across the empty bullpen and jumped through the fence. Once inside the tree line, Jack turned around to see if they were being followed. The destruction behind them was impressive. Flames leapt from the two burning buildings. There were men frantically trying to put out the fires, while others were clamoring around trying to rope an angry bull.

"No one is following," he told Hope. "Thank God you're okay. You are okay, aren't you?" For the first time he thought about the risk to them both during the escape.

The adrenaline rush of the battle and escape had subsided. Hope's face took on a serious, commanding expression. She put a finger on his chest and started advancing toward him, pressing him back into a tree trunk.

"Jack Banyan, don't you ever leave me again!" she commanded, then leaped into his arms, all smiles and kisses. "You are my hero, Jack. Thank you, Thank you, Thank you!"

"Alright, alright. Enough of that hero stuff. We aren't out of trouble yet. Come on, the horses are over this way." Jack took her hand with a firm grip that meant, Hope interpreted rightly, he had no intention of ever letting go of her.

28

Jack led Hope through the woods at a quick pace. He hadn't seen anyone following him but he wasn't taking any chances. He wanted to put as much distance between them and Bart as he could. Where they were headed, and what the next step in the plan was, he had not yet figured out. To be truthful, he didn't give much thought to planning the aftermath, because he never really gave himself much chance of getting Hope off Decker Ranch to begin with. She would be able to help figure out what to do about Bart once they were on the horses and away from here. Maybe they could get some help from the law. Surely kidnapping and attempted murder were against the law here. Actually, had Bart or his men attempted to murder anyone yet? Jack had been the one throwing explosives around, burning down houses filled with people. Jack decided to rethink inviting the law into this.

They had only to go about fifty yards into the forest to find the spot where the horses had been tied up. After he had gone at least 75 yards, Jack stopped and looked around. There were no horses in sight. He doubled back and found what was definitely the right spot. He could see the horse tracks, but they were gone. Jack cursed.

"The horses are gone," he told Hope. "Maybe I tied the rope too loosely, or someone made off with them." Hope could see that he was perplexed.

"Let's start walking then. If we stay in the forest, they won't be able to catch up to us on horseback."

"They won't need to catch up to you, Ma'am," a voice from the woods called out. "They's already caught up to you. Now git yer hands up in the air," the voice said. Jack and Hope raised their hands and watched Elijah come out from behind a tree pointing his pistol at them.

"Just where did you two think you were going? From the looks of Mr. Decker's ranch, you two been causing all sorts of trouble. Don't you know it is awful un-Christian-like to burn down a man's home? I'm guessin' he will be right pleased to see you two firestarters, and right pleased with me for catchin' ya." With that he fired two shots in the air. "Start walking."

Jack's mind was racing for ideas on how to get out of this one. He slowed his pace down to let Elijah get closer to him, but Elijah maintained his distance. He thought of making a run for it, but he couldn't be sure that Elijah would shoot at him and not Hope. No, he wasn't going to be able to make a physical escape, but maybe he could somehow talk Elijah out of it; outsmart him. He had to do it quickly though, as the gun shots had most likely been a signal for the men on the ranch to come running. Jack stopped and turned to face Elijah.

"You can't take us back to Bart," Jack said matter-of-factly.

Elijah raised his pistol some.

"Why the Hell not?"

"Because..." Jack's mind was a blank. Lack of sleep, coming down off of the adrenaline rush, whatever it was, Jack had nothing. "Because..." Jack started again, but before he could come up with whatever brilliance it was going to take to talk Elijah into doing the exact opposite of what he wanted to do, a six foot Indian lance with feathers streaming off the end of it whizzed by Jack's head and stuck into the ground at Elijah's feet with a 'Thunk'!

"Because the keeper of Manitou's Light say so," bellowed a deep Indian voice.

Elijah was completely startled. He dropped his gun to the ground. Three of the Indian braves came out of the woods carrying rifles. Toothless walked up behind Elijah and put the muzzle of his rifle at the back of Elijah's ear. Elijah looked like a mouse that knew it was about to be swallowed by a snake.

Hope greeted them and exchanged a few words with Tonkawa. Jack was looking at Elijah, who seemed to be more frightened with each passing second. Elijah was visibly shaking in his boots. "In my boots!" Jack realized.

Hope relayed her conversation with Tonkawa. She had thanked him and he said that they were free to go.

"Tell him I appreciate all that he has done for us, but that I need to get my boots from this man."

Hope translated, and giggled.

"Tonkawa says you had better hurry. Man who Whines Like a Squaw has wet himself!" Sure enough, Jack saw a spreading water stain on Elijah's pants.

"Take them off," Jack told Elijah. He sat down in the grass and removed the coveted boots. Jack reached over to grab the boots, then looked back to Hope.

"Tell him thanks" he said as he started to put them on. Hope and Tonkawa spoke for a second.

"Hold on Jack." He looked up at her questioningly. A few more exchanges and Hope told Jack, "Give him the boots, Jack."

"What? These are my boots. I am tired of losing them, Hope."

"Tonkawa says it would be a fair trade, your boots for a couple of fine horses he recently acquired. He says they followed the noisiest white man he has ever heard through these woods earlier today. The man left two horses free for the taking, which he would be willing to give to us in exchange for the boots. We need those horses, Jack. And we need to hurry."

"Okay, Okay. I know when I have been had." He put back on the old boots and handed the fancy boots over to Tonkawa. The fourth Indian emerged from the forest with Charley and the other horse. Tonkawa said something in Indian, which Hope translated for Jack.

"He says he has no idea how you beat him out of the boots the first time, but that isn't very likely to happen again. No more whiskey, he says."

Jack held up his hands and said "Fair enough. Enjoy them, Pal." Tonkawa smiled and melted away into the forest with the others.

They had marched close enough to the edge of the forest that they could see out of the tree line. Bart was leading a group of men on foot that was fast approaching. Hope and

Jack climbed up onto their horses. Jack couldn't resist the opportunity to poke a jab at Bart.

"Hey Bart," he yelled. "I hope you got fire insurance on that house. Did you forget to call 911?"

Bart stopped long enough to yell back. "You're gonna need 'life' insurance when I catch up to you, you son of a bitch!"

Jack yelled back. "Sorry to mess up your lunch plans. Are your business friends unhappy now?"

Bart's group had almost reached the tree line and slowed to avoid running into an ambush. Bart's reply came back in two parts. Part one was another shouted threat.

"Not as unhappy as your friends in that crappy little town are gonna be when I burn it to the ground!" The second part of his reply was a volley of gunfire that sent bullets whizzing by their heads. Hope and Jack turned their horses to ride off, leaving Elijah standing there still shaking in his socks. "Serves him right," Jack thought, wishing Elijah had a two mile walk in the dark ahead of him as Jack had done. As he rode by Elijah, Jack leaned down and told him, "You better get back there and get your brother out of Bart's underground torture chamber." Then they started toward the rendezvous point with Doc. The last thing they heard as they left was Bart shouting over and over again, "I'm coming for you Jack. I'm coming for you."

29

Jack and Hope met up with Doc at the rendezvous point. Doc was ecstatic to see Hope in one piece.

"Thank God you're okay!"

"Thank God, and my Jack," she answered proudly. "Thank you too, Doc."

"It was my pleasure. It was Jack's plan that got you out of there. It did feel good to give those people back a little of what they've been handing out. I don't think they'll forget us for quite some time."

Doc told Jack what happened at the front door. He was particularly descriptive of the blow he delivered to take out the sentry on the porch.

"I saw those business men pouring out of the house. They nearly passed me on the road they were in such a hurry to get away from that place. No doubt that whatever deal Bart had is lost."

"That's all good," responded Jack, "but now what do we do with Bart? I'm afraid we've stirred up a hornets' nest. He was pretty clear about what he intended to do to Dawson's Creek."

"Maybe we can get help from the sheriff in Denver," Hope suggested.

"That would take over a day to get there and back," answered Doc. "Do you think we have that kind of time, Jack?"

"How long do you suppose those horses will be sleeping?" Jack asked in response.

"Not more than five or six hours," Doc answered. "That medicine is meant for humans, not 1500 pound horses."

"There is your answer, Hope," Jack replied. "As mad as Bart is, I think we can expect him to attack as soon as he has his horses back."

"How many men do we think Bart can bring with him?" he directed back to Doc.

"I suppose 20 to 25," Doc guessed. "Less, of course, any that are too injured from today's fight. I don't think we'll be seeing the man whose nose I busted any time soon, unless it is for an office visit." He added, "Is it unethical for me to be drumming up my own business?"

"I guess we're on our own then," Hope said. "How are we going to stop them?"

There was a pregnant pause as all three of them considered the daunting task ahead of them.

"With a little luck, a little imagination, and a whole lot of determination," Jack answered with a reassuring smile.

Hope put a lot of stock in that smile. She had come to have complete confidence in her man. If Jack said it could be done, then that was all there was to it.

When they got to town, there was a bustle of activity as people were preparing for tomorrow's party. There were men building a wooden dance floor, and women hanging bunting and decorations all along and across the main street. Many others were inside, cooking and baking. There were even signs with slogans; 'We Love Bart' and 'Bart Decker The People's Man.'

"Those are going to have to come down," Hope said drily as they rode by.

Jack added, "I can think of a few replacement slogans that we can hang in their place." From there they fanned out to spread the word of a town meeting in front of Doc's office.

Soon they had the crowd they needed. Jack, Doc and Hope explained to the assembly the terrible events of last night and this morning. There were shocked faces in the crowd and several comments on Hope's ordeal.

"Poor thing."

"Are you all right, Honey?"

"Thank God you are all safe!"

Jack noted the conspicuous absence of any actual outrage. Had they not heard the words Hope was using; kidnapped? beating?

Finally Doc got around to the meat of the matter.

"Listen everyone. You haven't heard the worst part. Bart and his men are preparing, as we speak," he paused trying to think of the right words to use. "Bart's coming to burn the town to the ground," laying it out in his typically direct style.

That got the crowd fired up, but not in the way Jack had expected.

"What do you mean 'burn the town down? What did we do to him?"

"You mean he's coming after you three," someone else shouted. "He isn't coming after us. He wants those who burned his place down."

Doc responded. "Wait a minute. Weren't you listening? Yes he's coming after us. Yes we burned his place down, but we did it to rescue Hope. And we've destroyed Bart's plans to steal your land and make a fortune off the railroad, and then run for governor. Now nobody here could want that."

"I don't know about that," someone shouted. "He can't be any worse than what we have right now. Where are we going to go if he burns down our homes?"

What was it going to take to get these people up in arms? Jack knew that human nature was to avoid confrontation, but confrontation was coming whether these people liked it or not.

Jack stepped up.

"It doesn't matter what you want and it doesn't matter who you think Bart's coming after. All that matters is what Bart is going to do. He's an evil man. He doesn't care about any of you and he doesn't care about the law. He is going to march in here with his small army and he's going to burn this town to the ground. We can sit back and do nothing, put our heads in the sand and hide from the danger, or we can stand up for ourselves. We can stand up for law and order and what we believe in."

Jack stopped to see how it was being absorbed by the crowd. There were still plenty of blank faces.

Shouts came from somewhere in the crowd.

"This is your fight. You brought this down on us" and "Yeah, all he wants is your head."

The Baptist preacher came forward.

"Now listen everyone, we all heard Bart talk just this Sunday. I believe he can be a reasonable man if we just go to him and speak with him. We can help him rebuild his house and show him the Christian way."

There was a round of 'Yeah's' and a few 'Amen's'.

"Why don't we finish the party preparations? Father O'Leary and I will lead a delegation out to Decker Ranch and discuss this in a calm peaceful manner. Nobody has to get hurt."

This provided the 'safe' way out of the confrontation that most of the people wanted. The crowd started to dissipate back to their party preparations. Doc turned to Jack and shrugged his shoulders.

"I'm sorry Jack. I guess we gave it our best shot."

"Now just you hold on there. You people should be ashamed of yourselves!" Jack looked up to see Hope wagging a finger at the crowd. It was her voice, but it had a depth and command to it that he had not heard before. The crowd froze in its tracks.

"That's right, ashamed," she scolded. "Jack has risked his life for me and for all of you. Doc built this town from the ground up. How many of you have called on Doc in hard times and illness? Whenever we need him he is there for us. Now you're ready to turn your back, knowing that Bart is gunning for them? Ashamed you should be. I stood alone against Bart. It would have been easy to sell him my land and move on. For opposing him, I was kidnapped, and beaten, and he was going to kill me. If he'll do that to me, he'll do that to any of you when your time comes."

The crowd was paying attention now, but they weren't moved enough to defend themselves yet.

"Do you doubt me? Can any of you doubt what I'm saying? Quincy. Edgar. Doesn't Bart take what he wants, without paying? Hasn't he destroyed your saloon and your store?" Both men agreed.

"Ben Riley. Have you finished rebuilding your outhouse? Where is that wagon full of supplies that Bart's men tossed into the creek?"

"Mrs. Coors. How's your boy doing after Bart's man roughed him up? Have you forgotten that Jack risked being shot to drive them away?" Mrs. Coors pulled her son in close and nodded.

"Now these men are coming to town. They're after Doc and Jack and me now, but they've been after all of us for a long time. Only we've been turning the other cheek. The time for talk is gone, because if we do nothing, nothing is all we will have left."

"We owe Doc and we owe Jack the help that they need. More importantly, we owe it to ourselves and our children to provide a place to live where they don't have to be afraid to walk in the streets. We owe them that freedom. This is America in 1870. We have a right to that freedom!"

The crowd was clearly moved. Ben Riley and his wife came forward and asked what they could do to help. Quincy came forward also.

"It was costing me a fortune giving away all those free drinks to him and his gang anyway."

One by one the crowd pressed forward ready to help. Applause broke out. Hope pumped her fist in the air and shouted.

"Yes! All right! That's it!" She turned and gave Jack a little wink. "I threw that 1870 line in there for you," she smiled. "They're all yours."

Jack stood up to lay out the tactics of their defense.

"Okay, everybody listen up. We've got a lot to do and not much time to do it. The way I see it, they could come at us from any of three sides. That's too much territory to cover so will have to try to funnel them in to our fire zones. As we outnumber them quite handily, this should turn out pretty well." Jack reached out and grabbed the chain of Doc's pocket watch and looked at the time. "Right now it's almost 5 PM. We believe the soonest we could expect the attack is midnight." There were murmurs in the crowd.

"I want everyone to go home and get your guns and ammunition and bring them back here where we will outline our defense." A wave of silence crept over the crowd. Jack stopped speaking and surveyed their blank stares. He wasn't sure what it was he said that had caused this pregnant pause. Ammo shortage? Religious opposition to firearms? He had thought it was quite unusual that he hadn't seen anyone wearing a gun in a western town in 1870. He remembered thinking that Hollywood would sure be surprised that the town was not filled with gunfights and pistoleros. Mostly, Dawson's Creek was people peacefully going about their everyday business. Of course there was the occasional 'make the new guy dance in the street to gunfire' or "murder the sheriff' or even the 'bad guy brings thugs to town to burn it down'. All in all just your average, ordinary, everyday Wild West town. He looked at Hope and Doc but they wouldn't meet his eyes. He returned to the crowd.

"So is there something wrong with that? We're going to need every gun we can get." Nothing. Not a sound or movement. Just people looking down into the dirt or blank stares.

"Hope? Doc? What am I missing? I know this isn't a town of Quakers."

Doc took on the responsibility of sharing the bad news.

"We don't have any guns, Jack. We turned them all over to Bart months ago." Jack opened his mouth and tried to speak but he couldn't form any words. His head cocked to the left a little when he tried to speak again. His face had a quizzical look, and his head bounced back and forth between Doc and Hope and the crowd in short jerky motions, something like a chicken walking through the barnyard. It was a full minute before Jack found his voice.

"Why would anybody... what could Bart... who would...?" He still couldn't get out a full sentence. The world was a dangerous place. It was much more dangerous if you handed all of your weapons over to the enemy. Hope tried to ease him back down.

"We never thought it would come to something like this. We had a sheriff at the time, Jack. He thought it was a good idea to avoid getting anybody killed."

"Isn't that the same sheriff that ended up dead?" Jack asked incredulously. "This is America. Didn't anybody read the Constitution? No guns? No wonder Bart is so confident he can push you all around."

"What are we going to do?" someone in the crowd yelled out.

Another shaky voice added, "How are we going to defeat twenty guns?"

The crowd's unity was beginning to shake. Hope sensed their rising fear, and the amplifying effect that Jack's doubt had. She was amazed at how fast the fear was spreading.

"We'll defeat them with a little luck, a little imagination, and a whole lot of determination." She repeated Jack's words to the crowd while looking straight at him. It was just what Jack needed to get back on track. His smile reappeared.

"Dirty trick, using my own words against me," he joked with her, then turned back to the crowd.

"Okay, okay. Everyone settle down. Hope is right. We have everything we need to defend ourselves, even against twenty men with guns. They are going to come in here like the bullies they are, overconfident and expecting us back down. We will beat them by working together in teams. We can do this."

A young man, about 15, in the back of the crowd raised his hand to speak.

Jack pointed to him and said, "Go ahead, son. You don't have to raise your hand to speak out here."

"Does this mean there ain't gonna be no party tomorrow night?" Nervous laughter ran through the crowd. The young man felt the need to explain a little. "It's just because, well, I already asked Mary Burkhalter if I could escort her, and that was real hard, but she said 'Yes' and I really wanted to have that dance with her." Women in the crowd let out a low 'Ohhhhhhh'. The men continued to laugh.

"Buddy, there won't be any parties for Bart anytime soon, but if we can stop him from burning down this town, you will definitely be having that dance with Mary Burkhalter."

The young man smiled. "Alright then, let's get on with it!" he shouted. A pretty blonde girl on the other side of the crowd turned beet red.

"All right," Jack started. "We'll need you to divide yourselves up into working groups of ten or so." He looked down towards the blonde girl. "Mary Burkhalter, I think you ought to work in that young man's group. I don't think there's anybody on this earth that is going to do more to keep you safe than that gentleman right there." There were more 'Ohhhhh's' from the women in the crowd. The girl's face turned a little bit redder, but she ran over to stand beside her man. The rest of the crowd started to form up in groups.

Doc pulled Jack aside. "You know Jack, you don't have to stay and fight. I can help you get to back to the portal. This is the town's fight. Bart's men will be shooting real bullets and they will bring real death."

"Doc, you're not from here either. Why aren't you heading for the portal?"

"It's not the same thing, Jack. I threw my lot in with these people a long time ago. I have nothing to go back to. My life is here with them. If it has to end here with them, then that is just fine, too," he answered.

Jack eyes locked onto Hope. "It's exactly the same thing, Doc." He was looking directly into her eyes when he said, "I'm not headed for a portal. I'm not going anywhere."

30

Jack, Hope and Doc remained on the porch going over how they could best defend the town while the crowd waited anxiously. Hope wondered if they shouldn't lie in ambush on the road into town, to surprise the attackers before they got to the town with their torches.

"That leaves a lot of people out in the open once the gunfire starts," Jack said.

Doc added, "Besides, we can't be sure which way they will come in. I think we should defend inside the town. Why not divide up into equal sectors and cover each approach?"

Jack told them that would spread their forces out mighty thin. "If Bart came in from one direction, only a quarter of our forces would be engaged against his entire force. Some military genius said it best when he said 'to try to defend everything is to defend nothing'." Jack laughed at the thought that he may have just quoted somebody who hadn't been born yet.

Hope asked, "Doesn't that almost guarantee that some of the buildings will burn?"

"Yes it does," answered Jack. "It's not as if we're sacrificing things needlessly, but we have to realistically face the possibility that some buildings will burn down and that some people will likely be hurt or killed."

"Don't you think everyone will fight better if they feel their valuables are protected? Shouldn't we give everyone a chance to go home and protect their valuables?"

Jack was surprised he hadn't thought of that, and nodded his agreement.

"And I think we should send all the children in a group down to Haverhill. It's about forty miles away in the opposite direction from Decker Ranch. They can stay there until we send word that everything is all right." Again Jack just nodded

"Everybody that needs to," Hope addressed the crowd, "Go to your homes and businesses. Get the things that you can't live without, your most valuable items, and take them down by the creek. Please hurry and be back here in twenty minutes. We'll need to pick a few of us to take the children over to Haverhill, out of danger."

When Hope turned back around to Jack, he was smiling from ear to ear.

"What?" she asked indignantly.

"I just don't think I have ever been this close to a natural born leader," he answered.

"Back to the planning, General," Hope scoffed.

Jack did just that. "I think we should choose his most likely avenue of approach, set up our defenses in that section of town and fight as a group. We will be able to bring all of our force against them. It's also helpful when fighting with civilians to remain close together. There is security in numbers," he reassured them.

"Bart is no idiot but right now he's mad. He knows he has all the weapons. He may expect the town to be empty by the time he gets here. I expect him to come blazing into town with torches lit, overconfident and mad as Hell. We're going to use that against him."

Jack did then what military commanders for years have done to convey their battle plans to their forces. He stepped down off the porch, kneeled down to the ground, and began drawing in the dirt.

"Okay, here's the town. We've got the creek running along the backside here. It is pretty high and fast with all the rain we've had, so I don't think anyone will try to ford it and come in from behind. Decker Ranch is all the way over here. The most straightforward approach is to come right down through here," Jack said as he drew an arrow where the road from Decker Ranch to the town would lie. "Like I said before, I don't think Bart is worried too much about a bunch of shopkeepers and farmers with pitchforks. So we set up our defenses right through here. We'll put up some barriers on the flanks just in case he sends somebody around that way. We'll put some sentries out here, here and here to signal us when they catch sight of Bart. We'll do our best to funnel Bart's men into our defenses."

Having secured their treasures, the town reformed in front of the porch within twenty minutes. Hope had them standing in groups of ten to twelve people, forming a semicircle around the porch. Their faces were grim but determined.

"Alright everyone, we're going to lay a few ground rules," Jack addressed them. "These men are on their way here to do us harm. We are going to fight back with all that we have. It's going to be dangerous, and it won't be pretty. Some of them and some of us may not come out of this alive. I want you to do what it takes to protect your property and your loved ones. If that means one of the attackers ends up dead, then so be it. But we are not the murderers that they are. If we can do this without killing, then that's how we want to do it. We will capture and arrest as many as possible, but we will kill them if we must. Most importantly, do not take needless chances with your own safety. If it comes down to getting shot over letting a building burn, we can rebuild the building. Does everybody understand?"

There were head nods and yes's all-around. Jack led the groups over to the entrance of the town right along the path that he expected the attack. The element of surprise was going to be their only real advantage. The first sign of resistance would strip away that advantage, so he needed a surprise that stood a good chance of eliminating as much of the attacking force as possible.

"Right here, folks. We are going to dig us a pit and catch us a bunch of cowboys. Groups one and two, get all the shovels you can and start digging. We are going to tie a rope about a foot high across the street. When they come riding through here they will tumble right into our pit. We need it deep."

Jack pulled Doc aside.

"I want you to take groups three and four, and go up the street. Some of these men will get past the pit, and we need to contain them here in this section of town. They are cowboys, so they won't want to leave their horses. They might eventually, but I want them to flow back into our defenses. We'll need some trenches dug across the street that we can fill with kerosene. Once this thing starts, we can light the trenches on fire and force them back this way. Their horses will naturally avoid the fire."

"Okay, Jack. But what is to stop them from going between the buildings and around?"

"Put enough stuff in those gaps to block off their path. But leave several of them open, and make it obvious which ones are clear."

"Why is that? How are we going to keep them corralled?"

"We will have a hard time getting at them in the street, since they have guns. Between the buildings, potential energy will be in our favor."

Doc knew that potential energy was the energy an object at rest possessed if it were moved so that gravity would act on it. His face lit up. "We're gonna drop stuff on them, aren't we?"

"You bet," Jack confirmed. "The heavier the better. We'll put people on both sides of the rooftops. We'll roll barrels and buckets full of bricks down on them. Go set it up."

"Projectiles," Jack thought. "I need projectiles to force them out of the street and into the buildings. I need a catapult." The most mechanically inclined man in town had to be the owner of the hardware store.

"Edgar, take your group over to the store and figure out what you need to build a catapult. It doesn't have to be huge, just big enough to throw a ten pound rock halfway across town. Group five, we need rocks. Five to fifteen pounds, as many as you can find. Collect them and take them to the center of town."

"Group six, same thing, but you want throwing sized rocks. Not smooth stones, but jagged ones that will cut when they hit skin." Some of the women in the group looked a little queasy at that last comment. Too bad for them. That reticence would be gone at the first bullet that hit somewhere close to them or their loved ones. He hoped they wouldn't hesitate when the time came.

Jack had already sent group seven to build the catapult, so he called out group eight.

"Hope, I want you to split this group into two. Take them down the street to where Doc is coordinating the trenches. Tell him we need some good, stretchable tubing from his office. Then I want you to set up some giant sling shots just behind the fire trenches. You know what a sling shot is, right?" Jack wasn't sure when those were invented, but they must have been around for ages.

"Of course I know what a sling shot is. I got my backside whipped when I was ten years old for breaking out a window with one."

Jack smiled, because he couldn't help but think what a lovely backside that turned out to be. He mentally slapped himself. "World War III is about to start and you are still thinking about sex," he laughed to himself. Wait. It was only 1870. World War One-Half?

"Set your sling shots on either side of the road so that they can fire right down the middle of the street," he told her. "We are going to make it very dangerous for anyone to sit in the middle of the street and take pot shots at us. You are going to be our short range, direct fire artillery. It will take a lucky shot to put one of those cowboys completely out of action, but their horses are not going to sit there calmly and get pelted with rocks. They will either move back up the street or dismount and take shelter inside, where we'll be waiting."

"Group nine and ten, you are going to occupy some of these buildings along the street. Once the artillery has knocked those cowboys off of their horses, they are going to come looking for shelter. When they open the doors, you will be there to give them the wallop of their lives."

"Jack," one of the men said a little sheepishly, "I don't want to sound yellow or anything, but won't those men be coming in with their guns drawn?"

Jack recognized the smallish man that ran one of the general stores.

"I am certain of it, Tom. But we are going to set up a few equalizers. If our first blow doesn't take them out completely, they at least should knock away their guns. Then it will come down to hand to hand combat. Three or four of us against one of them might not sound like a fair fight, especially when we will all have clubs and pitchforks, but that is why the Marines always say the only 'fair' fight is one you walk away from."

The Catholic priest and what looked like the ladies choir made up the last group. "Father, I am going to ask for a big one from you. Bart has these men thinking that we are a bunch of sheep. I am sure he expects nothing more from us than to hole up in the church, praying and singing hymns. Not that there is anything wrong with that," he added to avoid offending the religious leader. "We are going to give him what he wants. You're going to need to get that player piano from the saloon down here."

"Yes, all right Jack. We are willing to sacrifice, but what if something happens to the church? Where will we worship?"

Jack held up one finger on his left hand, then put two of his right fingers to his mouth and sent a loud whistle up the street. He called the Baptist preacher over to their conversation and got right to the point.

"Pastor, the Catholics are worried about losing their building here. If this thing goes down like I expect it to, that is a real possibility. However, if they come in from the other side of town, you're likely to be without a meeting hall. What do you two say to agreeing to a little insurance? If only one church is standing, both congregations put their backs into rebuilding the other one. Until it is complete, you all can share the one good building. Baptists at 8 AM, Catholics at 10. Agreed?" Jack asked. Both men nodded their heads, then shook hands.

"There you go," said Jack. "Unity is a beautiful thing," as the men returned to their work. "Hell," he thought, "both those buildings are probably gonna go down, along with half the rest of this town built of matchsticks." At least he was living in interesting times, as the Chinese proverb went. For a moment he entertained the notion that the Chinese guy who said that had some insight into traveling around through time portals, then shrugged it off and went back to directing the town defense.

Night had crept up on them as they laid out their plans. Jack found Hope and asked her to send out several sentries with orders to signal Bart's approach back to the town. Jack spent the next couple of hours supervising the laying of the defenses. He went from group to group, offering advice and moral support. He helped the sling shot squads zero in their weapons, and showed them how they could quickly turn the weapons in the opposite direction if the assault came from the other side of town. He saw that Doc had the trench lines set, and had stationed all sorts of potential energy on the roof tops. He had taken some liberties with devising his own traps, and was a bit anxious to see how they might work. The groups inside the buildings needed help getting set up. Jack showed them how to saw through the porch posts and tie a rope so that the roof would come crashing down on top of a man. He showed them several other uses for springs and ropes before he set off to check on what he suspected would be the most difficult task, the catapult.

Jack got to the center of town and found the group hard at work. To his surprise, he had severely underestimated the engineering skills of the hardware store owner. Edgar had mounted the stands to a wide, flat frame. He'd built a cradle for the pivot arm, and had lashed a long thick board to act as the throwing arm to the pivot. Attached to both the bottom of the throwing arm and the back of the frame was a long steel spring.

"Jack! You are just in time. We were about to give this girl a test. Charlotte, hand me one of those rocks over there," Edgar said with the anxiousness of a kid getting to play with a Christmas toy for the first time.

"Whoa, down there, big fella," Jack said. "Maybe we should clear those people out of the way down range there. And why don't we try something a little less lethal on the test run?" Jack grabbed the nearest kid and sent him running to the store for a ten pound sack of flour, and sent another to clear the firing range. When the boy returned with the flour, Edgar took it and placed it into the carriage, then he and two other fire team members pulled the throwing arm back tight.

All eyes were downrange when Edgar, his eyes lit up with anticipation, yelled "Fire!"

The arm swung in a blurring arc. There was an immediate 'THUD!' followed by a flash of white that seemed to immerse the entire group into the depths of a winter blizzard. The sack of flour had impacted the ground not two feet in front of the catapult. Edgar got out a quiet, "Oh no" before Jack slapped him on the back, creating a puff of white flour.

"I think you're gonna need to raise that aim point a little, Edgar. Unless you are expecting some mighty close in fighting!"

Edgar appeared a little dejected, but his mind was already hard at work calculating the necessary adjustments.

"Seriously, keep trying. You'll get it." Jack went off to find Doc and Hope to gauge how they thought the defense was coming along.

Jack pulled Hope away from her sling shot practice. He could see from the broken windows all up and down the street that they had created an effective weapon. They met Doc and walked the short distance up to his office porch. Some of the ladies came by with sandwiches and tea. Hope had pulled them out of rock gathering duty earlier to prepare some dinner for everyone, and they were glad to help in a way that they felt was a more appropriate use of their talents. Jack hadn't realized how long it had been since he had eaten. He was famished. He thanked the ladies, and after the first bite of the sandwich, he called out to them as they continued down the street to tell them they had contributed mightily to the town's defense.

"Where do we stand," he mumbled over the top of a mouthful of roast beef. Hope told him the sling shots were ready, and that she had sent her groups out to gather weapons to keep close should they need them.

"Great. Good call on feeding the troops, and on gathering the weapons. Are you sure you didn't go through West Point?" he asked.

"That is an all male school, sir," she said, feigning indignance.

"Well, I am sure that you could teach them a thing or two about leading troops," Jack told her.

"Doc, take a breath between bites and fill me in, will you?"

Doc was as famished as Jack, maybe more so given his much rounder shape and size. He finished chewing a huge piece of beef before he started.

"Mostly complete on the trenches. We'll wait until we get the signal to fill them with the fuel."

Jack told him that as long as there was enough kerosene, to go ahead with the first pour in order to get the ground soaked well.

"Okay, will do. The alley ways are mostly blocked. There are a few on each side of the street that are open, and you can see them quite easily. We have a few surprises waiting for anyone that tries to get around behind us. I haven't checked in on the indoor teams or the church group...or the catapult."

"Good," said Jack. "The catapult needs work, but Edgar has a strong engineering mind. He'll get it working. You can see from all the flour dust on me that the test firing didn't go so well," Jack laughed.

"I saw that white dust cloud rising from down the street. That stuff sure spread out fast," Doc observed.

That put an idea into Jack's head for another nasty surprise.

"Best guess for how much time we have left?" Jack asked his two lieutenants. Hope shrugged, but Doc offered an answer of at least three hours, given the distance from the ranch and the effectiveness of the drug they had given the horses.

"I think you are right. Those horses aren't going to move too fast even after they wake up. Here is what we have left to do. Hope, get those sentries replaced every two hours. I don't want anyone falling asleep on watch. Then meet me back here. I am going to check on the catapult, then get some things I need from the store. Doc, you need to get these groups coordinated and ready for hand to hand combat. Everyone needs weapons to fight with, rocks to throw, rope to tie up prisoners. We will also need a couple of groups of strong men to hold in reserve. Their job will be to plug holes and fill in when any of our shooters go down. They will also have to handle any initial assaults on the other ends of town. I don't think Bart is smart enough to plan his attack out that well, but you never know."

Jack gave him instructions for the church group and the indoor groups, and finished with directions for hauling as much water up from the creek as possible. It was certain that there would be fires to fight, if and when fighting Bart's men had ended.

"Okay, any questions?"

"What do we do when we get finished with that," Doc asked.

"We wait for all Hell to break loose," Jack answered solemnly.

Jack headed back to the catapult, where Edgar was giving orders and making all sorts of adjustments. They had turned the catapult around so they could test fire without clearing the digging group out of the way. Their success in test firing was only marginally better. Jack could tell by the two or three gouges in the street that lay fifteen, twenty and thirty yards from the front of the catapult.

"You're getting better," Jack offered. Edgar looked up, none too happy.

"Not good enough, I'm afraid. We are having trouble getting the stone to release further back in the swing. We have plenty of power, though. See what I mean?" he asked, and pointed down the street. There, about even with the thirty yard gouge, but off to the right a few feet, was what was left of a horse watering trough. The stone had shattered the sturdily built wooden box. If it had been a human target, Jack might be able to see clear through him. Jack liked this weapon. He liked it a lot! They needed this one to work.

"Have you tried putting something up to stop the throwing arm?" he asked. Edgar just pointed to the splintered pile of wood pieces off to one side.

"How about raising the front...?" Jack could see Edgar shaking his head. "Well, we need this one. It is going to be a huge equalizer, and give us a range and fear advantage. It only takes once seeing a man get blown right off of his horse to scare the crap of everyone else. Keep trying," Jack said. He went over to the general store and picked up some supplies, then headed back over to meet Hope.

31

By the time Jack got back to Doc's office, Hope was there waiting for him.

"What is all this?" she asked, as she came forward to help him with some of the bottles and materials that were falling out of his arms.

"Just some ingredients I need to cook up a few nasty surprises for Bart. Let's go inside and you can help me put them together." They went into Doc's office and cleared off the table. Jack lined all the ingredients up and went through the directions for each of his homemade grenades.

That sat at the table in silence for a while, just enjoying the time alone together as they assembled the weapons.

The weight of Jack's guilt was bearing down hard on his chest as he finished the last one. He stood up and paced back and forth a few times before stopping by the door. "I'm sorry for the argument last night. I didn't do a very good job of explaining how I felt."

"Oh Jack. I am sorry, too. I don't ever want to argue with you again."

"I don't either, Hope. Last night, when I thought things were getting too emotional, I tried to put distance between us. That was a mistake."

"I shouldn't have yelled at you about the ink running. I wasn't really upset about that. I couldn't understand why you were so distant, why you didn't want me. Why you said you were leaving. I didn't know then, Jack. I didn't know where you were from and that you had to go back."

Jack was on unfamiliar ground; he had never even considered being completely honest with a woman. "I told myself that I couldn't let you get too attached to me. I had no idea how long I was going to be here, and I didn't feel it was right to take advantage of you."

Hope started to protest, but Jack stopped her. "No, let me finish. I told myself that, but what I was really doing was protecting myself. I've fallen in love with you, Hope and I don't know what to do. I am in the wrong time, the wrong place and I have never been in love before, and it is killing me not to pull you into my arms and do something about it."

Hope leaned way over next to Jack's ear, so close that he could feel the warmth of her breath as she whispered, "Then why don't you do it, Silly Boy?"

That was not an invitation Jack needed to hear twice. He reached out and pulled her in close, kissing her long and hard. They stood there kissing at the door, pouring their pent up emotion into each kiss. Jack reached around Hope, opened the door a crack, and flipped around the sign hanging from the door knob.

They lay there under the crisp white sheets on the operating table. Hope was tucked under Jack's arm and was rubbing his bare chest with her free hand. "Jack, I have to tell you something. I don't think I can go back to the ranch alone. Being with you now, here tonight... I just can't go back to that emptiness. After we stop Bart, I plan on spending whatever time we have left together tucked right under this arm. After you leave I'm going to sell that ranch and move on to California."

"Hope," Jack started slowly, "I don't belong in this time and I didn't set out to come here..."

Oh God, here it comes. He is leaving me. She knew he had to, but the confirmation of the empty void that her life was going to be was more than she could bear.

"...But there is nowhere in this world that I would want to be if you weren't in it. I don't know if it's possible for me to stay in this time forever, but Bart and Doc have both been here for months or years. There is nothing for me to go back to in my time as long as you are here in this time. I'm not going anywhere at all, so it looks like you are going to be tucked under that arm for quite a while."

Doc had been helping with the defenses for the last hour or so. He thought it might be a good idea to let Jack know how things were coming along. He hadn't seen Jack or Hope for some time. As he stepped onto the porch of his office and reached for the doorknob, he heard Hope's scream of gleeful delight at the knowledge that Jack was staying. He looked down and saw his own hand-painted sign hanging on the door knob:

OPERATING. Come back later!

Doc's smile stretched from ear-to-ear as he turned, tucked his hands into his pockets and walked away whistling the same instantly recognizable song about Cupid that he whistled the day he brought Jack in.

32

Soon enough, the sentry on the road that led to Decker Ranch could see torches coming around the bend. He tried to count them, then turned to his fire. He picked up his torch and quickly doused the rest of the fire with the bucket of water he had carried up the slope from the creek. He trotted off through the trees until he was out of sight of the oncoming riders, but could still be seen from the town, and started to waive the torch back and forth over his head. In the town, dozens of nervous eyes had been locked on him from the moment his fire had gone out. The defenders shared both a sense of relief that the waiting was over and dread that this could be their last, bloody night. The sentry rolled his torch in the dirt to extinguish it, then sprinted down the hill back into the town. He made it just as the torches became visible coming over the rise.

"There's a whole herd of them coming down the road!" he yelled to anyone that would listen. "I counted at least 25 torches, maybe more!" His voice had the rise in pitch that comes with anxiety and the heightened tension of an impending fight, and it was downright unsettling to most of the uninitiated warriors Jack had conscripted for this battle. Jack reached out and pulled him off the street, then said in a low, slow tone, "Stay calm, everybody. Count them yourself. It is the same twenty or so we expected. Just stick to the plan." Jack was right. 21 torches had come over the rise and were rapidly approaching the town. Scouts had been overestimating enemy forces since warfare began.

Jack was pinning a lot of their success on surprise. Beating twenty armed men would be nearly impossible if they were well trained soldiers entering battle with a plan. He had to hope that the pit would take out a good portion of them, and that the remaining battle would be against armed individuals not working in fire teams. Bart was following the script so far, bringing his entire force right down the middle of the ambush. After the digging was finished, the pit had been covered with tarps and sprinkled with dirt. It was almost undetectable on close inspection, and invisible to a rider coming in the dark night. Jack let himself have one confident thought that this might just work.

Bart was in the lead as his force loped toward the entrance to town. He could see only one light on, down near where the Catholic church was. He had already given directions to his men in a short, fiery speech.

"They didn't just burn down my home, they burned down your bunkhouse, too. They've taken away our shelter and our livelihood." He told them they had robbed him the previous night, showing them the wound on his head and concocting a story about missing money. Simply recovering the money she stole from him was the reason he gave for 'putting Hope under citizen's arrest. That sounded much tidier than the real story of why Jack and Hope had snuck into the house, why he'd had to kidnap Hope, and why the ranch had been attacked.

"No, we didn't start this war, but we're sure going to finish it." He had left out any specific directions for what to do beyond burning down the town. He knew that some of the locals would get hurt or die, but that didn't matter much in the big scheme of things. They were insignificant. He did make his preference known for what his men were to do with Hope and Jack. They were to be captured alive. Of course he intended to kill them, but that would be his privilege alone. Bart was confident that tonight would turn out the way he wanted. They might not be the brightest lot, but he had assembled a group of men that would carry out his orders without question. They were rough and tough, and enjoyed a good fight, especially one where they were the only ones armed. Bart could smell his revenge in the fumes of the torch he was carrying.

Then, just before they entered the town, Bart's gut started talking. Intuition is a funny thing. Maybe it was a shift in the wind. Perhaps his eyes saw something that his conscious mind didn't register. Whatever it was that caused his suspicion to overcome his thirst for fire and blood, it was intense. His gut told him there was something wrong; deeply wrong. He held his torch up high and pulled back hard on his reins, forcing his horse to come to an abrupt halt. The men behind him did the same, causing a few minor rear end collisions among the horses.

The town was quiet. Too quiet. Just one light could be seen. Bart was fighting an inner battle. He knew these sheep. These were the sheep that had handed over all of their weapons to him without a fight. They had been pushed into giving up more and more of their rights and freedoms, and their property, with the simplest strong arm tactics. Of course they would hide or run away. He turned in his saddle and looked back over his company of cutthroats and gunslingers. Bart couldn't actually blame the people for being afraid. He did blame them for helping that Banyan 'son of a bitch' and his pals burn down his ranch, though, and for that they would pay. What Bart's gut was telling him was that Jack was a wild card. Maybe he had shored up their backbones. What if they had rearmed? Was he riding straight into a trap?

"Damn it." Jack watched from one of the first few buildings along the street. What was Bart doing? He had been envisioning the entire attacking force piling up in the pit and the fight being over before it even started. Bart had pulled up some fifty feet in front of the trip line. Had he seen the rope? Jack held his breath as he waited for Bart's anger to take charge again and plunge his band of thugs right into the trap. He was trying to 'will' Bart into the trap. "Come on, Bart. You're angry. You're mad at me. Come on!"

No amount of mental energy that Jack could muster was going to overcome Bart's gut feeling. Bart called for one of his men.

"Frank, get on up here." Frank rode up from somewhere near the middle of the pack, where Bart knew he would be. Frank was one of Bart's favorites, not because he was very good at anything in particular, but because he was just smart enough to do what he was told and dumb enough to never question orders. That was Bart's ideal warrior.

"Frank, ride on up there and check it out."

"Okay, Boss," Frank answered as he started to nudge his horse forward, then stopped. Apparently he was smarter than Bart had estimated.

"Boss, what if they are sitting there waiting to take a shot at me? One guy riding up... I'm gonna make a pretty easy target."

"They are sheep, Frank. Besides, we have all their guns." Bart could feel the energy draining out of his assault force behind him. Even he knew that one man questioning orders could paralyze the attack. He hadn't worked these men into a frenzy just so that one chickenshit could scare them out of it. Besides, nobody questioned Bart Decker's orders.

"Just go check it out, Frank." Bart slapped Frank's horse on the haunch.

Frank's horse leapt forward in a gallop. Frank knew better than to counter Bart's order, so he turned his attention to the buildings looming up in front of him. He was wondering which window the rifle shot would come from that ended his life when everything seemed to slow down to dream speed. His horse slowly began to sink away from him, a sensation that he had no explanation for. Of course, he had no idea that the rope had stopped the horse's two front legs in their tracks, removing all vertical support the horse was expecting when it should have been landing on those legs. Bart and his men watched as the massively top heavy horse and rider sank gracefully to the ground. Their minds tried to make sense of the optical illusion of the dirt opening up and swallowing the falling pair. There was a loud 'Thud!' as Frank hit the far wall of the pit, then the horse hit Frank. A puff of dust rose in a cloud in what could only be explained in the witnesses' eyes as a belch from the hungry Earth. There was a moment of silence as everyone came to terms with what they had just seen.

Jack was pissed. He had been counting on the pit to even the odds some. Now he had lost his most important asset, surprise. Had it been too much to hope that these idiots would all ride into the pit on their own?

Bart and his men rode slowly up to the rope and peered over the edge of the pit. Frank was moaning, and his horse was screeching in an awful, painful wail.

"Ha Ha Ha Ha Ha," Bart started laughing. He liked it when he was right.

"A hole?" Bart yelled into the town. "Is that all you got, Banyan? A hole?" Bart kept on laughing, then had to stop as the screams of pain from the horse were rising out of the hole and drowning out the sound of his laughter. Frank was complaining too, about his 'broke' shoulder and needing help.

"Elijah, get down there and cut that rope." Elijah did just that, passing his torch to another man and cutting the rope with the knife that he kept in his belt. Once the rope had been cut, Bart added, "Now for God's sake, shoot that animal!"

Elijah looked at Bart, then down into the pit. He drew his pistol and pointed it down into the hole, then paused. His hand was trembling, and it was clear to those watching him that he was having a crisis of conscience. Zeke was afraid he was going to have to ride up and do it himself. Elijah seemed to steel himself to the task and took a deep breath.

A shaky voice rose from out of the pit. It was Frank, issuing a slow and stern order of his own.

"No, Elijah, he means the horse. Shoot the horse!" Elijah's eyes seemed to come out of their stupor. He adjusted his aim about fifteen degrees to the left and fired. The horrible cries from the horse stopped, and an audible sigh of relief rose from Frank down in the hole. Elijah looked back at the silent band of shocked cowboys. He put his pistol away and remounted.

"What!" he asked the stunned group. "Like you all knew what he meant."

Bart shook his head back and forth. "Someone throw a rope down to that man."

Mike threw a rope down to Frank, who winced in pain as Mike backed his horse to pull him out of the hole.

Bart yelled again to Jack. "Come on out Jack. We need to talk." Jack weighed the risk of walking out into the open and facing twenty guns, against the smug satisfaction Bart would derive from his hiding behind the door. Jack chose to deny Bart any satisfaction. He kissed Hope, then walked out the door and onto the street.

"What is it that we need to talk about, Bart?"

"Jack--- Buddy," Bart sang out in a sickeningly nice manner. "It doesn't have to end this way. I could use a man with your skills and..." Bart searched for the right word, "...innovation. You know where I'm from, and I know where you're from. I think we could really make a place for ourselves here."

"What, working for you, Bart? I hear there are certain health hazards for your employees."

Frank was sitting down off to the side of the road, moaning a little and sobbing some, trying not to move much when he breathed to avoid the sharp pains from his broken ribs and shoulder. Zeke felt a twinge of pain rising from both of his feet.

"Jack, it's not like that. You would be more like a junior partner. How does Vice President sound to you?"

"Still having delusions of grandeur, Bart? I have a feeling that those business friends of yours were a little discouraged by your... explosive personality. I don't think your political cronies are going to like it much, either." Jack felt like he was getting the better shots in, and it felt good.

"A temporary setback at most, Jack. Same plan, another place or time. Only you won't be there to stop me, will you?"

"Somebody will stop you. You don't seem to make friends very easily," Jack pointed out.

"This is a nasty trap you set here for me. Poor Frank there has a separated shoulder, for sure. Now why did you have to go and do that to a nice guy like Frank?"

"Maybe he should choose a nicer class of people to hang out with. That goes for all you boys. You can ride away now and save yourself a hanging." Another free shot. Bart was certainly not very good at this kind of debate.

"Seems like just the opposite is true here," Bart yelled back. "Any of you people hiding in there better take your opportunity now to run for it. I've got no quarrel with you all. I am only after those three that burned down my house for no reason."

That was about all that Hope could take. She burst out of the door to stand next to Jack, shouting as she walked.

"You're a no good snake of a man, Bart Decker! You sent those scoundrels to kidnap me from my home. You beat me. You were going to kill me. You deserved...," she stopped in mid-sentence. "Jack!" she shrieked, grabbing his arm and turning him around. Behind them, smoke and flames were rising from the other side of town.

"Damn it," Jack thought. "No wonder he was happy to sit here and chat." He heard Bart laughing behind him. When he turned back around, Bart had already drawn his gun.

"Thanks for the lively conversation, Jack. I wish we could go on, but I've got work to do."

33

Jack could feel Hope pulling on his arm, shouting something. All he could hear was Bart laughing at him. His pit had only taken one man out of action, there was another assault unchecked on the far side of town, and Bart was laughing at him. Jack didn't take losing well. He never had. Taking his ball and going home when he trailed by too much to come back and win on the playground. Quitting before his brother could get his last piece into the home space in whatever board game they were playing. Right up to the point of calling off his wedding with Rachel. He had done it because he was afraid she would call it off first. Losing sucked. Being laughed at sucked. Now he was losing the most important game there was. The stakes here were his life, and the lives of many others.

Gunfire brought him out of his state of shock. The dirt kicked up between him and Hope. Jack's feet started moving on their own, in the direction that Hope was pulling. Bart kept firing at them as they cleared the porch and dove through the door that Doc opened. Jack jumped up off of the floor, and turned to pull Hope along as they all rushed out the back door. They blocked the door with a barrel filled with dirt, then raced down the back alley to the next building set up for defense, the town assayer's office. That meant they were sacrificing the feed store to the fire, but things had changed. His initial plan was to initiate a small skirmish from there, then fall back further into town where his defenses were the strongest. Now that every one of Bart's men had seen them run into the feed store, the building would get hot very fast. Early on in Army training, Bart learned that good generals were great at planning, but great generals were good at adapting. Changes to the overall plan were inevitable. That was the first rule of military planning---"No plan survives first contact with the enemy."

Behind the assayer's office, Jack started issuing orders.

"Doc, take the men in the mobile reserve to the other side of town and do what you can to stop whoever is down there. Get back here as soon as you can. Light the blocking fire if you need to fall back. I am going to get those folks on the roof engaged and see if we can't put a dent into their numbers." Doc started out the back door.

"Be careful, Doc. There is nothing in those buildings that we need more than you and those men."

"You, too, Jack," Doc answered. "I think Bart has made it clear that he isn't leaving here tonight without your scalp."

Jack was already on the move. He went into the assayer's office and went to the front window to peer out into the street. Bart's men were going around the pit, riding up onto the porches of the buildings on either side. Both of those buildings were already burning from torches tossed into their windows or onto their roofs. That wasn't all bad. What the riders didn't know was that they had just locked themselves into the fire zone of multiple ranged weapons. Jack hoped that would count for something.

The riders poured into the street waiving burning torches and firing their guns randomly into the buildings. Wasted ammo that was not going to hit anyone. Unless, by chance, they were shooting into the candle shop...

Some of the riders could be seen trying to dart into the spaces between the buildings, but turning their horses away as their path was invariably blocked. Finally, one of them found a path unblocked. He turned and prodded his horse through the opening in a hurry. He wanted to circle around the front street and reenter farther down. So far everyone else was having all the fun. He hadn't been able to torch an untouched building yet, and he wanted to get a score of his own. He should have been thinking more about why this way was open and all the others blocked. That was probably too much to ask of a thug turned cowhand on a night ride to terrorize a town of innocents. In any case, this rider never saw the rope that came across his chest at the shoulders, sliding up under his chin as his horse carried him forward. The rope was securely fastened to solid wood in the walls on either side of him, and there was nothing to stop his horse from continuing on through the passage. The rope lifted the rider up and out of his saddle, his body rising to parallel the ground before upward momentum stopped and gravity became the dominant acting force. His body continued to pivot around the rope at his chin until the angle allowed the rope to snap back to its original line between the buildings, and the man continued to twist as his body fell forward and down. It was hard to say which part hit the ground first, since he had twisted all the way around in a most graceful 270 degree spin to face plant into the dirt. The impact to his chest and sternum resulted in a loud 'Whump!' which completely expelled all the air from his lungs. His one desire in life at this point was to somehow get oxygen back into his chest, but his lungs just wouldn't work. He was too occupied with trying to stave off suffocation to notice the gang of 6 women armed with clubs and other weapons rush into the passage from behind the buildings. They were on him in an instant, performing a perfect hog tie on his arms and legs. As the women dragged the thoroughly confused and completely helpless captive out of the passageway, another group of six took up position to await the next victim.

The shooters on the rooftops peered over the edges as the riders passed by. This was the hardest part, waiting for their turn in what was an intricate layer of defenses. Allowing armed men to ride past, threatening their friends and family further down the street was completely against their nature. Which is why Jack knew it would be completely unexpected by the attackers, and one more assault on their resolve. His experience in battle told him that men broke and fled not from one individual setback, but from the aggregate of several unexpected outcomes. If Bart's tough men were attacked all along their path, they would fight through each individual battle and push on. Jack was pinning his strategy on letting the riders think they had won through on an easy path, then getting their noses bloodied several times in succession. That, he thought, was the quickest way to get them to panic and look for their own exits from the war. Victories were the sum of smaller victories. So the men on the rooftops had to remain steady and trust the plan. And hope.

"Damn, this is fun!" Elijah shouted over to Zeke. Destroying things that other people had built was fun. It had always been that way. Zeke had shown him that all the time they were growing up. Every sand castle, tree fort or house of cards that Elijah had built, Zeke had loved tearing it apart. He still did, whenever he could. But that was the fun part of hanging out with Zeke. They got to destroy other people's stuff. Shoot things up. Burn things down. Just a twinge of guilt passed through Elijah's heart when he tossed a lit torch into a doorway as he wondered whose dreams he was burning down. Loud laughter of support from Zeke squashed any remorse that Elijah had let creep in. This WAS a good time.

The four men in the candle shop were getting tired, and they were feeling a little exposed. They were the fourth building along the street, and their position was isolated from the rest of the town. They had seen plenty of riders go by the windows, so they knew they were cut off from any help or support. If Bart's men got around behind them, their escape would be blocked. They had already doused two torches thrown through the windows, which was no small feat. Three men had to hold the tension on the springs while one man put out the torch. That was tiring work. When the third torch came flying through the window, the three men on the far side tightened their grip while the man on the end picked up the torch and tossed it back out the window.

That was the first sign of life in this town that Luke had seen. Burning stuff down was for little boys, real penny ante stuff. A torch flying back out the window meant there were people in there. That was the kind of fun Luke wanted. Bart had taken off all the restrictions again. It had been a thrill like he had never known the last time Bart let him loose. That sheriff hadn't even known he was going to die when

Luke had plunged the knife into his back. That sensation of taking a life had been on his mind ever since. He didn't know if he liked the feeling or not, but he knew he wanted more of it. Counting was never his strong suit, but he had shot six or seven Indians since then. That didn't really satisfy him like he thought it should. Probably because they were just savages. His entire body surged with power and expectation as he got off of his horse and climbed the steps. He didn't even try to hide the sounds of his boots climbing up the steps and across the porch. The sounds of the battle behind him dissipated as he approached the door. It was just him and what he hoped was a room full of people. He stopped for a moment when he realized he only had two guns with six bullets each. "Only eleven shots," he told himself. He reached around his belt and felt the hilt of his knife in his hand, then started forward again. This was too easy. Maybe he should try to find a fair fight, where the other guy was armed. Maybe next time. He reached out and grabbed the door handle with his left hand, gun in his right, and planned his bloodbath.

"As I get inside, I'll pull out the other gun with my left hand and give them both barrels at the same time. When the smoke clears, I'll switch to the knife for the mop up work."

"I am the Reaper!" he shouted as he pulled the door open and strode inside.

Grover thought that was a peculiar coincidence. On his "Now!" the four men released their hold on the bar. Although they were tired from keeping tension on the springs for so long, they had reached into their reserve strength and added an extra ten inches of pull tension on the springs when they heard the boot steps approaching the door. When they released their hold on the iron bar and stumbled backwards, the McCormick Horse Drawn Reaper springs returned to their natural state of compression with a force of hundreds of foot lbs. The 70 lb. iron bar struck Luke just above the elbow as he reached across his body to grab his second gun. Grover estimated that the impact damage from that heavy iron bar on a man's arm and chest would be...well, it would be a lot. He was right. The bar shattered Luke's arms and several of his ribs. He was lifted clean off the ground and propelled out into the street. The last thought Luke had before everything went black was disappointment that he wasn't going to be able to add the three men to his count.

The catapult arm sprang forward with a rush of air and a blur. Jack's instructions had been to let the larger portion of the riders get into range before he started firing, and to Edgar that seemed like right now. He had loaded a smaller stone into the basket to get some range. The stone carried much farther than any shot had gone all night in practice, clear past the pit and onto the road outside of town. The stone didn't hit anybody and it didn't cause any damage. It did scare the crap out of Frank as he sat outside of town nursing his broken ribs. Thinking he had been targeted individually by a cannon, he scrambled to his feet and ran off. Edgar beamed with the pride of a new father. He ordered a heavier stone loaded into the basket and the catapult team started firing as fast as they could reload. These heavier stones found their mark in and around the surprised riders. The first few didn't hit anyone but they certainly drew a lot of attention as they kicked up huge clouds of dirt. The fourth shot knocked one of the men completely off his horse. It had only been a glancing blow, but it made a lasting impact in the minds of the riders that saw it. They prodded their horses further along the street to get out of the fire zone of the terrorizing catapult.

The fuel oil had been poured into the trenches earlier when the sentry had signaled the approach of Bart and his men. Adolf waited until the riders were fast approaching before setting the oil ablaze. The firewall sprang from the ground in front of the riders as if summoned from the devil himself. The horses halted and reared. Confusion and fear began to reign in the street as the riders lost control of events. They were frozen with indecision. They could not spur their horses past the fire and they had no desire to return to the catapult killing zone. Absent direction, they circled their horses in the street looking for targets to shoot at. Hope and the slingshot crews leapt into action, peppering the riders and their horses with rocks. The rocks weren't travelling fast enough to penetrate like a bullet, but they were capable of raising very painful bruises and slashing cuts. When the rocks hit bones; elbows, knees, and skull, they were even more damaging. Hits in the face were the worst for the riders. Teeth were knocked out, faces cut and everyone feared losing an eye. It was impossible to remain in the line of fire. Not that many of the riders had much choice in the matter. Their horses were being pelted also, and they reacted in ways that most riders would have difficulty controlling. Those riders thrown from their horses scrambled to take cover in the adjacent buildings. Most of the horses turned and sprinted up the street, some still carrying their riders, who were holding on for their lives. Those riders that could control their horses looked for easy ways out of the streets between the buildings. Three riders found the way open between the general store and the saloon. However as they neared the end, a cart was pushed across the opening blocking their exit. They couldn't turn their horses around in the narrow passageway, and in the excitement were having a difficult time backing their horses up. A low rumbling noise above them caught their attention. The three looked up in unison just in time to see barrels of all sizes rolling off the rooftop and crashing onto their heads.

The men and women on top of the stable and surrounding buildings had been waiting and watching. They had watched several of their homes and businesses set afire, and felt an anger welling up inside of them. Finally, it was their turn to act. The confused riders had stopped short of the gouges in the street from the catapult, shooting at whatever moved in windows and on rooftops. The townspeople on the rooftops began throwing spears, rocks and some of Jack's homemade grenades. Dawson's Creek had only one citizen of Indian descent. He had joined the shooters on the rooftop carrying his bow and a quiver of arrows. Quincy the bartender watched Ten Bears' first three shots miss wildly.

"No offense Ten Bears, but just what kind of Indian are you?"

Ten Bears replied, "None taken. Shooting the bow is harder than it looks. If I was any good at it, I would still be shooting Army soldiers taking Indian lands." After a short pause, he added, "No offense."

"None taken," Quincy responded. "Keep shooting, Ten Bears. Just hit something!"

The only light in town was the lantern hanging in front of the Catholic Church. Elijah and Davey stopped their horses when they heard singing coming from the building. They dismounted and peered into the windows. Sitting in the pews they could see the heads of twenty or thirty people as they heard 'Nearer my Lord to Thee.' Bart shouted from behind them.

"Are you two planning on joining this fight anytime soon?"

"But Mr. Decker, there's a bunch of women in there singing hymns."

Bart had watched this battle unfold and wasn't enjoying the results. This should have been a cakewalk. He didn't care what it took, he was going to make these people pay. He was going to get that son of a bitch Banyan. Besides, with his plans up in smoke, what did he care? He wasn't going to be around long enough to worry about hanging.

"Block the damned door and burn that church down. I don't care if the whole Mormon Tabernacle Choir is in there. I'll shoot you and do it myself if I have to. Burn it down, damn it!"

Elijah and Davey moved to the side of the porch where a barrel sat. Davey started to move the heavy barrel toward the door. Elijah continued to move slowly away from the door. He had signed up with this outfit to make a little money and maybe raise a little Hell. He had no intention of going straight to Hell, which is where he was certain to be headed if he burned down a church full of women singing hymns. 'Nearer my Lord to Thee' had always been his favorite hymn, and they were singing it now as some sort of heavenly message sent straight to him. When he reached the end of the porch, he turned, jumped down from the porch and ran down the alleyway. Since he was on foot he ran completely under the rope between the two buildings. As he cleared the passageway and ran into the open space towards the creek, he saw to his left a group of women's behinds stacked up at the back door of the church. They were poking their heads into the door and singing as loud as they could.

Back at the front of the church, Davey had moved the barrel next to the door. He pulled the lantern down from its latch, looked at Bart to give him one more chance to call it off, then opened the door to throw in the lantern. As he pushed the door open a huge sack of flour came crashing down onto the floor right where he would have been standing had he entered the church. A huge cloud of white dust engulfed the front of the building and Davey. Thinking he had escaped a twenty pound sack of flour falling on his head, Davey started to laugh. Bart was laughing, also. Their laughing faces framed by the fire behind them, combined with the cacophony of yells and battle sounds, competed with the Choir's hymn in a nightmarish representation of the battle between good and evil. Their maniacal laughter rose to a crescendo as Davey raised the lantern and brought it crashing down inside the church door.

Farmers have known for years that aerated grain dust has explosive potential that rivals dynamite. Many a silo has been blown to bits with just the slightest spark. The blast that Davey created brought down the entire front half of the church. The pews, and their straw scarecrow occupants, were blown into the far wall. The fireball engulfed Davey, then belched him out all the way across the street. The blast knocked Bart onto his back. For a moment, the entire battle stopped as the blast shocked both sides. There was a deathly calm as Bart stood looking at the scarecrows that had been sitting in the pews, scattered and burning in the church. He looked around at the burning town, saw the remains of his small army, some lying unconscious in the street, others taking cover from the flying weapons. It was too much for a man with his temper to take.

"I'll kill you Banyan!" he shouted up and down the street. He seemed to have a protective field around him as projectiles flew by him from several directions.

"I'll kill you and I'll go back and I'll start all over again. You'll never win, you son of a bitch!"

Needing to rally his forces, Bart ran over to a group of his men taking cover under a porch. After a quick pep talk, mostly threats backed up by Bart's gun, the men started back up the street. They split into several groups with weapons drawn, intent on exacting some revenge while fighting a retreat. A group of three of them offered a juicy prize when they walked right onto the porch of the town's only law office. Two teenage boys were running this trap. David was on the ground in between the law office and the next building. He had the rope in hand tied to the post holding up the porch. The posts supporting the porch had all been cut through, and heavy iron fittings had been placed on top of the roof. David's sight line to the porch was blocked by the barrels that prevented riders from exiting this way, so Chester was on the roof of the building serving as a scout. The plan was for Chester to signal David when the porch was occupied. David would yank on the line, pulling the support from the awning, and hundreds of pounds of wood and iron would smash down onto the men below. That was the plan, anyway. When David yanked on the rope, however, the roof didn't fall. Chester had not been the obvious choice for someone that would climb up on top of a building. He had forever been left out of the gang when it came to climbing trees, or hills, or anything that required moving his very large frame off the ground. Today, however, David's fear of heights was the reason for the unusual assignment. Chester was happy to contribute in any way he could. He had been on the receiving end of all kinds of fat jokes from those Bowe brothers and their friends. He wanted revenge, and he wanted recognition. Was that too much to ask? That was what drove him to do the most courageous, and most stupid, thing of his short life. Seeing that the porch wasn't going to fall, he didn't think twice before he started in motion. He moved with catlike agility across the rooftop, albeit a very large cat. He made a graceful leap over the building facade, and came down onto the porch in a sitting position. Several hundred pounds of wood and iron, plus several hundred pounds of Chester dropped down onto the three men underneath. Their bodies actually cushioned the blow on Chester such that it was only a bit of a rough landing for him. For the men underneath, however, the fight was over. Chester let out a "Yee Haw" and thrust his fist into the air in a triumphant gesture. The rush into action had been as far as Chester had planned the attack. That part had gone superbly. Now, however, bullets started to kick up splinters around him. Chester looked up to see a cowboy on the other side of the street reloading his pistol. As he scrambled up from the entangling wreck of wood and iron, the cowboy finally found his mark, putting a bullet into Chester's shoulder and spinning him back down onto the deck in front of the door. Chester sat against the door, watching the cowboy draw down on him and waiting for the bullet that was going to end his life. Then, as if by magic, an arrow appeared in the cowboy's chest. The door opened behind Chester. He fell back into the hands of David and Sally Coors. They dragged him into the office and pulled him behind a desk. David put a bandana on the bullet wound while Sally wiped his face and neck with a wet cloth. She was gushing praise for Chester's heroic act.

"You were magnificent! I saw the whole thing. You moved so fast, those men didn't have a chance against you. Why Chester, I never knew you were so strong and brave!" Sally's attention eased whatever pain Chester was in. He hardly noticed the pain at all when he looked up at Sally's beautiful face. Chester had half a mind to go out there and find some more of those boys to tangle with, but that would mean leaving this angel holding his head in her lap. Wild horses couldn't have made him leave that office.

Jack had been all over town that night. He had stopped in to nearly every building or outpost to give guidance and encouragement to his troops. He'd only been yards away when the church exploded. He had heard Bart's ranting and could see that the pieces of his plan were falling into place. Not that everything had gone right. There were still fires rising from the other end of town, and he hadn't heard back from Doc yet. The backstop trenches hadn't been lit, so he had some hope that the threat had been contained. There were plenty of buildings ablaze on this end of town, and there were still cowboys with guns trying to get away. Once Bart had them reorganized, the real danger would be taking them out individually. They already had 14 or 15 of the riders out of action or hogtied down by the creek. They weren't dealing with mounted men shooting from the middle of the street anymore. The seven or so remaining cowboys, including Bart, had all lost their mounts, and had no desire to go anywhere near the fire zones. Jack could see that Bart was rapidly running out of options. He could try to mount a fighting retreat. There wasn't much the town could do about that, maybe get one or two more men as the rest fled. But that would be a loss for Bart. Jack was certain that Bart still thought he could take this town. Though it would be a pyrrhic victory in every sense, Bart wasn't thinking about conserving his forces to fight another day. That shout in the middle of the street told Jack all he needed to know about Bart's intentions. His temper was driving him now. Bart would keep fighting until he ran out of troops, like so many bad generals throughout history. Of course, he would slink off into the shadows once the battle was lost. That is what Jack could not let happen. Whatever happened from this point forward, Bart must not be allowed to escape.

Jack was in the hardware store now. He had a fire team assembled there, and the team was making terrific use of a spring loaded bolo ball launcher, shooting through the windows as what was left of Bart's army came running by on their way out of town. They had knocked down and entangled two men already. In their zeal for clearing out the bad guys in front of them, they never heard the back door open.

"Where are my boots?"

Jack and the three men turned around to see Zeke, pistol in hand, bleeding and bruised all over from rock strikes, and hobbling on his two very sore feet. He was injured and desperate, and clearly very mad. And he wanted those boots.

"I asked you a question. You ain't wearin 'em, so where are they?" He thrust his gun forward a little for emphasis.

"Why don't you ask your brother, Zeke?" was all Jack could come up with. He needed to buy a little time to get his hand around the makeshift concussion grenade sitting on the table. He would still need to find a way to get over to the candle to light it, but first things first. "Didn't he take them from you?"

"That little weasel couldn't take nothing from me. He found them somewhere, that's all."

"For a little weasel, he must have done something right. I sent him to pull you out of that fire. He must have saved your life. He's a real hero, isn't he Zeke?" Jack had the grenade under his hand, and was plotting how he could get to the candle.

"He ain't no hero. He... " Zeke stopped mid-sentence. "Bart, in here!" Zeke had seen Bart running by the window. Bart came through the door and saw victory in his grasp.

"Well, well, well. Nice work, Zeke. It looks like you have caught a very big fish." Bart walked around to stand next to Zeke. Both men were pointing their guns at Jack.

"Looks like I will get what I want tonight, doesn't it, Jack?"

Jack was out of options. He needed to get that fuse lit. He had seen it work in the movies, but the diving distance between him and the candle looked like a long shot. At this point, though, a long shot seemed preferable to a gun shot.

He looked up past the two gunmen at the back door. "Thank God your here! Cover these two." Zeke took the bait and turned, lowering his pistol. Jack took a two step diving leap to the table across the room, reaching out and grabbing the candle as he dove. Bart had only scowled at Jack's ruse, and at Zeke for falling for it. He fired twice before Jack disappeared behind the table. Jack felt a sharp stinging in his side, but was more concerned with getting his grenade lit. He had knocked the table over, breaking a kerosene lantern on the floor. The candle had ignited the spreading pool of kerosene across the floor and up the curtains. Jack had no trouble lighting the grenade in the growing fire and tossed it over the table next to where Bart and Zeke were standing. He could just see around the end of the table where the grenade landed with the fuse burning. Then he saw a boot come down and stomp the fuse out, followed by that slow laughter again. He was really getting tired of hearing that laugh.

"Come on out from behind there, Banyan. I don't think we will be blowing up any time soon." Jack stood up slowly, partly from disappointment that Bart and Zeke weren't going to be blowing up, and partly from the pain in his side.

"Looks like my shooting was close enough, huh Banyan?"

Jack looked down to see several wood fragments jutting out from a growing red stain on his shirt.

"Now where were we? Oh, that's right. I was saying that it looks like I am going to win tonight. Isn't that right, Jack? More importantly, that means that you lose, doesn't it?"

Jack just glared at the pair holding their weapons. This was it? This was how he was going out of this world? Gunned down by the Devil and his moron apprentice? Bart was right. Jack had lost, and that was the worst part of it.

"What's the matter, Banyan?" Bart continued poking at Jack. "Cat got your tongue? Where is all that witty repartee that we started the night off with? Where is it now, Jack?"

Jack looked up to give Bart a piece of his mind. If he was going to go out, it might as well be in good form. But something stopped him before he started speaking. A slow smile spread across his face.

"I think you boys will want to be putting those guns down now."

"Jack, you're stalling. Come on, you can do better than that. If you can't come up with something new, I'm just gonna have to kill you. I suppose I ought to get on with it. That fire is getting a little out of hand."

"I'm telling you boys, we have the drop on you. Put your guns down." He said it with the straight face of a poker player holding aces.

Bart smiled, and his thumb slowly pulled the hammer back on his pistol.

"I don't think so, Jack. See you in Hell."

There was gunfire again, only this blast was much louder and came from off to the left. Jack blinked, and when he opened his eyes, where the two pistols had been pointed at him there were only two red stumps at the ends of arms. Zeke and Bart were too shocked to comprehend what had just happened. Old Ben Riley was standing in the window, holding the biggest, baddest looking shotgun Jack had ever seen. There was a wisp of white smoke rising up from the barrel.

"Where did that thing come from?" Jack asked incredulously.

"This old thing?" Ben asked as he patted the gun. "I kept this one hidden when they rounded up everybody's guns, just in case. Zeke there would have tasted this lead sooner if I'd had it in the outhouse with me."

Everyone but Zeke and Bart laughed in relief at the turnaround in their fortunes. Then Ben asked, with some concern in his voice, "Say Jack, what are those white things burning in the fire there?"

Jack looked down to see that several of his concussion grenades had fallen with the table, and were now engulfed in flames. Everyone in the room recognized them for the danger that they were. Ben fell back away from the window, the bolo gun operators and Jack dove toward the front door, while Zeke and Bart recovered enough to dive toward the back of the store. The string of explosions destroyed what was left of that side of the hardware store.

Hope had made her way forward, following the crowd of defenders as they chased the remaining cowboys out of town. They scooped up the injured ones, tying them and treating their wounds so that they would live to stand trial. She had just made it to the hardware store when she saw Jack and his fire team jumping, or being blasted, out the front door. She hadn't seen Jack for the last half of the battle and had been worried that he was hurt.

Jack's forehead had a gash and a knot rising up from some flying debris in the blast, and it took him a few seconds to gather himself enough to stand.

"Thank God you're all right!" Hope said as she helped him up off the ground, then nearly knocked him back down with her elated kisses. "We did it, Jack! We did it!" Jack's emotions were more muted. He surveyed the battle field around him. There were buildings on fire all around. There were bruised and bleeding people and horses getting medical help. Doc was down the street attending to the wounded. It was worse than anything he had seen in Iraq. Jack was shaken up, but he could still see that there were things that needed to be done.

"I see Doc down there. Did they take care of the threat on the other side of town?"

"Yes," Hope answered, "He and the reserves found two men setting fire to buildings on that side of town. They used your grenades and that harpoon gun contraption to stop them. Jack reached down and felt the wood splinters jutting out from his side.

"Jack! You've been shot!" Hope shrieked. She saw for the first time the gruesome splinters rising out of the blood soaked circle on his shirt. Jack felt a little woozy at the reawakening of his pain, but brushed her concerns aside.

"Not shot, exactly," he told her. "Maybe I'll have Doc take a look at it later. Can you get the fire brigades organized? I need to find Zeke and Bart in this rubble and make sure they live to stand trial."

"Are you sure you are okay?" she asked.

"Yes. Absolutely," Jack responded. There was a slight hesitation between the words as a hot flash of pain seared in his side. He turned to the men that had been blasted out of the store with him. "Come on, fellas. We need to drag those two one armed bandits out of this rubble and see about patching them up." He leaned over to help one of the men up off the ground. Just as they stood up together, several shots were fired and the man slumped back down into the dirt. Jack looked up to see Bart, astride a horse twenty feet away. He was sweating profusely, his right arm wrapped in a blood soaked cloth. He was pointing the pistol in his left hand at Jack. He was pulling the trigger, but getting only a clicking noise.

"Damn it!" Bart yelled. He threw the gun at Jack in an awkward, left handed throwing motion that nearly toppled him out of the saddle. Then he grabbed the reins with his one good hand and spurred his horse into a gallop out of town.

Jack ran to the nearest horse. He started to mount, but was pulled back down by his belt.

"No Jack. Let him go. We've won," Hope begged him.

"I can't do that, Hope. We haven't won anything if he gets away. You heard him say it himself. He'll just start the plan all over again somewhere else. I have to finish it now, tonight."

"Jack, please don't go?" Her voice was trembling, and tears were welling up in her eyes. "I can't live without you in my life. I love you, Jack."

Jack reached his hand up to the back of Hope's head and pulled her in to a kiss that spoke louder than any words he could have used.

"Hope, we'll be alright. I plan on living a long and happy life with you in it. I love you."

He turned, put his foot into the stirrup, and pulled himself up into the saddle. His face was away from Hope as he grimaced in pain and nausea from his wounds. He wondered if the splinters had punctured some internal organ. One of the men passed a pistol up to him. "That should even the odds a bit for you," he said. Jack tucked the gun into his belt and took one last look at Hope. She was tired and disheveled from the battle, but she looked angelic to him. "So this is what love feels like," he thought as he mouthed "I love you" to her. He prodded the horse and started off at a fast trot, which was a lot considering his riding skills were only recently acquired. Not exactly the Lone Ranger standing Trigger up on two legs, but she still might be impressed just a little. He had gotten pretty good at this horse riding thing.

Hope watched him disappear into the night. She wanted to believe otherwise, but she couldn't shake the feeling that Fate was not going to let her have this man. Watching him ride off only added to her fears. "Good Lord, he is going to fall off that horse and break his neck," she worried.

34

Jack didn't have much trouble following Bart, since Doc had told him where the portal was. Jack wasn't sure himself why he hadn't come back here. He could have left at any time after he had rescued Hope, so why had he stayed? Hope, of course, was the obvious answer. He belonged here with her. They would live a long happy life together on her ranch. That would be enough to make any man want to stay. It was more than that, though. Deep down, he realized that he would have chosen to stay even if there had not been the love of his life. Like Doc, he had made a difference here. He could still make a difference here. Was it like the SciFi shows, where time travelers were always disturbing the space-time continuum? Would staying here in the past change historic events? Jack laughed at that one. Who was having delusions of grandeur now? It didn't matter. He could only control what was in his realm of possibilities. He would live his life here in the past, without taking advantage of his knowledge of the future, at least not intentionally. If what he did here was going to have some effect on the future, that cat was already out of the barn door, or however the proverb went. He had led two battles, injured some people, and probably saved some lives. If he was going to make a world-affecting change, it was already in the works. Whatever he did from here out would be minor in comparison.

His horse had no trouble seeing in the moonlight, so Jack sped up to a gallop. He had to catch up to Bart. Bart was a cold blooded killer who would be a real danger to whatever world he was in. Jack would be dead now if it weren't for Ben Riley and that beautiful shotgun of his. Jack reached into his belt to feel the pistol that Luther had handed to him. What was it the Army used to say about taking weapons into battle? Check your weapons, then check them again. Jack drew the pistol out of his belt to check the drum. He could see the brass circles of the loaded bullets. He hoped it didn't come down to his needing to use it, but it was sure nice to have a gun. He had used a nine millimeter Beretta automatic in the Army, but was unfamiliar with revolvers. Same basic principle, he figured. Point and shoot, but only six times. How tough could it be? The bloody stain on Jack's shirt had not stopped growing, and the jarring ride was taking a toll. He felt light headed a couple of times, but forced himself to push through and clear his mind. He had work to do.

Bart could see Jack riding behind him. He had turned off of the road, in a perpendicular direction headed toward the hills. Jack had slowed to a trot and taken the 45 degree angle to cut Bart off. Bart still managed to reach the rocky slope leading up to the cave entrance well before Jack. Bart had left his horse and started the difficult traverse, using his one good hand to steady himself. It was slow going, but not impossible. He turned to see Jack getting closer. Bart let out a short laugh and continued climbing.

Jack got to the bottom of the slope and started climbing as soon as he was off his horse. Although he had two hands, he was hampered by weakness from his loss of blood. Bart had already disappeared over the rise leading into the cave. The light headedness was with him full time now. Everything seemed to slow down. By concentrating only on the single task at hand, Jack was able to make it up to the plateau. He stopped just below the edge to catch his breath, and more importantly, to refocus his mind on the next step. He couldn't be sure what path Bart had chosen...Go straight into the cave and make a run for it, or lie in wait to kill Jack first. After thinking about it for only a second, Jack decided it would be prudent to place his bets on option two. He peeked over the edge of the rise. Sure enough, Bart was sitting on a crate at the entrance to the cave. He was taking deep swigs of whiskey out of a bottle, probably to kill the pain from his severed hand. Jack ducked back down beneath the ridge. He fought off a dizzy spell from moving too quickly, then worked his way around the edge of the rise.

If he could put one of those bushes between him and Bart, he might be able to get over the ridge and on him before... Jack didn't get to finish his thought. The rock he had placed his foot on gave way and Jack slid a few feet down the slope in a small avalanche. His body and mind were only working at three-quarters speed.

"This would be a fantastic gunfight at the OK corral," he thought. "Drunk guy shooting left handed vs. Dazed man losing blood." He knew his situation would only get worse the longer he waited. He climbed up to the edge of the slope and peered over the edge again. He had worked his way around to a spot behind a bush, so he couldn't see if Bart was still sitting on the crate. He pulled himself up over the ledge and in close behind the bush. When he peeked around the side, Bart was nowhere to be seen. Jack stopped to listen, and heard the crunch of rocks beneath a boot on the other side of his bush. Jack pulled his gun from his belt and stepped out into the open.

"Don't move," he commanded. His gun was pointed right between Bart's shoulder blades. The pistol was heavy, and it wavered a bit as he tried to keep it pointed at Bart. Bart turned slowly to face him. He held a gun in his hand, hanging down at his side.

"Well Jack, fancy seeing you here," he said sarcastically. "Right back where we both started. Poetic that we should die here, don't you think?"

Jack didn't like the talk of dying. "Drop the gun."

Bart didn't take orders very well, and didn't appear to be too inclined to drop his gun. Jack backed up a little to put some space between them.

"Drop the gun. It's over, Bart." For emphasis, Jack decided he could spare one of those six bullets in a warning shot. He pointed the gun off to the side and squeezed off a round. 'Blam!' should have been the sound Jack heard. It was only 'Click.' Jack pulled the trigger again. 'Click.' Jack stared down at the useless gun in his hand. Click. Click. Click. Then he heard it. That evil, penetrating laugh. There it was again. He had been sure that he was never going to have to suffer it again. Damn it, what was wrong with the gun?

It didn't really matter anymore. When Jack looked back up at Bart, he was laughing and pointing his gun right at Jack's chest.

"Jack, Jack, Jack. Do me a favor. Take a look at the bullets in the barrel of your pistol." Jack looked. They were all right there. It should have fired.

"Look a little closer, Jack. Do you see a little dent in each one? Like it has already been fired? Ha Ha Ha!" Bart was enjoying Jack's mistake.

Jack looked closer and saw the hammer strike dented into each of the brass shells. He hadn't been able to see them when he checked the gun while riding the horse. Maybe that was why the Army motto was to check, then check AGAIN!

He looked up, expecting to hear the roar of Bart's gun at any moment. Looking past Bart and down into the valley, Jack could see lights bouncing up the road. The posse was coming, but it was going to be too late.

"Yeah, I saw those lights, too," Bart said. "All in all, I would prefer not to bring them up here with a gunshot. Why don't you just do what you're told and maybe we can avoid that unpleasantness?" Jack's first thought was that Bart would knife him in the back, and that he had let Hope down. To Bart's credit, he had no intention of anything so messy. He would simply wait until they were out the other side of the cave, then shoot Jack. Bart directed him over to the cave.

"Pick up that box, Jack. You are gonna be my mule. I have a nice collection of items in these boxes here. Should make a lot of money where we're going. I dropped it off up here while we were waiting for the rest of our horses to wake up. That was a nice touch, putting most of my horses out of action. Gave you enough time to scurry back to your rat hole of a town and set all of those traps. How you got those sheep to defend themselves I'll never know. You almost won, Jack. Almost."

Jack felt the sting of losing to a bastard like Bart too strongly to offer a response.

Bart kept on. "I was sitting here trying to figure out how I was going to carry all of this stuff through the portal. Lucky thing you showed up and volunteered to carry it for me. Only fitting since you're the reason I'm shorthanded." He laughed at his little play on words, then added grimly, "You'll pay for that later."

He wagged his gun at Jack. "Go on, pick up that rope."

Jack grabbed the rope. It was tied to a sled of sorts, with several boxes lashed to it.

"Now start walking." Bart let Jack get several yards into the cave, then struck a match and lit the end of a long fuse.

"That's a thirty minute fuse. It should let that posse get a long way from here before it goes off. Hold on to that rope tight. There won't be any coming back for anything that falls off of the truck. This is one Hell of a ride, and it is a one way ticket." Bart followed Jack into the cave and past the case of dynamite.

35

Jack opened his eyes slowly. This was about the worst headache he could remember, and he'd had some killer ones of late. The sunlight pouring in through his pupils exacerbated that pain. The world was a bright, blurry blob that kept changing from light to shade. Sound started to filter into his head. He could hear a voice, a man speaking. He had a vague recollection of a similar event, only then that someone speaking had been God, and he had been riding in the back of a wagon. His head had hurt then, too. The voice was a little clearer now.

"Mister? Hey Mister? Come on out of it... that's it."

Jack tried to keep his eyes open and focus, but that light was an ice pick in his eye. Even with his eyelids closed, he was in pain. His mouth was really dry, too. Then the shade came back and he cracked his eyelids just a bit.

"There you go. Jack, isn't it? What hurts? Can you tell me where it hurts, Jack?"

Jack could see a face ringed by sunlight. He recognized that face, and the voice, but he couldn't remember from where. Just the slightest twist of his head brought on enough pain to make him nauseous.

"Everywhere," he mumbled through dry lips. It was really a fair answer to the question. Splitting headache, parched throat and mouth, nauseous, his side hurt. He wasn't sure he could even feel his legs.

A woman's voice said "Don't move him. He will be paralyzed forever. Then you'll have a Hell of lawsuit on your hands."

There followed a conversation about head and neck injuries, and Good Samaritan laws, and how there was this guy, in Indiana, or Iowa, that had just been trying to help and ended up getting sued.

None of that made any sense to Jack, and he couldn't care less about the guy from Indiana, or Iowa, but he didn't like that 'paralyzed' word much. He pushed himself up and asked Darrell for some water.

"Sure Buddy. We'll get you some water. Listen, you're banged up pretty bad. We should get you to a hospital."

Darrell! That was it! Darrell the show off. The boy-faced lead of the trail ride. Memory was flooding into Jack's head now like it was coming out of a fire hose. The dude ranch. Bart. Where was Bart? Obviously not here, because I'm not dead. Then the big one…Hope! His eyes opened wide. Hope! He had left her in the chase for Bart. He had to get back to her. He had made a promise. No more worries about Bart and what havoc he might wreak onto this world. Jack had to get back to Hope. He reached out and grabbed Darrell by the shoulder, and Darrell helped pull him to his feet. He twisted as he rose to look back at the hills where he knew the cave had to be. Jack caught a glimpse of the hills, which then started to shrink and seemed to get further away. He could just hear Darrell asking him who the man was riding away on Diablo before they rode up. Then the blood in Jack's head drained away from his brain, his eyes rolled back into his head, and his world went black again.

When Jack next woke up, the light was there again. This time it was a woman's voice he heard.

"I don't know who she is, but you sure seem to want that girl pretty badly. Who is Hope?" the woman asked.

Jack opened his eyes to the sterile environment of a hospital room. Standing over him was the nurse that had asked the question.

"Water?" was all Jack could force out of his raspy throat.

"How about some ice?" The nurse put some ice chips up to Jack's lips. "You are getting fluids through the IV, but I know you still feel dehydrated. Just suck on these for a bit. How do you feel?"

He took a bodily inventory, and all in all felt a lot better than the last time he had done so. "Okay"

"You took a nasty fall from that horse. Quite a bump on the forehead. A concussion. It's a wonder that you didn't break your neck. You lost a lot of blood from those wood splinters in your side, too. That's why you feel so dehydrated. You should have seen yourself the first day you came in. You were as pale as I have ever seen a patient."

That statement caught Jack's attention.

"First day? How long have I been in here?"

She turned and drew open the shades as she spoke. "Oh, that was Sunday. Today is Wednesday, almost evening. I think you've gotten past the worst part of it. You should be out of here in no time. Can I call this 'Hope' for you? You've been calling out for her in your sleep."

That was enough to get him going. He tried to sit up, but fell back instantly onto the bed, out of breath and light headed. The nurse rushed back to the bed and handed Jack the remote control.

"Slow down there. You aren't going anywhere for a while. Just use this button to raise and lower the bed."

"I have to get back to Hope. I promised her..." his voice trailed off as he tried to collect his senses. Again he tried to rise. The nurse gently, but firmly, pushed him back down onto the bed.

"She is going to have to come visit you here, I'm afraid."

Now that was going to be one Hell of a trick. He had to get out of there and find that cave. He could feel his heart rate accelerating, and the increased pressure was pounding in his head. He looked around for his clothes, then back to the nurse. She was pulling something out of the IV line leading into the back of his hand.

"That should calm you down some. You just try to relax, and we will have a nice talk with the attending physician when you wake up."

Almost immediately he felt a gentle warmth emanate from his hand up through his arm and throughout his body. The warm glow and euphoria he felt induced a vision of Hope's face smiling up at him from the sheets after they had made love. That was the last conscious thought he had as he went back into his deep sleep.

The next two days were frantic for Jack. He was increasingly anxious to get out of the hospital and find his way back to Hope. None of the nurses or doctors seemed to know much about how he had gotten to the hospital. Of course, they all knew that he had fallen off of a horse, but they were all in the dark about who had brought him in and the dude ranch itself. He had deflected most of the questions about Hope and why he had been calling out her name, and he was happy to further their assumptions that his injuries had come from his fall off of Diablo. His condition slowly improved such that by Friday, he was capable of leaving. The hospital staff disagreed. The doctors and nurses all tried to convince him that he needed a few more days rest. They even made several attempts to 'lose' or 'delay' his checkout paper work to gain more time to convince him he was too weak to leave. By noon, Jack had had enough. After waiting 45 minutes for a nurse who was supposed to remove his IV, he simply pulled it out himself and slapped on a bandage. The clothes and gear he had taken to the dude ranch were in the closet. He was dressed and out the door in fifteen minutes.

The better part of a week had gone by since he had left Hope. His promise to return, to never leave her again, burned in his every waking thought. He was headed straight back to that cave as fast as he could get there. Jack's gut had been churning all week over the fuse that Bart had lit as they entered the cave. He had no idea if the portal even existed any longer, but that thought had been too painful to contemplate, so he decided to focus on the positive. He would get back to the dude ranch, find the cave, the portal would be working, and he would be back with Hope as he was meant to be.

He spent the rest of that Friday trying to get back to the Bar None Dude Ranch. He had come to the Bar None in a van, and had been dropped off at the Emergency Room by Darrell, so he had to take a cab back to his apartment to get his car. The hospital had been on the outskirts of the city, so he had been on the road for several hours before he got back to the vicinity of the dude ranch. Jack spent those three hours trying to make sense of the timeline. He had arrived at the Bar None on Sunday. He had fallen off of

Diablo and entered the cave around two in the afternoon. He had spent five days in Dawson's Creek, and had returned to the cave around one in the morning. Yet Darrell and the trail riders had found him recovering right where he had fallen from Diablo, less than an hour after he had left the riding trail. How could the clock have stood still the entire time he had been with Hope? It hurt his head to think about the mechanics of time travel, but he assured himself that it was possible that time somehow went at different speeds. Did that mean Bart and Doc could return, and it would only be minutes after they had left? How then was it possible for Bart to come back through the portal with Jack, but he was not on the trail ride originally? And did his being in the hospital for a week mean that years had passed in Hope's life? All he really cared about was finding the portal and getting back to where Hope was waiting for him. A mental image of his returning to Dawson's Creek, only to be greeted by a 90 year old Hope, passed through his mind. He stepped on the accelerator. Screw the tickets... every minute counted!

36

He had arrived back to where the dude ranch should have been. He had followed the directions on the flyer, but they seemed to be written by the same guy that writes the instruction manuals on all those electronics from China. "This hot iron not to be used while wearing clothing." Were they telling him not to iron clothes while he was wearing them, or not wear any clothes while he did the ironing? Neither interpretation made much sense, and the dude ranch flyer was no better. Jack searched for the ranch for hours, driving along roads that seemed familiar, but not, at the same time. If only he had paid a little more attention on the first trip. If not for the two kids and their bickering, anyway. He tried calling the Bar None for directions, but got no answer at the number he found in the useless flyer. He started asking gas station attendants and store clerks if any of them knew the location. Most just shook their heads or said they had never heard of it. Two of the clerks said they thought they had been asked that same question before, but no, they did not know where it was.

When darkness came, Jack found the nearest motel and booked a room for the night. He used the hotel's Wi-Fi connection to search the Bar None on the internet. It was unusual that any business these days could be anonymous on the internet, but he could find no mention of the Bar None. He tried scanning through the satellite mapping utility, but the remoteness of the area meant the photos were years old. He could find nothing that looked like a dude ranch on the images. He tried searches on Dawson's Creek, Hope Sugar, Doc Welby. Nothing on any of those except a web page for fans of the TV doctor. Even the web address printed right on the Bar None flyer returned a 'Domain Name Available' page. When Jack finally got a search hit, it was to his query 'Bart Decker'. There were several news stories and an online article from 'Coin Collectors World' about Bart selling some mint condition Confederate States of America currency. The story highlighted the fact that while after 1865 the currency would have been useless, today they sold for over $50,000.

"Great," Jack thought. "Bart goes there and back again, twice, and makes a fortune off of it, and here I am screwed. I can't even find the portal. Bad guy profits, good guy loses the girl." As Bart drifted off to sleep in his chair, he could not get those last words off of his mind..."Hope, we'll be alright. I plan on living a long and happy life with you in it. I love you."

Jack spent the rest of that weekend driving, asking for directions, and walking in the hills searching for a way back. The terrain was the same, but he could not get a solid feel for where his adventure had been. Late Sunday, he did come across some land that was familiar, but it only made his heart ache. He was in a small valley near a stream. It was overlooked by a hill that Jack climbed, where he lost his breath looking at the Rockies in the distance. This was the same view he had shared with Hope on their picnic. At least he wanted to believe it was where he had stared breathless at her.

Jack was confused and tired. There was nothing to show for the time he had spent in the past, the very real time he had spent with Hope...Doc...saving the town. He had continually fought down the attempts by his brain to explain it all, to neatly package it.

"You hit your head when you fell off the horse."

"It was all a dream."

"It never happened."

The longer he looked and found nothing, the stronger his doubts became. As darkness fell on Sunday night, Jack drove silently back to his apartment. He returned to work on Monday to an office that had not changed in any way. Several of his coworkers asked him about his vacation week at the ranch, and Jack just gave them the cursory, "It was fine. Very relaxing." Even Stephanie left her office in Finance to stop by and flirt with him, coyly telling him how boring the office had been without him for a week. Jack shooed her off, telling her he had a ton of email to catch up on. He actually tried to go through the email that had piled up, but could not bring his thoughts away from Hope. How was he going to get back to that portal? He knew it existed. It had to. Then he realized what he had been missing all along. Bart had the information he needed! Bart knew exactly where the portal was. He had been there four times now in his travels back and forth. Jack just needed to have a short conversation with Bart. There was only the small matter of finding him. And getting the information out of him. And somehow walking away from the conversation alive.

37

A quick internet search got Jack the name of the reporter who had done the story for 'Coin Collectors World' magazine. A few phone calls later and a BS story about being Bart's former business partner got Jack the name of the hospital where the interview had taken place. Jack grabbed his keys and headed out the door. At the hospital, he ducked into the gift shop to pick up a flower arrangement and some 'Get Well Soon' balloons. A pretty girl, of the type Jack had dated dozens, sat behind the hospital reception counter reading a romance novel.

"Hi there. Can you give me a number?" he asked with that confident smile that had worked so well in the past. She looked up from her book, took notice of Jack, and smiled back.

"I don't usually give out my number so quickly," she answered with a coy smile of her own.

"Oh, no. I certainly didn't mean to...Let me start over. Hi, I'm Jack," he said, extending the hand holding the balloons. She shook his hand over the desk.

"Brittany. What can I do for you?"

"Well, Brittany, you can take this as an apology." Jack pulled one of the flowers out of the bouquet and presented it to her. "I'm here to see my roommate from law school. He lost his hand in an accident... Bart Decker." She sniffed the flower and laid it on the counter, obviously impressed with Jack and his newly created pedigree. She started tapping away at the keyboard.

"I'm sorry. It looks like he has already been discharged."

"Oh no. I spoke to him here Wednesday. When he said he was going to be in Denver for a few more days, I assumed he would still be in the hospital." Jack let the flowers hang down at his side, looking quite deflated. "I don't suppose he left an address?"

She winced. "I can't give out patient addresses."

"No, and I would never want you to get into trouble. I just have no idea how to find him. He doesn't live here and I have no address for him. We used to play a lot of golf, and I thought he might need some emotional support, what with losing his hand and all." Jack nodded to the balloons and flowers as he scrunched his lower lip up into the upper one. Brittany started tapping again at the computer.

"I can't give you his address, but this might help." She took out a hospital business card and spoke while she wrote on the back. "Everybody could use a friend like you." She smiled and met his gaze as she handed the card over the counter to Jack.

Jack looked at the card. 'Rocky Mountain Hotel' was written over 'Brittany 303-555-1108.'

"Thanks. You're awesome, Brittany." Once outside and in the parking lot, he gave the bouquet and balloons to an older woman on her way inside to visit someone. He crumpled the card into a ball and tossed it into the trash can. Brittany was a nice girl, but he knew where the only girl he wanted was. The trick was figuring out how to get there. He tapped 'Rocky Mountain Hotel' into his car GPS system and had the map up before he got out of the parking lot. He drove the thirty minutes to the hotel and waited in his car. The hotel was a two story, L shaped building with outdoor stairs and entrances. It wasn't long before he watched Bart emerge from a room on the second floor and head for the parking lot. He still had a massive bandage over his right wrist. Once Bart left, Jack slipped up the staircase and walked by the room. He could hear the television playing inside. He continued down the walkway to the maid's cart outside the room two doors down. He cautiously avoided the open doorway while trying to find her pass key. He wasn't cautious enough, though, as a tap on the shoulder startled him.

"Room service?" the maid asked in a heavy Latino accent.

Jack paused for a moment. He hadn't thought this one through.

"I was just looking for some...some more towels. I took a shower earlier and got water all over the floor in my room, and now I wanted to go down by the pool, but I don't have any dry towels, you see?" It was weak, but it was all he had on the spur of the moment. The maid's expression never changed.

"No Ingles. Room Service?"

Whew. Not as busted as he thought. "Mas towels." He took a couple of towels off of the cart and smiled as he walked back to Bart's door. He continued to make eye contact and sheepishly smiled as he walked. He made a show of searching for his room key for the maid, then put on his most embarrassed looking expression. Using his one semester of high school Spanish class to its utmost, he looked back at the maid and said "Yo no remembero mi key?" while he pantomimed inserting his key in the door. The maid had to laugh at this point. She walked over to the door, unleashed a monologue of Spanish, and inserted the pass key attached to a string around her neck into the keycard slider. Jack opened the door and backed in, all the while intermixing gracias' and thank you's.

Once inside, Jack closed the door and took stock of the room. He was hoping to find the cache of antiques, thinking he could use them as leverage to get the portal information from Bart. No such luck. He found a map of the area in the desk drawer covering a 9mm automatic pistol. Now that was a weapon he was familiar with. Jack spread the map out on the desk, but couldn't find anything that looked like a cave with a time portal. Not that he expected there to be some kind of standard map symbol for that. He felt a little silly for hoping that Bart might have marked this map as he had the one in Dawson's Creek. He sat down in the uncomfortable motel chair on the other side of the bed and watched the television as he waited for Bart to show up.

"Coming up on News 4, a major change in our weather pattern and the FBI is looking for leads in the string of arson's that has left two dead and has the entire community clamoring for action."

Jack let the TV drone on as he tried to come up with a way to get Bart to tell him how to get back to the portal. He thought briefly about pointing the gun at Bart and demanding the information. He cast that thought aside. Bart would know that Jack would never shoot him in cold blood in a motel room. Besides, it would be awfully hard to find his way back to Hope while serving 15 years in the state pen. No, he would have to get Bart to volunteer the information. The sound of a room key sliding in the electronic lock and a beep interrupted his planning process. In walked Bart, holding the room key in his left hand, a fast food sack in his teeth and cradling a large soda between his shorter arm and his ribs. He stopped in his tracks when he saw Jack sitting in the chair. His expression went from startled, to angry, then finally settled on confident when he saw that Jack was unarmed.

"Jack. What a surprise to see you." Bart said after dropping his dinner bag from his mouth onto the desk.

"How did you find me?" Before Jack could answer, Bart held up his gauze wrapped wrist. "The coins I sold to pay for this?"

Jack nodded his head.

"I suppose you came looking for answers, like why I didn't kill you when I had the opportunity. It would've been easy you know. I could have shot you before I rode off."

"Why didn't you then?"

"Call it a temporary onset of compassion, if you like. You were lying there almost dead anyway. Seemed like a shame to waste a bullet. Turned out to be a wise move, not shooting you. Those people rode up just as I was leaving. Might have been hard to explain, shooting a man as he lay unconscious."

"I guess you're just an old softy, aren't you, Bart?"

"Yeah maybe. What makes think I won't kill you now? What are you doing here? Looking to steal my antiques and make a little profit for yourself?"

"Hardly. I want you to tell me where the portal is. I know you can find your way back to it."

Bart laughed at what seemed like an insane request. "Why would I do that? Besides, I blew it to high heaven before we left. You're never going back. Nobody is."

"Just the same, you're gonna tell me where it is," Jack confidently told him. "I can make things pretty uncomfortable for you here. I know where all that stuff came from."

"Yeah, but that doesn't help you get it across to the police, now does it? You might find it hard to convince them that I brought it back from 1870 through a time portal. That still doesn't explain why you want to go back. Got a soft spot in your heart for that girl, do you?"

"It's none of your business why I want to go back. All you've got to do is show me where the portal is and you're home free. That's the cost of keeping me quiet."

"Maybe I can keep you quiet for the cost of one bullet," Bart said as he reached into the drawer and pulled out the gun.

Jack stood up. "Go ahead, shoot me. You'd only be putting me out of my misery. I know that there is no way the portal will still work. I just have to see it for myself. I can't live without her." Jack walked over and stood within arm's length of Bart, the gun barrel just touching his chest.

Once again, Jack had to endure Bart's laughter.

"You are pathetic, Banyan. No woman is worth that. Pathetic!" Bart kept on laughing as Jack lowered his eyes.

"I think I will let you live, Jack. It'll be worth it to see you miserable. In fact, maybe you do need to see that the portal is destroyed. Right here," Bart said as he tapped the gun to a spot on the map. "Right here is the source of your misery for years to come. Maybe you can put up a little shrine there," he laughed.

Jack studied the point on the map. He said nothing, and turned to leave. He had just put his hand on the doorknob when he heard the unmistakable cocking of an automatic pistol behind him.

"What, Jack? Not even going to say thank you?"

Jack stopped. Without turning he answered, "Never in a million years."

"Then I believe I've changed my mind. I think I will kill you, Jack."

"You're going to have to shoot me in the back, Bart. That's gonna have an impact on your new reputation as a softy." Jack turned the doorknob.

"A chance I'm willing to take to get you out of the way for good."

Jack started to pull the door open. There was a 'Click'. Jack smiled as he continued out the door and down the walkway to the stairs. Once he was to his car, he reached into his pocket and pulled out the bullets he had removed earlier from Bart's clip. He held his hand out the car window so that Bart could see the shiny brass from where he leaned against the second floor railing. Bart's cursing slowly faded as Jack rolled the window back up and drove away. He had sure been convincing when he was playing Bart back there. Wasn't it all true, though? Could he live without her? At least Bart had helped to solidify the reality of the entire thing. It was funny how his mind wanted to retreat back into a dull world of denial.

"Self-protection at its highest," he said aloud.

Jack wasn't sure how he'd missed that spot on the map in his earlier searching. He knew right where he was going now and it didn't take long to find the place. The first thing he recognized was the ranch house. He stopped and knocked at the door. The woman who opened the door had never heard of the Bar None and claimed that she and her family had owned the ranch for years. By the time Jack gathered himself enough to apologize, the woman was nearly as distraught as he was. He continued on down the road as his surroundings grew more and more familiar. He stopped his car where the road came nearest to the point he believed the cave had been. He continued on foot until he crossed the riding trail, which he followed to the 'Y' where he had separated from the group. There he began his own mad dash through the underbrush looking for the point where he and Diablo parted company. The hills ahead of him took on a roughly familiar look, and he used them to find the point where he had fallen off Diablo. There were plenty of horse tracks and boot prints around the spot and even a scratched up area in the dirt where he imagined he had struck the ground. He bounded up the hill to where the cave should have been. There was nothing but a rounded, weathered hilltop, similar to the rest of the hills he could see. He had expected to see fresh dirt and rocks from the explosion, and had hoped that he could dig his way through to the portal. Reality struck him as he stood on top of the hill. Of course there wouldn't be fresh dirt and rocks. The portal had been blown up 140 years ago. It was gone, weathered over by a century of wind and rain. Bart was right. There would be no going back. This would be the site of his misery for years to come. He sat in solitude on top of the hill thinking of Hope. She had told him that she couldn't go on without him. He could not imagine a life without her in it. Depressed and feeling utterly alone in the world, he trudged back down the hill. As he passed the horse tracks, a silver glint caught his eye. It was the sun reflecting off something metal under a bush. Jack walked over and picked up his cell phone. The battery was dead and the screen was shattered. That seemed like a perfect commentary on the situation. He thrust it into his pocket and made his way back to the car.

38

The rest of that week was Hell on Earth for Jack. He spent some time sitting alone in their picnic spot, and even made an offer to the owner of the land to purchase it. He took his cell phone to the repair shop. He was completely useless at work. He spent most of his days researching time travel and the history of the area. He could find nothing of a town called Dawson's Creek, a frontier doctor named Marcus Welby, or a landowner named Hope Sugar. There was no record of any of them ever existing. Jack was good at finding solutions to problems, but this one was beyond his ability. The days drifted into weeks with no change. Nothing useful in his study of time travel. No information in the census books or land documents. Most importantly, no change in the dark, despair-filled ache that was Jack's heart.

His newly purchased ranch land brought him some consolation. It had taken all of his savings and a lot of convincing to get the current owner to part with it, but it provided a link to Hope that was tangible and comforting. He searched animal shelters all across Denver until he found one that reminded him of Hope's Lab. He named the dog Charley, hoping the dog would give him less trouble than the horse had. He ate meals often at their picnic spot, watching sunsets over the Rockies and pondering with Charley what life with Hope would have been like.

After a few weeks of solitude, Jack had gotten used to the routine. He and Charley were inside, unpacking the last few moving boxes on a stormy summer day. Jack heard a car pull up in front and shortly after, a knock on the door. Charley barked a few times then went strangely quiet. Jack looked down at Charley and back up at the door. The ranch was remote, and Jack no longer had a social life. There had not been a knock on the door since he bought the place. He had been wondering how long it would take Bart to figure out where he was. Jack had known since they parted at the motel that Bart could not let him remain a risk at large. Jack walked toward the door. What did he have to lose? Maybe this would be the one that finally put Bart away for good.

"Come on, Charley. Let's go meet our fate."

Jack pulled open the door and said "I've been expecting you."

"Jack!"

In a blur Jack was pinned up against the wall. Hope was pressed up against him so tightly that he could scarcely breathe. She was showering kisses on him and saying his name over and over. Her lips and hair were wet from the rain just as they were that night in the wagon. Charley was barking, the rain was roaring on the roof and the thunder was crashing outside. It was almost too much for Jack's mind to take. Good God, could it be her for real? She was real. He could feel her, smell her, taste her sweet lips. He came to his senses and held her at arm's length looking her over.

"Hope! Is it really you? I thought I'd never see you again." Jack stared at her in disbelief. He spun her around, then pressed her up against the wall. He planted a long, wet, hard kiss on her.

"I tried to come back. I tried."

"I know you did," she said between kisses. She was running her fingers through his hair and tugging at it to be sure he was real. Her body was shaking and tears started to fall.

"I can't believe I found you."

"How did you?" he asked. "How did you get here?"

"Doc. Doc helped me get through the portal. He brought me here." She looked past Jack through the open doorway. Jack turned and saw the Mustang on the dirt road in front of the house. Doc sat in the driver's seat watching them. He rolled the window down to stick out his arm and wave.

"Take care of her Jack!" He blasted the horn twice and yelled, "See you two kids later!" Doc floored it and the engine roared. The Mustang fishtailed forward along the wet dirt road. The tires threw mud twenty feet behind the Pony car as it sped out of sight into the gray mist and rain.

"Why didn't he stay?" Jack still had her pinned up against the wall. He ran his hands along her neck, shoulders and arms. He could not touch her enough.

"Oh Jack, he has helped me so much. He said he wanted to come in and say hello, but that we would probably want some time alone together." She said that last bit while staring up into his eyes.

"Doc was never more right in his life," Jack agreed as he reached down and placed his arm behind her knees. He lifted her and carried her into the bedroom, never losing the lock his eyes had on hers. He laid her on the bed and lay down next to her, stroking her cheek. He slid his hand behind her neck and pulled her face into his. Their mouths met in a full wet kiss, one that signaled the transition from reunion to passion and desire.

They laid there in the sheets, arms and legs fully entangled, soaking in each other's warmth and listening to the rain.

"I feel so complete when we are together, Jack. I love you."

"I love you, too," he answered. "I know what you mean. Like everything is right in the world. Like we've always belonged together."

Jack told her about the fight at the cave, his time in the hospital and his search for the portal.

"I couldn't find it, and when I did find the place where the cave had been, it was completely gone. I've been back there dozens of times trying to figure out how to recover it. How did you two manage to find a way to get back through?"

"We were only minutes behind you that night, Jack. We saw the explosion on the hill. When we got there you were gone. I was in tears. I thought you were dead. Doc pulled me aside and told me he thought that the two of you had gone through this portal and that something had destroyed it. I told him to 'fix it, fix it now'! He said that he couldn't fix it, crushing the sliver of hope that he'd given me. He told me not to worry, that you and I would be together again. That we were meant to be together. At first I thought he meant in Heaven. I told him I wasn't willing to wait that long. He assured me that wasn't what he intended. We spent the days together after that. He told me all about your world and drew pictures of the things in it. I learned about air-planes and cars. Re-Frigid-aters." Hope said these words distinctly, as things that were entirely foreign to her.

"E-mails." She looked at him sternly. "Or fancy telegrams," scolding him for his made up answer to that question back in Dawson's Creek. I thought we were just passing time at first, but then I realized he was coaching me for coming here to be with you. Today he came to get me and said it was time to go. He promised that Adolf would take care of the animals. We rode in the wagon for a while and went through that awful cave. When I woke up Doc was there waiting for me, holding an umbrella over me. That 'car' of his was already there. He brought me here in that thing. I have to admit it took a while to get here. I kept having to make him slow down. People could get killed in that thing," she smiled.

"I'm so happy you're here with me now," Jack told her. "So how well a job did Doc do in preparing you, I wonder? Let's give you a little test." He pointed to the digital alarm clock and asked her what it was. While Doc had not coached her on it specifically, she was quick enough to guess that it was a clock like the one in the car. He pointed through the open bathroom door at the toilet.

"Ha!" she said, Doc told me specifically about that one. "That is an indoor outhouse."

"Okay, okay. Not bad."

Hope took up the challenge. She pointed to the ceiling and announced, "And that is an electric light blob!" Jack figured he could wait to correct that one.

"How about that black box hanging on the wall there?" he asked.

"Television?" Hope said tentatively. "But Doc said it was full of moving pictures, like plays?"

Jack reached across her to the bedside stand and grabbed the remote.

"Only when you turn it on by pushing this button." The TV sprang to life, and so did Hope. She sat up to get a good look at the screen. Jack wondered how she would handle all the amazing things she would discover in the coming days. He thought back to how hard it was for him to accept his transition and knew that he would need to help her. Hope sat transfixed by the TV as the evening news started.

The newscasters were introduced as the opening music played. "That's a Negro woman!" Hope exclaimed.

"Women, and all the races, are treated equally now," Jack explained. "Mostly," he added.

"High time," she said matter-of-factly, without taking her eyes off the image.

The woman opened the newscast. "There has been an arrest in the series of church arsons that have plagued the black community in recent weeks. The Federal Bureau of Investigation announced the arrest today." The image changed to an FBI agent speaking in front of a podium. "The FBI placed under arrest today Bartholomew Allen Decker..." Hope turned to look at Jack in amazement. Jack was smiling.

"... in connection with the arsons and firebombing of six churches in Colorado, and the murders of two people killed inside one of those churches." The picture shifted to the scene as FBI agents marched a handcuffed Bart Decker into a vehicle. Hope gave a shriek when she saw Bart's image and clamped onto Jack.

"Its okay, Honey," Jack calmed her. "He's in jail now. He can't hurt us." The image switched back to the agent behind the podium.

"We are in possession of video evidence from an anonymous source that clearly ties Mr. Decker to the crimes. We would ask that the anonymous source come forward to help us with our investigation." Once more the image changed. There was Bart, framed by the night sky, his angry face glowing in firelight as he shouted, "Block the damned door and burn that church down! I don't care if the whole Mormon Tabernacle Choir is in there. I'll shoot you and do it myself if I have to. Burn it down, damn it!" The newscaster came back on the screen.

"The FBI is investigating leads in trying to identify the accomplices involved in the crimes. Anyone with information is encouraged to call the FBI tip line."

Hope turned to Jack with a puzzled look.

"When...? How did you...?" Jack sat speechless, returning only a smug smile.

"Out with it," she directed as she poked him in his ticklish side.

"Okay, okay! There's another piece of technology that Doc might not have told you about." He reached back over to the nightstand and came back up with his cell phone. He thought about going through all of the functions available on a modern-day smart phone, but he thought it better to just cut to the chase and give her the basic functions.

"This is a cellular telephone. It is basically a portable telegraph station that sends voice signals instead of dots and dashes."

"Yes, Doc told me about telephones," Hope answered.

"This is a special telephone, because it is mobile. It doesn't require a cable connection to work. It does have to be within range of a working antenna tower. It was useless to me in Dawson's Creek as a telephone. But it also has a camera that can take those pictures that you see on TV...television," he quickly corrected himself. "It stores them inside. Do you understand so far?"

"Yes, I think so."

"I took that video, those pictures, the night of the battle in Dawson's Creek. The trip back through the portal damaged my phone. Once it was repaired, I sent those pictures of Bart to the FBI...sorry, the Federal Bureau of Investigation."

"Yes, but can he be arrested for burning a church over a hundred years ago?" she asked.

"Arrested, Yes. Convicted, No," Jack answered. "The FBI will figure that out pretty quickly and move back to looking for the actual perpetrators of the arsons."

"But then Bart will go free!" That look of fright returned to her face. Jack took comfort in seeing that she considered it dangerous to be here with him, but was still willing to take that risk.

"Maybe he will. They won't be able to pin the church burnings on him. Funny thing is, Bart told me himself how to put him away for good. When I was trying to get him to show me the portal location, he laughed at me. When I threatened to tell the police where he got his antiques, he just laughed at the thought of me describing a trip to 1870 and back. So now he gets to try to explain it. He's going to have one Hell of a time trying to answer where that video came from. Where he's been over the last few years. Where he got all of those Confederate antiques that he has been selling. The FBI is pretty thorough when they start investigating someone. Even if he can provide plausible answers to all of those questions, unless I'm guessing wrong, they'll find something in Bart's long history to nail him for. I think we have seen the last of Bart Decker."

This time Hope let out a squeal of happiness.

"Jack, you're brilliant!" She sat quietly for a moment, her eyes looking upward as though she was thinking through something.

"So what other pictures do you have on there?" She playfully grabbed the phone out of his hand. Pressing random buttons got her nowhere. "Show me," she commanded.

He laughed as he took the phone back and played the videos and pictures for her. He showed her the video he took as he chased Charley, trying to catch hold of the reins after he'd been thrown off. Jack didn't look so brilliant as he cursed each time Charley bolted. That was before they had come to their mutual understanding.

"I miss that old horse," he told her. "We'll need to get some horses for our ranch."

She smiled at that comforting thought. "Keep going."

He showed her a picture of the two snarling, barking dogs taken from under the porch of the servant's quarters.

"I was hoping that the flash bulb would scare them off. No such luck." Then he brought up a video of Zeus and Apollo cuddled together, snoring as they slept in the hallway of Bart's ranch. "Sleeping tonic did the trick." There was another of Jack whispering a narrative as he laced up his boots, then walked backwards away from the drunk, sleeping Indians. There was a still photo of Hope standing over unconscious Bart being attended to by the cook, the broken vase handle hanging from Hope's hand. He zoomed the picture in on her face and they both laughed at her look of righteous indignation and sweet satisfaction. There was a photo of the cow and bull kissing through the gate. Mostly there were innocuous tourist photos that Jack wanted to click through quickly. Hope slowed him down as she pored over each seemingly meaningless photo of the town, the surrounding countryside, and Hope's ranch. She stopped the longest on photos of the people in town going about their everyday business.

"Oh thank you Jack. Thank you so much. This is greater than any treasure to me," she said of the pictures of her friends and her past.

"Won't you miss them?" Jack worried. "Can you be happy here with me?"

"I'm back with you now, Jack, and I couldn't be happier," she declared. "Of course I'll miss them. It will take some time to get used to all the new things in your world, but you'll help me, won't you Jack? Easy Peasy, right?"

"Sure, Honey. Easy Peasy."

39

The rain was still falling from dark gray skies as Doc and Darrell walked along the country road under umbrellas. Each was still dressed in his western attire.

"How long we been doing this?" Doc asked.

"Longer than I can remember. Why?"

"I don't know. Sometimes I think maybe I've had enough. Time to move on, you know?"

"What? Retire?"

"Yeah, maybe. That ranch sure looked peaceful. Long morning rides. Sunsets over the mountains. No worries..."

"That doesn't sound so bad. But you could never do it, my friend. Not in a million years."

They folded up their umbrellas as the rain stopped almost instantaneously. The warm light of the sun pushed through puffy white clouds. The two friends looked fresh as spring in their all white suits and pastel ties. Their white shoes crunched the pebbles on the road beneath their feet.

"You're wrong there. I could do it easy."

"You'd like to think you could do it. But you would miss righting the wrongs. Aligning matched souls. Trumping the Tyranny of Time!" he announced with fanfare. "I can see it in your eyes every time our clients have that first meeting, where that one look is all it takes for them to know they will spend the rest of Time together. You look like you're reliving your first meeting every time. Don't give me that retirement baloney. Bringing together soul mates out of time synch is what keeps you young."

"No, seriously. I could use a rest."

"That might be true. You stepped way outside the boundaries on this one. You know we aren't supposed to get physically involved. You crushed that guy's nose with that iron bar up your sleeve. And what on Earth were you doing setting fires and traps in that town? That won't go over very well when we file our closing report. You know what a stickler for the rules they can be."

"I know, I know. I just felt like one man against twenty seemed like a bit much. Besides, I wanted to participate a little this time. It was fun, too. Reminded me of the old days."

"You know the Boss is already mad about losing one of his portals. Do you know what those things cost? How hard it was to get another one brought in on spec?"

"There's not much I can do about that now. I sure as heck didn't expect Decker to blow the darned thing up."

"That's what I'm saying. If you weren't having so much fun participating in the story, you might have seen that one coming. I'll bet they dock your pay for that thing. It will take years to pay it off."

"Then it will have been worth it. Did you see the look in their eyes? That might have been my best one yet."

"I had my doubts about him at first. He seemed pretty self-centered to me. How did you know he wouldn't head straight for the portal as soon as you told him where it was?"

"I didn't. Sometimes you just have to have faith. He came through in the end, didn't he?"

"See, that's what I am trying to tell you. You won't ever retire. No way. You live for this stuff."

"Like you don't? You're right, though. Every time I see that I go back to another place, another time."

"There you go again. Don't go getting all wispy on me. Where to now?"

"Next one is going to be kind of fun." He pulled a faded notebook out of the inside pocket of his jacket. He opened it to the page marked by a rubber band looped around the back cover of the notebook.

"Looks like a World War One doughboy and a single mom from the seventies." After a few more steps, Doc pointed to the side of the road. "Here we are." He pulled the tail of his simple white linen smock out of the way and put the notebook into the back pocket of his loose fitting, white pajama pants. They walked off of the road toward a thick line of bushes separating the roadway from the forest. He pulled some branches back, opening a pathway for them to enter. Doc adjusted his bandana headband a little, then held up two fingers in a 'V'.

"Peace, man. Wipe your sandals before you go in."

To learn more about Bill and his books, visit Bill's Amazon Author page
https://www.amazon.com/author/billapplewhite